THE MINNESOTA KINGSTONS | BOOK FIVE

STEINBECK

THE MINNESOTA KINGSTONS | BOOK FIVE

STEINBECK

SUSAN MAY WARREN

Steinbeck
The Minnesota Kingstons, Book 5

Print ISBN: 978-1-962036-59-7
Ebook ISBN: 978-1-962036-60-3

For more information about Susan May Warren, please access the author's website at the following address: www.susanmaywarren.com.

Published in the United States of America.

Cover design by Emilie Haney, eahcreative.com

For Your glory, Lord

ONE

W HAT IF THIS WAS THE REST OF HIS LIFE?
Sweaty, covered in grime, reeking of frustration, rooting around the dungeon of his father's workshop, hunting for, well, in this case, a battery.

But Steinbeck might as well have been hunting for his future.
For hope. For anything that could jostle loose a fragment of a lead
as to where—

"You find it yet?"

His brother Jack stood in the open doorway, an outline against
the bright light of the hot August day, the scant breeze off the lake
not enough to stir the heat of the old shed. Humidity sheened
Jack's skin, plastering to it the sawdust and woodchips that also
littered Stein's slickened skin. The place smelled of its vintage,
humble beginnings as a wooden garage built in the thirties.

Stein longed for the fresh, salty breezes of the ocean. "No. Are
you sure Dad kept the extra battery in here?"

In here might have been a vague term, given the mess of tools
that were scattered across the worn, chipped workbench, inter-

mingling with old gum wrappers, rusty nails, oily bolts, crumpled sandpaper, and tangled wire.

"He said it's here."

Steinbeck shook his head, pushing against the old drawer until it groaned against its runner, caught, and wedged sideways.

He gave it another shove, but it only jerked and stuck again, and he bit back a word as he lifted his hands in surrender.

"For the love. I don't know how he can find anything in this disaster." He pulled the drawer back out and reworked it in. Then opened the one below it. "This is like walking into a time warp. Grandpa's been gone for years, and still"—he pulled out an after-market service manual of a 1973 Alfa Romeo Spider, the pages coffee stained and wrinkled, as if the old man had set one of his cracked *I Love Minnesota* mugs on it while studying the schematic of the dual side-draft carburetor that had endlessly plagued him—"it smells like stale coffee and old oil in here."

"And varnish and dirt. Grandpa must have spent thousands of hours in here. Wow, I miss him." Jack came into the room, shirtless, wearing a pair of paint-stained khaki shorts and beat-up runners. "Forget the battery. We'll recharge the one we have."

"I wanted to get the table done today." Steinbeck closed the drawer and shoved past Jack into the sunlight and beyond, to the shade of the towering cottonwoods and birch that arched over the maintenance area of the King's Inn compound.

A twelve-foot table, handmade, stained white, awaiting a second layer of sanding, stood on the cracked concrete driveway.

The story of Steinbeck's life—another unfinished project.

Finally a breeze, and he stopped, hands on his hips, staring out across the impossibly lush, meticulously kept back lawn—*good job, Jack*—to the deep indigo lake, where a handful of guests sat on the long dock or in lounge chairs on the sandy beach.

The perfect getaway. Or prison, depending on your view.

The wind skimmed over his body, the scent, just barely lifting from the lake, carrying with it not only the white pine but the aroma of his mother's fresh-baked bread in the kitchen of the nearby Victorian home-slash-inn.

Steinbeck's stomach growled.

"You're a real peach today," Jack said, turning his ball cap around. Stein's brother needed a haircut and maybe a shave, but he'd been spending long hours at a nearby rented garage, working hard remodeling a city-bus-turned-mobile-home, so maybe he didn't care about his appearance. Stein could nearly smell the wanderlust emanating from his older brother.

"No word on your missing friend?" Jack asked.

Missing. Friend. Two words that didn't exactly describe Phoenix. First—not missing but *captured*. Imprisoned, and yes, missing because, according to his contacts, no one had seen her since she landed in Cuban custody nearly a month ago.

His gut tightened. She was valuable. And tough. And would hold out—

Nope. He blew out a breath. "She's not my *friend*. We worked together."

Jack had walked over to the table, started to wipe off the last layer of sawdust with a clean rag. "Yep."

"Really. We knew each other—well, in a different life."

"When you were active duty."

Steinbeck grabbed a thermos of water, took a drink. It went down cool in his throat, loosened the simmer in his chest. "Yeah. Met her on an op in Poland."

Jack stood up. "Wait—not the—"

"Yes. That one." Stein capped the bottle. "The one with the bomb and where I woke up in Germany, my knees blown out." Only when his body soaked in the sun, like now, could anyone see the straight-line scars down both knees.

"Was she there?" Jack had stood up, shaking out the rag. "At the bombing?"

"Yep." Stein ran his hand along the tabletop. It needed at least two more coats of stain, plus sanding, but his mother would have the outside table she'd hoped for when she'd plunked down the plans to her oldest sons last weekend.

Maybe he'd finish one project. And he was determined to finish it today, if he could just find that battery in all this mess.

Jack had retrieved his water too. He had spent the last few years as a hero, searching for the lost, before returning home last winter. And now he was sticking around to take over maintenance duties at the inn while their younger brother Doyle found a fresh wind down in the Caribbean, finally restarting his life.

Out of all of them, Doyle deserved a happy ending.

"So you ran into her again?" Jack said after taking a drink.

"Down in Mariposa when I was working for Declan, and then yeah, a month ago when I went to visit Austen." Not entirely true, but he *had* seen Austen. Well, more than seen her. He'd helped rescue her from Cuban pirates, and maybe gotten in over his head in said country, an escapade that had ended poorly.

And landed Phoenix in Cuban custody. It wasn't his fault, maybe, but . . . "Let's just say . . ."

"No man left behind." Jack met his gaze. "She means something to you."

"No. She's . . . Like you said, I don't leave people behind."

"Mm-hmm," Jack said.

"I just need to find her. Make sure she's safe. That's all."

"That's all." Jack smiled. "So, you're right. Not a friend." He took another drink.

Stein shook his head, but for a second, he stood in the shadows of a Spanish-style hotel in Old Havana, Phoenix's voice soft. *"I think you should kiss me."*

No, *no*, he should not—

"You okay, bro? You look like you just got bodychecked." Jack was staring at him.

Right. "Yeah. The fact is, I've run into a dead end. I can't find her. And I know . . . just know she's in trouble."

Jack's mouth tightened. "Okay, let me see what you've got."

Stein stilled. "Yeah?" And maybe he shouldn't turn to his brother with so many secrets—but it wasn't like trouble, as in any of the Russians he suspected of taking her, would show up in Minnesota, at the door of the King's Inn.

"Okay. My computer is back at the Norbert."

Jack's house, a.k.a. private family quarters, a.k.a. part of the family parcel of four homes that encompassed the entirety of the King's Inn property. All Victorian homes built by their great-great-grandfather, a newspaper baron back in the Gilded Age.

Stein climbed into the driver's seat of the golf cart, and Jack hopped in on the other side, and they rumbled over to the Norbert, smaller than the main house, but with the same charming apron porch, a turret, five bedrooms, and a small top-floor ballroom, of course.

They pulled up, and Stein headed inside, then up the stairs to his room, the one with the alcove window that overlooked the lake, and grabbed his computer from the writing desk. He went back downstairs to the kitchen with the oval oak table, where Jack was slathering mayo on bread, making himself a ham sandwich.

"I'll take one of those," Stein said and sat at the table, booting up his computer. Then he got up and pulled an ice pack from the freezer, wrapped it in a towel, and set it on one of his knees. The cold seeped in and eased the swelling.

He pulled up his latest scan of the Havana port shipyards, looking like a grainy 1970s movie scene, complete with swarthy dockworkers, old Russian GAZ trucks, and ragged palm trees. He half expected Hemingway to saunter onto the screen.

Jack came over, leaned down over his shoulder. "What's that?"

"I have a hacker friend who got me into a feed of the port. I've been going over footage, trying to find a glimpse of her."

"Why?" Jack returned to the counter.

"I thought she was arrested by Cuban officials, but there's no record of her arrest." He opened another file, clicked on the video feed of the few days after she was detained. "Declan used all of his political power, and I even tapped"—well, maybe Jack didn't need to know that their cousin Colt worked for an off-the-books government agency—"a friend who has connections. She's not in the system, period."

"So where is she?" Jack set a sandwich on a napkin in front of Stein.

"Thanks. Not sure. She might have escaped, but my gut says she was taken by the Russian mob. Maybe put on a ship."

Silence, a whole beat, and he glanced at Jack as he picked up the sandwich.

"To Russia?" Jack said. "The mob? Really?"

"Mm-hmm." Stein took a bite, let the video scroll. Grainy and black-and-white. Mostly forklifts moving crates down the long pier, another shot of cranes lifting shipping containers onto cargo ships.

Please, God, don't let her be in one of those containers.

"We ran into mob-types in our escape from Cuba, and they even pirated Declan's ship—"

"Your life is like an action movie."

He glanced at Jack. "You do see me in the kitchen, eating lunch, icing my knee, covered in sawdust?" He raised an eyebrow.

"It's a time-out."

"My entire life reduced to waiting for a battery to charge." He glanced at the screen. "She's gone. Vanished into the cogs of the Russian Mafia and . . . I'm sitting here eating a ham sandwich."

"Wow. You're a head case. But I get it. You run into a dead end and you start circling the drain. The key is to keep trying leads, no matter how desperate."

"I thought about trying to find her sister, but frankly, Phoenix isn't even her real name, so . . ." He lifted a shoulder.

"Okay, let's think. Where are those ships going?" Jack had opened a can of pop and now handed another to Stein, who held it against his other knee for a second before opening it.

It frothed out over his hand, and he sucked off the foam. "I don't know. Anywhere."

Jack sat across from him. "Probably an international port. And if it's a Russian ship and they carry 'illicit' cargo"—he finger quoted the word—"they'd want a country friendly to Russian interests."

"Like?"

"Well, Russia and Brazil are part of BRICS, so . . ." He lifted a shoulder, took a drink. Set it down. "And on the European side, you have the Baltic states."

Stein studied the port video. "What about Portugal?"

"Why Portugal?"

Stein pointed to the screen. "I think that cargo ship is flying a Portuguese flag." He didn't know why he hadn't seen it before. He turned the computer toward Jack, who peered at it.

"Yeah, maybe. Not a lot of countries have the coat of arms in the middle of their banner. Spain. Albania. But Spanish flags have horizontal stripes. And Albania has the two-headed eagle. This flag has two sections, with the coat of arms in the middle. You're right. That's definitely Portuguese. And Portugal has been pretty friendly with the Russians in past years."

"I don't know how you know these things." Steinbeck turned his computer back. Paused the video and searched for the IMO number.

"Maybe your hacker friend could find the ship's log, or a bill of landing. See where it ended up." Jack finished his sandwich.

"How long does it take to cross the ocean?"

"In a cargo ship? I don't know. Eight, ten, twelve days? Depends on how often it stops."

Which meant she was probably long gone into the labyrinth of the Russian gulag system.

If she was even still alive.

"What did you say her name was?" Jack got up, pulling out his cell phone to retrieve a text. He threw his pop can into the recycling bin.

"Phoenix. But again, that's not her real name—"

Jack looked at his phone.

"I got a ping from our King's Inn website contact form. It has a booking request for a woman named Firebird. Except the dates are all wrong. It's for December 14, 2005." He turned the phone around. "Twelve, fourteen, two-zero-five. It's missing a year digit."

"Or not." Steinbeck took the phone. "Maybe it's European dating. Fourteen, twelve, two-zero-five. Which would be one, four, one, two, two, zero five. Seven digits." He studied the screen. "The IMO number on the ship is seven digits."

"The IMO?" Jack said.

"International Maritime Organization. They have a global shipping information system that keeps a record of all the locations of ships at sea by their number."

"And you know this—"

"SEALs don't just bang down doors," Stein said. He opened a new tab and did a search. "Found it. It's a container ship. Registered to . . . bam, Portugal." He held up a fist, his gaze still on the screen.

Jack bumped it.

"It's a Panamax. Big ship—about nine hundred feet long, a hundred plus feet wide. Draft maybe forty feet." He leaned back, made a wry face. "She's about 190 feet tall above the water."

"Hard to board a ship like that at sea, in case you're thinking like a SEAL."

Stein nodded. "She's still at sea, port of call, Lisbon." He didn't want to think of where they'd kept Phoenix for the past month.

"ETA, three days from now." He ran a hand over his mouth. "If this message *is* from Phoenix, then . . ."

"Then you're all done sanding, bro."

———•———•———

Her prison even came with a view. And if Emberly looked long and hard enough, maybe she could even make out her apartment on the hills above the Tagus River, in the Santa Catarina neighborhood of Lisbon. Students would be basking in the grass of the nearby Miradouro park with the Adamastor, the epic literary sea-monster statue, maybe watching as her container ship churned into port.

Over a month off the grid—Nimue would be crazy with worry.

Please let her plan work.

Sunny blue skies, a cloudless day, the distant Serra da Arrábida a sleeping hunchback in the far southern horizon. Across the gray-blue of the water, the city of Lisbon climbed up the hillside, with ocher and whitewashed buildings, red clay roofs, streetcars motoring up the cobbled streets, the sidewalks lined with slick and shiny black basalt. Ahead of her, the 25 de Abril Bridge spanned the river, golden sun turning the metal to blood red, now glistening on the water. That same sunset splashed over the rebuilt limestone Tower of Belém at the seashore, a reminder of the explorers who left the shores, along with the resilience of a rebuilt city.

Maybe that's why she'd picked Lisbon and her tucked-away two-room flat. She loved to sit on the balcony that caught the salty winds off the sea, winds that stirred into the city air the scent of lush stone pine, fragrant eucalyptus, and even hints of the cork oak that had once overrun the city.

So close, and yet so far.

Staring out the window of her bare crew-quarters cell, Emberly nearly groaned for a taste of a fried bifana or a beefy prego. Maybe a plate of crispy-rice paella with shrimp, mussels, and crab—and now she was just torturing herself.

Most likely, her captors would shove her onto a plane headed for some remote Siberian gulag. With a stopover in Moscow just so they could have another go-round of interrogation.

She'd have the same nothing to say this time around. She didn't have the jump drive that contained the Axiom program, and in the bonus round, no, she didn't know where the shipment of obsidite had ended up.

Didn't know anything except that the thugs who'd taken her belonged to the Petrov Bratva. A piece of information she tucked away to tell her boss.

If she ever escaped.

Stay calm. Think.

Emberly sat back on the twin bed and drew up her bare feet—she should have scored better shoes back before . . .

Well, before her foolish heart had decided to defect from her brains and stick around to help a guy who'd abandoned her.

"I'll be right behind you! I promise!"

Aw. Her stupid words.

She touched her forehead to her knees even as the boat's horn sounded, alerting the harbor of their arrival. She couldn't blame Steinbeck for abandoning her—he had his own life, his sister's life, even Declan's life to protect.

She was an afterthought, at best. So maybe she shouldn't have put so much hope into her desperate shout for help.

If only the stupid cell phone she'd taken off one of the crew who'd delivered her dinner four days ago had had more than a wink of juice left, she might have been able to make a call to her boss when they got closer to port. Instead, in the fading life of the battery, Emberly had connected to the Internet and taken a chance.

A drastic, reckless chance.

She'd left a message on the contact form of the King's Inn. Because of course she couldn't dredge up Steinbeck's cell number—had she even gotten it? And the idea of connecting with Nimue and maybe having some Russian hacker trace the connection put a fist in her gut. So yeah, she hoped Stein was still the savvy SEAL he'd once been.

Probably hoped too much. Steinbeck Kingston wasn't going to be waiting with some magnificent plan as the Bratva dragged her off the ship and into the trunk of some old Lada. He wasn't going to overpower Igor and Boris, the rather grumpy men who had guarded her at the home of some Cuban official, or any of the other Ivans who'd watched over Prisoner 24601 in the crew cabin in the aft superstructure of the boat.

Steinbeck wasn't a superhero. Just . . .

Well, he was her *only* hero. And even that might be going too far.

He had too many reasons not to rescue her, not to trust her, and if it weren't for his response to her words *I think you should kiss me* . . . Her words shifted again in her head, but really, she'd probably lived too long on and read too much into the way his mouth had curved into a smile, the way his blue eyes had roamed her face. His sardonic words before he'd taken her up on her suggestion.

"Really? I feel like we've been here before."

Oh, they had. Once, in an alleyway in the city of Krakow. Quickly in a mine tunnel on a Caribbean island. And over and over and painfully over in her head for the past three years.

But in real life, she'd ghosted him. Also over and over . . .

No. Steinbeck wouldn't come for her.

Still, her entire body seemed to thrum with a sort of radar, an anticipation, when the door to her quarters opened and Boris stood there. "Poydem."

Right. "Let's go."

His beefy hand gripped her upper arm, the mouth of a gun pressed to her spine as he marched her down the portside gangway.

They hit the dock, a long concrete pier that jutted into the water, and she glanced at the IMO number on the hull of the ship. Please let her have typed it right.

The sun baked her skin through the worn clothing she'd stolen from some liveaboard trawler over a month ago. Thankfully, her cabin had come with a shower, but please let her not die in a pair of salt-soaked, baggy, and ripped cargo pants and a white T-shirt that said *Stay Positive*.

Good life advice, maybe. Especially for a woman heading to the tundra.

She couldn't help, however, scanning the wharf for a tallish, scruffy blond sailor, maybe in sunglasses, and perhaps pretending to be one of the dockworkers who drove forklifts and trucks or operated any of the giant cranes overhead. The redolence of diesel fuel and the briny tang of the rusty, bleeding metal fouled the salty air and bored into her bones.

Run.

Mooring lines snapped, and the growl of machinery overhead could mask a small scuffle, probably, but Boris's hand viced her arm, the handgun still burrowed into her spine, and now Igor flanked her other side.

She was a thief, not a fighter.

So she walked and hoped, and jerked when a container landed on the wharf with a thunderous boom, and even then—

No hero.

Another ship sat docked beside them, its shadow cool as she walked into it, the darkness momentarily blinding her—

Now, Stein! And she even tensed in Boris's grip, just in case.

He yanked her, hard, against himself and laughed. "They said you were a fireball."

Firebird, hello. The name she'd left burned a trail through her throat and into her chest. Oh, she'd been too full of hope. Too—

Gunshots.

She flinched, looked—

A barrel rolled across the pier, a sailor chasing after it—dark hair, skinny.

Not gunshots—just her head, her heart, hoping.

A Ford Kuga sat at the end of the pier, motor running, and instead of throwing her in the back, Boris opened up the rear passenger seat. "Get in."

No handcuffs? This she could work with.

She slid in.

Stilled.

A man sat in the opposite seat. Lean, not overbearing, he looked at her with green eyes that seemed more amused than lethal. Sharp Slavic nose, trimmed brown hair, he wore a pair of khakis and a short-sleeved seersucker shirt, a pair of white boat shoes.

Hardly the mafioso she'd expected of the man named Tomas, head of the Petrov Bratva, at least here in Europe.

"You know me," he said quietly, and smiled.

"Of course." Pictures, surveillance, and a file sent from Mystique, her boss at the start of her op nearly a year ago. Up close, he smelled of aftershave, as if this were a date.

"I suppose you would." He drew in a breath. "Where is it?"

She shrugged. "I left it on Declan's ship." Surely he knew what ship she meant.

"Too bad said ship blew up."

She stilled. *What?*

Oh—she hadn't considered . . .

What if Steinbeck never got the message because he'd—and her chest squeezed—been lost at sea?

"But we're not stupid. We know you made a copy, parked it somewhere for safety."

Yeah, that would have been smart but, "When would I have done that? I was trapped on an island without Internet, and then on a boat that was boarded by pirates. I barely escaped. So?" She held up her hands.

He stared at her so hard she put her hands down and braced herself.

He didn't need to know that she'd worn the drive strapped to her body in a waterproof case for most of her crazy trip.

Until she'd taken a header off a Cuban fishing boat.

Right now, the world's most dangerous hard drive lay in the silt of the Havana harbor. So, that was nice.

"We'll see," he said then and motioned to the driver.

We'll see what? But Tomas got out and Boris slid in next to her, Igor in the front, and the locks clicked.

And still, Steinbeck didn't show up.

They drove through the city, up the Avenida da Liberdade, past cafés and shops, through the dappled sunlight as it cast through the tall Canary Island date palms and fan palms, waiting for streetcars, and maybe she didn't care about the gun anymore.

She tried the handle. Child locks. "Where are we going?"

Silence from her captors.

They left the city, passed small villages and patches of forest, heading toward . . .

Sintra. The palace city of Portugal, perched on a mountain, shot round with twisty roads and lush pine and cork oak trees. A mist hung below the protruding towers of the tallest castle, almost a mystical protection for the kings who once resided there, like in an old-time fairy tale. The old town nestled into the side of the mountain, locals who hawked porcelain tile, lace, and pottery and baked the delicious pastel de nata.

Her mouth nearly watered with the memory of the sweet pastry. As they drove closer, she spotted the jutting ocher cupola and battlements of Pena Palace. Rising out of the greenery to perch atop the mountain, a wall with proper crenelations surrounded the former monastery, and a burnt-red cathedral with a central tower rose from the compound against the fading sunlight.

Glorious, breathtaking, and . . . impenetrable.

They drove through the cobblestone town, the side streets too small for even a European car, and past the National Palace, a white Moorish building with two gnome-hat parapets that sat in the center square.

They pulled up behind a small building, one of the village houses embedded in the hill, and the doors unlocked.

Run. This time the urge swept her up and turned to fire in her veins, but Igor got out and opened her door and grabbed her arm, and even a well-placed kick would have netted her nothing in the narrow space.

She gave a fight nonetheless as he wrestled her out and shoved her against a plastered building. He leaned low, his cigarette breath on her neck, his words in Russian. "Stop. Or I will make you stop."

She didn't scare easily, but . . .

Then he led her up the narrow street to a door in the stone wall of the battlement. The white stone rose three stories, maybe more, and the door opened to a tunnel, the cool, musty breath eking past her, darkness beyond.

Her skin raised gooseflesh.

Boris stepped inside and flicked on a light. A wire ran across the ceiling, like some old-time mine or catacombs, and she became the dead, walking to some underground tomb. Igor pushed her from behind, not gently.

"Where—" But the stone ate her words, the chill seeping into her skin. Tiny alcoves were etched into the walls, many of them with bars, and the cold now ran all the way to her bones.

A real dungeon.

They reached a wider room, this one circular, and facing the center was a collection of cells, all scraped out from the outer ring. They each held nothing but darkness, a bucket, and a drain in the pitted stone floor.

Except for one.

A man sat in the shadow of one of the cells. He wore a dark

beard, shaggy hair, didn't even glance at her. She looked away as Boris stopped before the neighboring cell.

No.

Boris opened the door and Igor pushed her in. She stumbled and turned just as the door closed with a clang, a knell that nearly collapsed her. Dampness rose off the floor. An odor she couldn't place permeated the walls. Despair, perhaps. "Wait—"

Boris smiled. Igor stood at the entry. "Do svidaniya."

Goodbye?

She rushed the cell door. "Wait—I—"

Boris stopped. "You will wait. Until you are ready."

"Ready for what? I don't have the program!"

Boris walked down the tunnel and she closed her eyes.

He didn't come.

Steinbeck hadn't stepped out of the shadows to yank her away from her captors. Hadn't forced his way into the car, hadn't . . .

Maybe he hadn't even gotten her message.

Because he was dead.

And if not, probably he simply didn't care.

She stepped back, found the wall, and slid down against it, the dampness and chill of the stone seeping into her flimsy clothing.

Then the lights went out and left her in darkness.

Don't cry.

Black Swans didn't cry. Didn't—

"Took you long enough, Phoenix," said a male voice, soft, almost gentle, a bit of laughter on the end, as if . . .

And her heart jolted, jump-started, exploded inside her.

"Steinbeck?"

"Who else do you think? Wanna get out of here?"

TWO

I T WORKED.

Steinbeck's crazy, thrown-together, call-it-chance, good-luck, not-to-mention-decent-intel plan had actually *worked*.

The tremor in her voice in the pitch darkness, the way Phoenix's breath caught at his words . . . Clearly she hadn't believed he'd actually show up.

"Seriously?" The voice on the other side of the wall seemed almost frail, nothing of the woman he'd met three years ago while on an op in Poland—tough, in control. Although, when she added a snarky "I hate to mention this, but you're locked in here with me." Yeah, it sounded like Phoenix.

He gave a laugh, a spark, the heat of it a warm flame igniting inside. "Please." Then he reached into the pocket of the ratty pants he couldn't wait to get out of and pulled out a key.

A helpful souvenir from the guard outside the tunnel door, currently snoozing in Stein's rented Fiat Panda.

He moved over to the lock, inserted the key. The door whined open. Then he pulled on a headlamp and flicked it on. The beam cast over her cell, over her.

She stood at the ready, her hands clutching the bars. She wore the same baggy green cargo pants and a grimier version of the same white T-shirt as a month ago. Bare feet, so clearly she'd lost her flip-flops along the way. Her hair glowed, copper red under his light, and her green eyes settled on him, wide. "It really is you." Her voice had cut to almost a whisper, as if he were an apparition, or maybe just a dream, losing all sense of her earlier bravado.

He swallowed back the same ethereal feeling, found words as he approached her lock. "Who else would deliberately sneak into a dark tunnel, get trapped in a cell, and show up smelly and dog tired to rescue a woman who might only get him into trouble?"

She cocked her head. "So many feelings for a guy whose biggest response is usually a grunt."

And she was back.

He grunted and opened her cell.

And then she stood there, in the opening, three feet from him, just . . . staring. As if—

"Phoenix?"

She launched herself at him. A full-on, legs-around-his-waist, arms-around-his-neck embrace, holding on as if he were a pillar in a flood, her only hope.

His arms went around her, and he had to take a step back to keep from falling, his knees hurting just a little from all the ruckus a few hours earlier, but he held her.

Held *on to* her. He'd never realized, really, how petite her frame felt against his. Small, strong, a bobcat more than a tiger, but also broken maybe—because her body shook a little, belying her tough demeanor.

"You okay?"

She leaned her forehead into his shoulder; then her entire body exhaled and she let go, first her legs, then her arms releasing.

He lowered her to her feet and met her eyes. They seemed to be—"Phoenix, are you crying?"

"What? No. Just . . . I'm cold." She wrapped her arms around herself, then looked away. "Let's get out of here."

Mm-hmm. "Good idea. I don't know how long we have until the Russians figure out that their guy at the door isn't on a chai break."

She frowned, and he resisted the urge to pull her back into his arms.

Even kiss her.

Yeah, shoot, he'd been harboring that version of their reunion for the last seventy-two hours.

Clearly, relief was not the same as *"Oh Steinbeck, I've missed you so much."* This was an op, one still very much in peril.

Still, he grabbed her hand, put it on his belt behind him, and said, "Hold on. It's dark."

"That's a newsflash."

Ah, the woman was coming back to herself. He headed down the tunnel toward the entrance, some thirty feet away.

"I don't understand—how did—"

"No. You first. What happened in Cuba?" Because he'd woken up too many times over the past month with her words— *"I'll be right behind you"*—in his head. Words that he'd let himself believe. And then he'd spend the rest of the night wrestling away the *what-ifs* and *please, no's* of the terror that he imagined befell her

"The scooter wouldn't start, and the cops caught up to me on foot."

He felt her hand on his belt. If she let go, even once, he was taking her hand.

"They didn't even bother to take me to the Cuban police, though, so I'm not sure they were official cops. I ended up locked in the guest room of the home of a government official."

"The guy from the consulate?"

"No, someone else. Cuban. With Russian friends. They were after the program." Her voice dropped a little then, and even as he kept them moving, his light dragging over the rutted, scarred rocky surface, his chest tightened. He didn't want to ask—

"They didn't hurt me."

He couldn't speak.

"Much."

He credited himself for not stopping, not turning and giving in to the urge to again pull her to himself. Never let go.

And okay, maybe that was overstated, but he was tired, cold, grimy, and lacking sleep.

"Where is the program?"

"You were there. It drowned."

He did stop then. "Seriously?"

"Keep going, and yes. I didn't get a chance to upload it—I know, stupid, but this entire op has been a comedy of chaos. I'm back to zero. They put me on a boat; I swiped a cell phone with low battery and got a message out. Bam, your turn. What happened after you got away? I heard—" Her voice hitched then.

Interesting.

"They said the yacht blew up."

Who was *they*? But he just nodded, then, "Tactical error. The Russians hadn't left the ship, so we had a small shootout on the boat. Dec and I disembarked into the cool waters of the gulf."

She snorted. "Pre-explosion."

"Sort of. And to be clear, I looked for you in Cuba. Good job with the message. Jack, my brother, got it and asked me about it, and I knew it was from you. Clever, giving me the IMO number."

"Clever, you figuring it out."

With that, the old dance, a sort of camaraderie, settled into his bones.

They just might make it out of here.

"But that's a long way from you showing up in a dungeon in Portugal."

"I called my cousin Colt. He works with the Caleb Group."

"That's convenient."

"About as convenient as the fact that, apparently, your sneaky little group of Black Swans occasionally works with the Caleb Group."

"Sometimes they just need a woman's touch."

"Please. You're all highly trained thieves."

"Covert specialists in retrieving hard-to-obtain items."

He let out a grunt. "Yeah, well, Colt's boss, Logan, hooked me up with intel and a guy on this side of the pond named Roy. Apparently, he knows the Petrov Bratva and especially their hideouts. Once we figured out where your ship was heading, Roy put a tail on Tomas, their leader. He owns an estate near here with an airstrip. Our best guess was that they were going to move you."

"And what—the dungeon in Sintra is the international lounge? It needs a buffet, maybe drink service."

They reached the door, and he glanced back at her, again casting the light upon her. "Roy and I put a tracker on the Petrov car, and his hacker, Coco, tapped into the camera on the wharf. They picked you up getting into Petrov's car, and when you headed out of the city, Roy stayed on your tail while I took a shortcut to Sintra. I found the dungeon, tranqed the guard—left him in my car—and sneaked into the prison."

"Lots of what-ifs there, Ethan Hunt. I could have ended up on a plane."

Her words only tightened the coil in his gut. "I took a chance." He kept out the part where he and Roy nearly had a throwdown in the hotel room where Roy told him the plan.

He'd wanted to storm the wharf, but with too many sailors on the Russian dole . . . "This plan had the best odds for survival."

Then he opened the door.

The twilight streamed in, and his eyes blinked hard against it. He cupped a hand over his eyes and eased into the cobblestone alleyway.

Phoenix still gripped his belt.

He pulled out a handgun, secreted to him by Roy. Steinbeck had a whole list of questions for the spy, but he'd pocketed them in favor of a thanks and a what-I-don't-know-can't-hurt.

They came out of the alley to a set of stone stairs, and he pulled off his grimy wig. Then he grabbed her hand and a baseball cap that he shoved onto his head.

"What look are you going for, there, Tom Hanks? Because you look like you've been on a desert island for half a decade. Nice wig and beard."

He glanced at her. "I think there are things crawling in it. But I'm not the only one who needs a shower."

Her mouth opened.

He smiled and found his Panda at the bottom of the stairs, secluded in another tiny alleyway.

Opening the back door, he grabbed the Russian, still zonked—so hopefully still alive—and pulled him out, leaving him propped in a corner.

"How much sleepy juice did you give him?" Phoenix got into the front passenger side.

"The entire shot," Stein said as he slid into the driver's seat.

"He's breathing, right?"

"Had a pulse, so yes." The engine turned over. "You ready to get out of here?"

She looked at him, blinked hard, her mouth opening, and *shoot,* he flashed back to the words he'd spoken to her three years ago as they'd left their safe house in Krakow.

Right before his world had blown up.

And right before she'd betrayed him.

She nodded, and he ignored the terrible stone lodged in his chest.

That was then. This was now. Him—oh no—trusting her. Again. *Please, please . . .*

"Let's go back to my place," she said as he pulled out. "They don't know I'm gone yet. We have time, and I have security."

"I think we're living on borrowed time, but if it has a shower and grub, I'm in." He held up a fist.

She bumped it.

He drove them off the mountain, past the lush estates and wineries, to the farmlands on the outskirts of Sintra. Postcard country.

"Why Lisbon?" He glanced at her. She'd ridden in silence since they'd left Sintra. He noticed a fading bruise on her cheek and didn't want to ask about it.

"It's off the radar. Whenever people think about clandestine hubs, the last place they think is Lisbon. It's all London or Berlin or even Paris. Besides, I love the smell of the ocean."

"You live on the Tagus River."

"Close enough." She glanced at him. "For a girl who grew up in South Dakota, the ocean is any decent body of water."

He said nothing to her revelation about the life she'd had before joining an international spy ring. Once upon a time, she'd mentioned a single mom, moving around a lot. "Why didn't you contact your sister?"

Heavy sigh from the passenger seat. "I was afraid they'd trace the signal and . . ."

"And find her. And use her."

She nodded. "I mentioned the fading cell signal too, right? I had to make a choice."

"Harder to track an Internet search than a cell call."

"I didn't think they'd make any connection to you. You're still scrubbed from the Internet, thanks to your SEAL past."

"Maybe. Hopefully."

They'd reached the outskirts of Lisbon. "How do we get to your place?"

"Have we been followed?"

He glanced in the rearview mirror again. "Nope."

"I live near Bairro Alto." She directed him off the highway, into a neighborhood. They passed milky white stone and red-brick apartment buildings, the streets lined with olive and linden trees that bordered boulevards and parks. As they drove toward the center, the roads turned to cobblestone and the architecture went from modern to historic, the buildings more Renaissance and classical.

"I love the ancient architecture of Europe."

"Don't be fooled. These buildings are only two or three hundred years old. An earthquake and a tsunami wiped out the entire city back in the late seventeen hundreds. It's not Rome or anything."

"You talk like you're not from America. Admit it—everything in Europe is old."

She smirked, and he didn't know why the smile hung on to him, took root. *Hello. Just. An. Op.*

As in Operation Free Phoenix and Make Sure Declan's AI Program Hasn't Fallen into the Wrong Hands.

"Maybe that's why I like Lisbon. The city was completely destroyed and they rebuilt it from nothing. I like fresh starts."

Interesting. She directed him deeper into the city, finally pulling up to a creamy white Renaissance-style building with narrow Romanesque balconies and a clay-tile roof. A streetcar rang as it rumbled by them. The night arched high, cloudless, a thousand stars watching them.

He shut off the car. "You sure this is a good idea?"

She keyed in a code to a gated door. "My sister is a security expert. I promise—anyone tries to break in, we'll know. We'll be safe here."

He grabbed his burner phone, then a backpack from the back, and followed her inside a narrow entry, then up three flights of stairs to an apartment with a keyless entrance.

The inside was exactly like what he'd expect from a woman who lived out of a suitcase. Or a backpack.

Not a big place—the kitchen attached to the main room, with

two tall balcony doors that let in the darkness through sheer white linen drapes. A hallway with a door at the end, and one near the front. Wood floors, a black leather sectional, a round Formica table with two chairs, faux plants, and a bookcase. He set his backpack on the floor and walked over to the bookcase. It took up the entire wall, jammed full of books. "You read fantasy?"

"It's epic. And not real. And maybe I'd like a world where you could time travel or conjure up magic or even fly." She walked over to the kitchen and picked up a hot pot. "I'm making tea. I think there are probably biscuits in the pantry."

He picked up a book, paged through it. It was about a slave trying to reclaim his kingdom. That might be a story he could read. "You sound British."

"I'm anything I need to be." She set the pot on to boil. "Except clean. I'm going to hop into the shower." She pointed to the nearest bedroom. "There are two bedrooms, two bathrooms. Make yourself at home."

Just like that? "You sure one of us shouldn't stand watch?"

She pointed to a flat-panel screen on the wall in her kitchen. It showed four camera views—one from the balcony, one in the hallway outside her landing, one in the alleyway below her balcony, probably, and one near the front door. "I'll set the alarm. Don't worry—if it sounds, you'll have two minutes to grab a towel before anyone can get in." She winked.

Clearly, she'd shaken off the tremble from the dungeon on their drive into the city.

She headed down the hall to the bedroom in the back.

Okay then.

He found the room spare but clean, a double bed with a cotton blanket, a side table, a reading lamp, a wooden chair. And a full bathroom.

The heat of the shower turned his bones from brittle to revived. He pulled off the itchy fake beard, washed his face, shampooed out the itch from his hair, then pulled out his kit and shaved. He dumped the clothes in the garbage can, then found a clean pair of cargo pants and a T-shirt in his duffel.

Pulling them on, he stepped to the window and surveyed the view. The lights of the city burned, and he eased open the balcony door, let in the ocean—er, river—smells.

He could like it here. And maybe, once this was over—

Stop. So what if she'd clung to him? Of course she had—he would have been freaked out too if he'd been shoved into an underground hole on his way to Russia.

But it stayed with him, the shape of her body against his, the sense that she'd needed him.

Had reached out to him, *thank you very much*, in her hour of need.

He was brushing his teeth when he heard the beeping.

He spat and ran out into the hallway in his bare feet, his heart thundering.

Phoenix's door hung open at the end of the hall, the scent of a shower lingering in the air. The beeping emitted from the panel in the kitchen, and he walked over.

He'd triggered the alarm when he opened the balcony door, it seemed. "Phoenix!" No answer. He pressed reset.

The beeping died. And that's when he read the panel alert. *Street entrance accessed.*

"Phoenix?"

He turned, headed back to her room. Pushed the half-open door.

The bedside light splashed over a double bed, a canvas picture of the ocean on the wall. The scent of lavender lifted from the bathroom. He took a chance and looked inside.

Nothing except a wet towel hanging on a warmer, and her grimy clothing in the garbage can too.

He rounded and headed back to the flatscreen and rewound the feed.

And watched as Miss Thank You for Saving Me strolled right up to the door, keyed in her code, flung a backpack over her shoulder, and walked out into the night.

●————————————————●

He wouldn't even notice she was gone.

Emberly stood in the shadows, breathing in the city, the smell of simmering oil and seasoned pork seeping out into the darkness, the scents of pastries fresh from the ovens of late-night bakeries, and even the savory treats of prego and the chouriço assado ablaze at a vendor across the square. The city sang after dark—music from local cafés, streetcars clanging, people laughing at nearby bistros.

"Calm down, Nim. I'm fine."

Really. The shaking had stopped, mostly, and after a shower that loosened all the damp grime and potential crawlies from her hair and pores, she wasn't lying.

Mostly. Because in her apartment right now was trouble. Big trouble.

What had she been thinking, inviting Steinbeck, the man who only complicated—that should probably be in all caps—her life, into her . . . well, her *domain*?

Her secret flat.

Her safe space.

"Two months, Emberly. Two. *Months* since you went dark. I was out of my mind." Nimue's voice pinched tight and low, the way she got when life felt too big, when she had to find a way to corral it and reduce it to ones and zeros. To a computer program she could manipulate and control. The skills she'd acquired being a world-class white-hat hacker.

"I'm sorry. The Internet on the island cut out after the earth-quake—"

"Not an earthquake," Nimue said, a little more calm in her voice. "A landslide triggered by an explosion on the island. I looked into it."

Her sister was probably sitting on the porch of her beach house in Florida, the small cottage nestled in the seagrass and sand dunes, overlooking a silver-tipped ocean, the scent of salt in her shoulder-length brown hair. Dark freckles kissing her sandy-hued skin. And wearing a pair of cutoff jeans and a T-shirt that read *sudo rm -rf /**.

"Right. Well, then I hopped on a yacht. It belonged to Declan Stone and, of course, was attacked by Russian pirates," Emberly said as she walked toward a nearby food vendor.

"I don't think I can hear this."

"We got away—but then while I was rescuing Declan from Cuba—"

"Seriously?"

"I've been held for the last month by the Russian Mafia. But I'm okay. Steinbeck rescued me."

Silence. So long that—"Nim?"

"Steinbeck. Declan Stone's bodyguard. The Navy SEAL from Krakow. The guy you left for dead—"

"Yes, him. Okay. We sort of . . . became friends?" Yeah, that sounded weird, even to Emberly's ears.

Nimue echoed it. "Friends?"

"I don't know what we are," Emberly said as the man at the prego counter nodded at her, holding a couple of greasy wrapped pregos in papo seco rolls, slices of cheese melting from the ends. She had popped in an earbud and now dropped her phone into her pocket, paid and took the sandwiches. "It's a long story, but . . . listen, he rescued me. And he didn't have to, so I guess, yes. Friends." She garnished the sandwiches with mustard and garlic, then wrapped both of them in napkins and set them inside her backpack, along with the two cold bottles of pineapple Sumol.

"So now what?"

Now Emberly tried not to jump back into his arms, tried to put her head on straight and untangle the mess of this mission. "I still need to get Declan's program. For all I know, the Russians have it, and if they don't . . . well, it won't be long before some rogue nation gets their hands on it and uses it for their own nefarious purposes."

"Which means you need to develop the virus."

"Yes. In other words, back to the mission."

"And your next step?"

She sighed, waiting to cross the road. Lamplight puddled on the dark volcanic rock that lined the streets, and around her, from the cafés in the square, jazz spilled out, turning the night magical.

"I don't know. My guess is that the program is still with Declan. Maybe back in Mariposa. Maybe somewhere else."

The streetcar passed and the light changed, and she crossed the street, hugging the shadows as she walked up to her gated door. "I should have uploaded it directly to you when I broke into his safe on the island—"

"Hard to do when you're trapped underground."

"Details." She laughed. "I promise, when this is done, I'm coming to Florida."

"Good, because I'm learning how to surf. And I want to teach you too."

She punched in the code to her apartment entrance. "I don't know. You always loved the ocean more than I do."

"No, Em. You were the one who put this dream inside me. We'd lay in our tiny little bed and you'd tell me stories of how someday we'd have the sand in our toes, the salt on our lips."

She took the stairs up. "I blame that book I stole from the library—"

"*Island of the Blue Dolphins.* I still have it. Come and get it."

Emberly laughed. "I miss you."

"You can fix that. There's a bedroom here that's unused, just for you."

"Roger that. I'll be there as soon as I can."

"Don't make me wait another two months. I . . . was really scared."

Me too. Emberly stopped at the door. "I'll be okay, Nim. You know me. Survival over smarts."

"Em—"

"Gotta go. Love you." She clicked off before her throat tightened. Then she keyed in the code and opened the door.

An arm snagged around her waist, whisking her back from the door, which slammed behind her. Then Steinbeck pushed her against the wall. Clearly she was still off her game, because he had her cornered, just like that.

Stormy blue eyes, a grim slash to his mouth, and his breaths escaped as if—

"Wait. Were you worried?"

"Where were you?" He stood, one arm over her shoulder, his hand braced against the wall.

The other held his handgun.

"Um."

He was terribly close, the smell of his shower lifting off his skin. He'd shaved too, and cleaned up from that wretched beard, his hair tousled and dark blond again. He wore a white T-shirt that outlined his shoulders and his trim torso, and the way he looked at her turned her entire body into a snarl of . . .

Oops. Friend, friend, friend!

Except, why not? She'd kissed him before and—

"Are you trying to get yourself killed?"

She blinked at him, her gaze on his lips, then back on those intense blue eyes.

He seemed to notice, because his eyes roamed her face too. Then he swallowed, blew out a breath, and stepped back.

Because, friend.

Even *frenemy*, if he stood in her way of getting what she needed from Declan. To her knowledge, Stein didn't work for the billionaire anymore, but things could change while a girl was locked up on a ship.

"You . . ."

"I scared you?" She raised an eyebrow.

"No." His mouth tightened along the edges as he put the gun into his belt, in the back. "I thought . . ."

She stilled. *Oh.* "You thought I'd ditched you."

"It's happened before." He raised a shoulder. "Let's see, there was the ocean—"

"That was panic."

"And the shooting in Mariposa—"

"I dragged your body to the hospital!" She walked over, put her pack on the table.

"And—oh wait, the running part in Barcelona."

Her mouth pinched.

"And what about the dance floor at Boo's wedding?"

She grinned. "Who knew you were such a good dancer?"

"You took Declan's phone and slipped it into my pocket."

He was just *now* figuring that out?

"And we haven't even mentioned Krakow."

"Do we have to?" She opened the pack. "We've been over this. I had a mission to complete. Not to mention, I *tried* to get you away from danger."

Silence, and she glanced at him.

He stood in the dim light of her under-cupboard kitchen lights, a tired and raw expression darkening his face. She'd taken out the drinks and now set them on her table. Turned to him.

Swallowed.

He took a breath, and the look in his eyes matched the urge inside her, the woman who really just wanted to eat a prego with the man under a star-strewn Lisbon sky and forget . . .

"I'm sorry."

He blinked, raised an eyebrow. "What?"

"I'm sorry I, uh . . . left you. I had to call my sister. And I got us steak sandwiches." She pulled out the napkin-wrapped street food. "Except they're a little flattened, thank you so much, Jason Bourne."

He frowned, then took the proffered sandwich. "You got food?"

She grabbed a bottle opener and her own sandwich, then opened the balcony door. "Of course. I know you."

He made a little grunt, which made her smile as she stepped over the doorframe onto the narrow space and sat on the concrete on one end.

He came out and squeezed himself down on the other end, his legs crossed in front of him.

She crossed her legs on the other side of his and spread out their dinner. "I hope you like mustard."

He bit into the sandwich, made a sound of hunger and delight that did strange things to her insides. "This is fantastic. Reminds me of a panino con la salamella—it's a sandwich with onions and peppers made from salamella, a sort of sausage—"

"From northern Italy. I'm familiar with it." She took a bite. "And you're right. Although it's not as good as manti from—"

"Kazakhstan."

"Almaty?" She lifted her bottle of Sumol in a toast.

He met her bottle with a clink. "Astana."

"While you were on the teams?"

He lifted the bottle to his mouth and said nothing. But his blue eyes sparked.

Oh, maybe this was a bad, very bad idea. They couldn't be teammates, especially not friends. She did not have room in her life for

Mr. Devastating Blue Eyes. "I remember you saying you missed being an operator, back in Cuba, when we were staking out the embassy."

He cocked his head.

"I had a lot of time to think while I crossed the deep blue sea." She took another bite.

His mouth tightened. "It's going to kill me, but I have to know, Phoenix. How badly—"

She held up her hand. "Listen. After they figured out I didn't know anything—or wasn't going to give them anything—they locked me in a room at the estate and left me alone. Same with the boat. I just had the one scuffle, during which I grabbed the phone."

He considered her, the slightest pull in his jaw. But he nodded. Set his sandwich down. "I should not have left you in Cuba."

"You need to let that go. I *told* you to leave. You had Declan and your sister to protect. I knew I could take care of myself." She swallowed when she said it, however, because—

"I know."

She looked up at the stars, sighed. Looked back at him. "Listen. You didn't have to come for me. And I don't know why you did, but . . ." She nodded. "This isn't over, Steinbeck. I need that program. And—"

"I know."

She stilled.

"I get it. After . . ." His mouth tightened. "After we left you in Cuba, we got back on the yacht only to have it be overrun with Russians—"

"Tomas said it exploded."

He raised an eyebrow.

"The Petrov boss and I had a chatty-chat down at the wharf. You might have caught it on video."

"Right. And yes. Declan and I blew up his yacht. Got lost at sea for a day or so."

"Austen?"

"Safe."

She leaned back. Exhaled.

"What you don't know is that Declan wasn't a bad guy, just like I said."

She eyed him.

"He was working with the Caleb Group."

Her mouth opened. "No. No, he wasn't—"

Stein held up a hand. "Absolute truth. He hijacked the ship with the obsidite the Russians stole from the island and routed it to a processing plant in America."

"Not a terrorist."

"Not. A terrorist."

She gave him a wry smile. "Okay, but we still need that program. It can still fall into the wrong hands, including the United States'. I can't let the US be the only country that has access to the virus that can shut down his AI program."

"Agreed."

She stared at him. "Okay, did you get hit in the head when the yacht blew up?"

He met her gaze then, and under the velvety dark sky, the stars shining in his eyes . . .

A beat of silence fell between them, thunderous. She swallowed. *Friends.* Maybe comrades in arms.

His voice turned a little rough when he finally spoke. "I came for you because I couldn't . . . because the thought of something happening to you—"

"Stop, Stein. Just—" She shook her head. "It can't work." Oh, now *her* voice roughened. "In a different life . . ."

He stared at her for so long that she thought maybe he hadn't heard her. Then, softly, "What kind of different life?"

His gaze made her entire body ache. "A life where . . . when I look at you, I don't see my mistakes. The things I've done. And where you don't look at me and see . . . regret. And anger. And . . . the truth is, I'm just not built for anything real, Stein. I'm not a team player. I'm a solo act. And I'm built to survive. That's all. I should have told you that from the beginning. But—"

"But in the beginning, you were just trying to survive."

She nodded.

He swallowed, sighed, his chest rising and falling, the lights of the city sparkling around them. "So was I. But . . . I don't know. Maybe we can figure out how to get past survival together?"

Did he not hear her?

"Stein—"

The alarm shrieked, a blaring shot into the night, and she jumped to her feet.

"Two minutes," he said and took off for his room.

She looked down into the alleyway. Nothing amiss. Sweeping up her pack, she took off for her room.

From a shelf in her closet, she retrieved her go bag and a tactical vest, then climbed onto her bed, pushed aside the canvas picture, and sprung open the latch that revealed the compartment behind it.

She grabbed one of the two Glock 19s and a SIG Sauer P226. Shoved them into her tactical vest.

Stein came charging in. "You have a bunker above your bed?" He snatched up the other Glock. "You do realize how sexy that is, right?"

She stared at him, her eyes wide, and he grinned, winked. "One survivor to the next." He grabbed a radio from her stash in the compartment and tossed it to her, then the other. "Let's roll."

He took off down the hallway, stopped at the door while she checked the monitor. A man stood in the hallway. And he was armed.

"C'mon. We'll take the balcony." She headed for the doors, opening her ottoman on the way.

"You have a fire ladder."

She nodded, turned, and headed outside. Hooked the ladder on the side of the rail and let it fall.

"Let's—"

He wasn't behind her.

She stepped back inside and stilled as she watched Steinbeck unlatch the door, stand back, and let the enemy into her home.

THREE

S TEIN WASN'T A TOTAL IDIOT. OF COURSE HE had his SIG Sauer out as he opened the door. Not for the man on the other side, but for the unknown woman who'd stepped up behind him.

Mid-thirties, maybe, brown eyes, blonde hair pulled back, wearing a black jacket, a pair of black pants, she held her own weapon, although she now tucked it away under her jacket.

"What are you doing here?" Stein said to Roy as the man lowered his gun and held up a hand. The dim hall light half obscured the man's features, but Stein had glanced at the flatscreen in the kitchen and made out Roy's outline, and maybe just in time, because Phoenix had fully planned on flinging herself over the balcony's edge.

And he would have been right behind her, casting himself fully into her chaos.

"Maybe we can figure out how to get past survival together?"

Yeah, he'd said that. Not sure why, but really, *really*, he didn't want this life.

Honest. Cross his heart and . . . well, all the things.

His words to Jack even filtered back. *"I just need to find her. Make sure she's safe. That's all."*

Clearly that wasn't all, because yes, here he was, gun in hand, ready to go mano y mano with whoever stood on the other side of the door.

The woman behind Roy said, "I need to talk to Emberly."

Who?

Oh. Phoenix. And it might be another alias, but it felt weirdly real. Right. She just kept reappearing, reigniting the fire inside him.

Not to mention rare and beautiful.

He turned just in time to see Phoenix-Emberly charge him from the balcony. "What are you doing?" she shouted.

Roy walked into the room and she stepped back, pulled her Glock.

"Phoenix! It's Roy—don't shoot." Stein held up his hand and stepped in front of Roy.

Phoenix—no, *Emberly*—hesitated for a second, her green-eyed gaze hard on Roy.

Then the blonde entered, and Emberly's mouth opened, her eyes widened. "What are you doing here?"

He glanced at the duo and shut the door. "Okay, everybody just calm down. Ph—Emberly, this is Roy." Maybe she needed the Emberly name as cover. He didn't know—but he didn't want to blow it.

And now she directed her gaped look at Steinbeck. "How—"

"That's on me, Em," said the blonde. "I dropped your real name."

Real name. Oh, he knew it.

Emberly finally lowered her gun. "Oh joy." She set the gun on a nearby side table. "Again, my question. Why are you here, Mystique? And with—" She gestured to Roy. "Thanks, by the way."

Dark hair, tall, a former operator according to Colt, Roy had a quiet presence, a solemn sturdiness, and now just nodded.

"We have a problem," Mystique said.

Steinbeck cut a look at Emberly, who put her hands on her hips and backed up, a set to her jaw. "Yeah, we do. Never mind that you would have let me be shipped off to a Russian gulag—"

"You went off-grid. And you know the rules."

Rules? What rules?

Emberly nodded, a tiny pinch on the side of her mouth.

"But I am glad Roy and . . ." Mystique glanced at Stein.

"Steinbeck Kingston," he said, filling in the gap.

She frowned for just a second, then nodded. "Right. Boo's brother."

Huh?

Then she turned back to Emberly. "I'm glad they got you out. You're okay?"

"I'll live," she said and took off her backpack. Then she stepped onto the balcony and reeled in the fire ladder.

Roy had walked farther into the room and now stood, arms akimbo.

Steinbeck turned to him. "How'd you find us?"

"Mystique reached out. She heard via Logan about our op. You run into any trouble?"

"No." Which maybe seemed a little odd but, "You get a tail on Tomas?"

"Yes. He boarded a flight for Moldova a few hours ago."

"Moldova?" This from Emberly.

"It's the new HQ for the Petrov Bratva," said Mystique. Pretty, she exuded a disarming calmness and bore a hint of a British accent. The strangest sense of familiarity about her nudged him.

Wait—she knew *Boo*? Which meant—"Were you at my sister's wedding?"

"Right. That's where I know you from."

"I don't—"

"I'm on your sister's Air One Rescue team," she said and gave a wry smile. "Day job."

"That's a thing?"

"For some of us." She glanced at Emberly. "Some of us can compartmentalize, separate our lives."

And some couldn't.

"In a different life . . ."

A *completely* different life, maybe. Because he got it. He'd always been an all-in, get-the-job-done guy too, unable to make room for anything but the mission.

Emberly dropped the ladder back into its spot in the ottoman. Then she turned to Mystique. "What's on fire now?"

Mystique's expression turned grim. "Luis is missing."

Luis?

"What do you mean *missing*?" Emberly said.

"His panic alarm went off two days ago. I arrived yesterday and got ahold of the video footage. Looks like the Bratva might have taken him. We saw them entering his home."

"Why?"

Wait—"Our Luis?" Stein said to Emberly. It might take him a millisecond or two to get used to that name. He rather preferred Phoenix. Emberly made her . . . well, maybe down-to-earth. Even vulnerable.

And only fed the *maybe* inside him.

She raised a brow to his words. "*Our* Luis?"

"You know what I mean."

She nodded, her mouth quirking. "Yes. Our Luis."

The Portuguese computer scientist they'd fought over in Krakow.

"He was living up in Porto, under our protection," Mystique said.

Steinbeck remembered her name now. "London," he said. "You were with a guy—"

"Shep, yes," she said and turned back to Emberly. "We think the Bratva got their hands on Axiom, or maybe a version of it—"

"How? I promise it was destroyed."

"Maybe there's a leak in the DOD," Stein said. "I know Declan sold it to them."

London-Mystique held up her hand. "It doesn't matter. The truth is, it's not when the program gets out into the wild, it's how many governments will get their hands on it."

"We need that virus," Emberly said quietly.

"Yes," London said, now perching on the arm of the sofa. "Which means we need the program."

"And Luis." Emberly folded her arms. "You think they're forcing him to corrupt it?"

"I don't know. But we'll find him. I'm on that." She pointed to Emberly. "You need to get that program from Declan."

"Wait a hot minute," Steinbeck said. "You're not suggesting another heist, right? How about we just *ask* him for the program?" He shot a look at Roy. "He was Dark Horse. Alosha. The infamous spy who took down the Russian cybertech lab in Vladivostok."

Roy nodded. "Yes, he was. Still is."

"Wait. What? I don't know who—" Emberly looked at London. "You said he was a terrorist."

"To be fair, we didn't realize that the Caleb Group had reactivated his cover and had pulled him in to spy on the Bratva when you set out to get the program," London said.

Steinbeck glanced at Roy.

Roy held up a hand. "I'm just a chess piece. I don't control the board."

As opposed to Steinbeck, who clearly watched from the gallery. "Okay, so we get the program and then what?"

"*Emberly* gets the program," London said. "You go home."

His mouth opened. Closed. "Over my dead body."

"That's what I'm trying to prevent." London took a breath, shook her head. "The last thing I want is for Boo to lose her brother."

"You're kidding me, right? I was a *SEAL*. She's well aware of the risks."

London's mouth tightened. "You haven't been vetted—"

"I was Declan's bodyguard. I have top-secret clearance. And I sprang Miss Pants on Fire here from a Russian dungeon. I feel like that qualifies for vetted." And yes, he meant to raise his voice.

Aw, who was he kidding? Since Emberly had stepped back into his life, and he into hers, something had awakened inside him. No, *ignited.*

Phoenix, indeed. She was a live coal inside him, and he wasn't going to let it die.

And *that* he didn't want to look at too closely. "Listen. Clearly she needs someone watching her back—"

"What?"

"And Declan trusts me." He glanced at Emberly.

"That hurts."

"He works for the Caleb Group," London said. "He'll give us Axiom."

"Maybe," Stein said. "But let's remember that Emberly attacked him in Barcelona—"

"That's a little overstated." She rolled her eyes.

He ignored her. "And even if Declan does hand over Axiom—what if the Russians don't have the program? They could be watching her." He cast a look at Roy. "Maybe that's why we walked away so easily from Sintra."

Silence.

"Black Swans work alone," Emberly said softly.

He met her green eyes. "Not anymore."

Her jaw tightened as she looked away.

"We'll track down Luis," said London. "You guys get Axiom."

"Then what?" Steinbeck said.

"Stay out of trouble and wait to hear from us."

"You *have* met her, right?" He grinned when her mouth opened.

London laughed. "Try not to kill each other."

"Been there, done that," Stein growled.

Emberly folded her arms, shook her head. "He's slow. And annoying. And—"

"And just maybe, Emberly Hart, you've met the one man who can keep up with you. Try to keep him alive." London pointed at Stein. "Don't make me regret this."

"Mystique—"

"You either," London said as she turned back to Emberly. "I don't want to lose one of my best operatives, so try to play nicely."

Emberly rolled her eyes.

"I'm not sure where Declan is," Steinbeck said. "My guess is Minnesota."

"Great," London said. "I'll arrange a flight for you in the morning. Check into the server for details. And get some sleep." She turned to Roy. "Let's go."

Roy smirked and clamped Stein on the shoulder as he left. "Heaven save us from Black Swans."

Stein locked the door behind them. Turned. "Emberly?"

She sighed. "Phoenix to you, bub."

"That's what you think."

A beat, then she picked up her backpack. "I'm going to bed. But . . ." She also picked up her handgun. "Next time, maybe you let me shoot them."

He laughed as she closed the door at the end of the hallway.

Then he grabbed the pillow off the bed and set up a perch on the sofa.

Just in case.

●————————————●

Her new teammate had full, enviably long eyelashes a woman would die for, dark and closed against his handsome face. Frankly, he might be *too* handsome, because she needed a guy who didn't attract attention, blended in.

More, Stein exuded *warrior*. Even fully asleep, he still possessed a lethal energy, strength captured but not at rest.

Like this morning, when Emberly had walked out of her bedroom and found him sprawled on the sofa, one foot on the floor as if poised to run.

After her, maybe. So much for trust, although that had never been a thing between them. Except briefly, maybe in Cuba, staking out the embassy. A dangerous liaison, destined for pain.

No, this was not going to end well.

He'd awakened abruptly just by her soft footfalls on the wooden floor, sat up fully alert, and she'd raised her hands with an "It's me, Phoenix" at the threat in his eyes.

Maybe he'd been having a nightmare. She'd tossed a few hours away staring at the ceiling and reliving the past month in her blotchy dreams.

"Emberly," he'd said, and she'd decided to wage that war later as she made coffee.

He'd taken the proffered cup once it finished seeping in the French press and now took it out to the balcony, leaning a hip on the railing.

She joined him, refusing to think about last night, the moment of maybes on the balcony.

Maybe was too far away for either of them to consider.

"I got Mystique's message. She arranged a flight out in a couple hours."

"Private plane? And for the record, I know her as London."

"The Swans have resources. Mystique is her code name, but yes, I know her as London too."

He nodded, staring past her toward the square and maybe beyond, to the sea. The sky arched azure and cloudless above them, and in the golden tones of the morning, he seemed impossibly tan, his eyes terribly blue, and all she could hear was *"Swans work alone."*

This could be a very bad idea. It was one thing to worry about Nimue and some rogue player rounding back on her and enacting some kind of personal vengeance.

Completely another to let her heart get tied up with someone who . . . Well, she didn't mind risking her own life, but . . .

"This isn't going to work."

He glanced at her, frowned. "Believe me, sweetheart, I can keep up with you."

"Oh great, now we're in a spitting contest."

"You did say I was slow."

"And don't forget annoying."

His mouth opened, but she held up her hand. "Just . . . don't get hurt."

He raised an eyebrow, but she left him there and headed to her room. An hour later, he waited for her by the door. They grabbed an Uber and headed to Cascais Municipal Aerodrome.

She didn't know who actually owned the Gulfstream G650, but with only her and Steinbeck as passengers, she found herself on one long sofa, Stein on the other. Where he'd stretched out and fallen dead asleep, finally, to the world.

She didn't want to believe that he'd only relaxed because he knew she couldn't ditch him.

He did make for an interesting study as he slept. Clearly he'd worked himself back into shape after the devastating accident in Krakow—she'd seen that, of course, over the past eight-plus months and definitely when they were on the run in Cuba. He didn't even seem phased by the gunshot wound from this past summer—and frankly, at the time, she had worried that he might expire waiting for help outside the Mariposa clinic.

She put her hands to her lips, the whisper of his kiss still lingering there.

Oh boy. She sighed, got up, made coffee, helped herself to a protein bar, and okay, might have been trying to figure out how she could ditch him, when he roused. Sat up, scrubbed his face, and stood.

"I'm going to need an IV of that coffee."

She glanced up at him. Whiskers scraped across his chin, his hair was tousled, a sort of sleepy warmth radiating off him.

"All I have are mugs," she said and found one in the cupboard. Poured him coffee. "And a peanut butter protein bar."

He took the bar. Read the ingredients. "I could have a Snickers bar for all the protein in this." But he opened the wrapper. "I'd prefer ramen."

She blinked at him. "You remember."

He smiled. "Your obsession with Snickers bars? Yes. And by the way, best ramen I've ever eaten was in Poland."

His smile hit her entire body like sunshine and warmed her all the way to her core.

Oh my.

She managed to nod, to swallow, and made a beeline back to the sofa.

He followed, sat opposite her. Blew on his coffee, softly, gently, the cup cradled between his hands. "I liked that trick—milk and a piece of cheese in the ramen."

"My mom used to make it that way." Now she was telling him stories? *Stop*—"She had a dozen different ways to make ramen. Learned it from one of her boyfriends."

She couldn't seem to contain herself.

"My favorite was Ernesto. He made the best pizza. He worked at a restaurant where my mom waitressed, and sometimes on the weekends, he'd make me and Nim—"

Her breath caught.

Stein sat listening, no reaction to the name-drop of her sister.

"—my sister, personal pizzas. Sometimes he made faces with the pepperoni."

"My mom did that for us on family movie nights," he said quietly.

She'd bet their family movie night looked a lot different from hers.

"Yeah, well, she caught him cheating on her with a different waitress, kicked him out, and we didn't eat pizza for years after that."

He raised an eyebrow.

"My mom was . . . she struggled."

"Struggled?"

"Alcohol, drugs, boyfriends . . . Nimue and I learned early to . . ."

"Survive." He met her eyes.

She lifted a shoulder.

"Nimue. I've never heard of that name."

"It's after the Lady of the Lake, who gave Arthur Excalibur."

"Really?"

"Nimue's dad was a professor of English at Black Hills State University. I don't remember him, but Mom had pictures. He died in a motorcycle accident."

"And your dad?"

"A smokejumper, back in the day when Mom was obsessed with firefighters. She lived for a while in a town in Montana called Ember. Hence . . . the name."

"Emberly." He said it softly, and hearing it from him that way unlatched something forbidden inside her.

No. She did not want to be known—

"Don't panic. I can call you Phoenix if you want."

"I wasn't panicking—"

"You were. You have a tell. Your eyes sort of widen, just for a second, and the tiny gold flecks in your eyes flash. It's totally panic." He took a sip of his coffee. "Why don't you like the name Emberly?"

"I . . . Emberly is a dreamer and the person I can be when I don't have to look over my shoulder." She drew in a breath. "It's been a very long time since I saw myself as Emberly."

"Your handler does."

"That's because she knew me back when I started. She likes to remind me of who I was, I think."

"Who were you?"

"Eager. Hopeful. I saw a chance at a new life, and I grabbed it."

"Why did you need a new life?"

"You're very nosy."

"It's a nine-hour flight."

"You already slept through half of it there, Sleeping Beauty."

One side of his mouth lifted. "Listen, I get it." He leaned back. "Fair is fair—ask me anything."

Outside, the clouds tufted around them, jockeying for space, the sunlight falling onto the ocean below, an endless blue. She looked back at him. "If you could do anything, restart your life, what would you do?"

He shrugged. "Nothing."

"Not even shoot me and not look back?"

His mouth opened. Closed. "What?"

"I cost you everything, Stein. Your SEAL career. It's because you trusted me. And yet here you are . . . " She shook her head.

He stared at his coffee, back at her, his shoulders rising and falling. "Okay, yes, I hated you. I hated that you betrayed me, and maybe . . . somewhere deep inside I don't trust you."

"Wow. That's . . . Maybe let's go back to talking about food."

His mouth made a grim smile. "Fail early, fail often, but always fail forward."

"SEAL talk?"

"Grover Kingston. My dad loved to quote John Maxwell."

"And this is you failing forward?"

"Maybe I don't want everything we've been through to be for nothing." He took another sip of coffee. "Besides. I think you *are* trustworthy, Emberly Hart. More than you want to admit."

She made a face. "So you'd change nothing?"

He met her eyes, held them. "I'd change the moment in Cuba when I let you go."

And what was she supposed to do with that? She set her coffee down, crossed her legs. "I needed a new life because my old one was going to land me in jail. Or get me killed."

He didn't move.

She sighed. "I started stealing from my mom's boyfriends when I was seven. At first, just coins, then a few dollars. By the time I was ten, I was figuring out how to use their credit cards online. Nimue learned fast—that's probably how she learned her hacker skills." She sighed. "We moved around a lot, and my mom got a little desperate for money. She started working for our landlord for rent . . . " She made a face.

Steinbeck drew in a breath, leaned back. "She ever bring any of her clients home?"

"No. But he held on to her money. And I figured he probably owed her more than what the rent was, so I decided to collect. I broke into his office one night, and it triggered a silent alarm. Nimue activated the fire alarm and helped me escape, but I realized that it wouldn't be long before I did something that really got her in trouble. I left home a few days later."

He'd fixed his gaze on her, unmoving, a sort of compassion in his expression.

"Nimue was removed from my mom's custody and spent the next three years in foster care while I tried to figure out how I could rescue her."

"And did you?"

"Yes. I lived in Rapid City and hooked up with a gang of bikers who weren't as dangerous as you might think. I learned how to pickpocket tourists, and in exchange for the cash, they kept me away from the cops, gave me a place to sleep, and . . . well, I pocketed my share of the money, ran credit cards, and basically learned the ways of a thief."

He didn't even flinch. *Huh.*

"When I turned eighteen, I came back for Nim. I'd purchased a secondhand pickup with a camper bed—not anything fancy, but enough for us to leave Rapid City. We got as far as a rest area south of Nashville when the entire rig just sort of blew up. The radiator exploded, the head cooked, and there we were, broke and a couple of teenagers with nothing. I saw my life spooling out like my mother's, and . . . I got desperate."

She drew up her knees, wrapped her arms around them. "A family had stopped at the rest area to walk their dog—there was a whole horde of kids. And they were traveling in this conversion van, and I don't know why but I thought, yeah, that was a good idea. So I dragged Nim over to the van, jumped in, and . . ."

"You stole the car."

She nodded.

"That's grand theft."

"Yeah."

She didn't know why her eyes filled. *Sheesh,* she'd put this so far behind her. Maybe because, "I was caught. And then the man, the dad, Boz Davidson, whose van we stole . . ." She looked at Stein. "He lied. He said that he'd given permission for us to use it. That he'd made a mistake and didn't realize we'd taken it. I don't know why—but he made up this story. He even said that we were his foster children." She shook her head. "He bought us dinner. Asked where we were going."

"Where were you going?"

"Florida. The ocean. I read this book to Nim when we were kids. I stole it from the library—"

He laughed. And it wasn't harsh or brutal, just a chuckle. "We all have a library-book theft in our background."

Oh. But his laughter burrowed into her, loosened the story's terrible grip. "It was called *Island of the Blue Dolphins*. It's about a girl who spent eighteen years alone on an island off California. It sort of made us—*me*—believe that I could survive on my own." She sighed. "And maybe I could have, but I had Nim, so . . ."

"What happened?"

"Mr. and Mrs. Davidson took us in. See, he really was a foster parent—all those kids weren't his. But they were, sort of, because he treated Nim and me like we were too. He was—is—a good man. Raised horses. Lived on a farm. It was perfect . . . "

Silence, and in it, too many memories, so she sighed. "I stayed for a while, but in the end I was too angry and scared and I . . ." She shook her head. "I left Nim there, and I ran. Boz caught up with me. And instead of bringing me back to the farm, he introduced me to a man named Pike Maguire. He founded the Black Swans."

"How old were you?"

"Nineteen. And suddenly, I had a job and a future and a sister-hood, and I became a Swan."

"And you never looked back."

Never? But she nodded. "So, see. Emberly is . . . complicated, and broken and needy, and Phoenix is strong and capable and . . ."

"A survivor." He had finished his coffee. He considered her. "But it's Emberly who gave Phoenix the skills and courage to be the Swan she is today."

She had nothing for that as he went to the kitchen area and re-filled his mug. When he returned, he held a couple bags of Doritos. Tossed one to her. "Here you go, partner."

She caught it. Stared at him. "You did hear me, right? I don't do . . . partners. Look at what happened in Cuba—already you're regretting our . . . whatever that was."

"Teamwork." He crunched a chip. "And that's not what I regret."

He had such piercing eyes, she had to look away.

"This is going to end badly," she said softly, almost to herself.

"As long as I don't get blown up, we'll be fine."

She looked at him and must have worn horror on her face, because he grinned.

Oh, for the—"Stein. Don't kid yourself. Sure, we have . . . moments."

He raised one sexy eyebrow.

"But this"—she gestured between them—"you, me. We can't work. We're like—"

"Fireworks." He put a chip in his mouth.

"I was going to say a cluster bomb. With lots of shrapnel and internal injuries."

"That's dramatic."

"How about this?" She leaned forward and enunciated each word. "It. Can't. Work. Steinbeck."

He stopped, a chip halfway to his mouth. "Don't make that bet quite yet, *Emberly*." Then he winked.

She leaned back and looked out the window. Hated the way his wink stirred up all the wrong feelings.

Very wrong, inconvenient feelings.

He grinned at her, still crunching.

Oh, this was going to be a long, very long, trip.

"There's no need for a blindfold."

Harper stood in the opening of the oversized garage in the town of Duck Lake, the early September night warm on her skin, stars winking overhead.

"I don't want you to peek." Jack stood behind her, his soft voice close to her ear, casting over her, raising just the right amount of tingles.

Tonight was the night, she knew it in her soul, and when Jack had shown up on her doorstep, showered, shaved, smelling like a man with a plan, yeah, this was *it*.

He was going to propose. *Finally and hallelujah.*

Although she might have picked a picnic by the lake or on the dock of his family's lakeside inn. Maybe in town, a fancy dinner at the Paddle House.

Or they could have flown down to his place in Melbourne Beach, and he could have bent the knee in the sand, the ocean as witness.

She'd even have been thrilled if he'd simply popped the question on the patio of her mother's home, where she was staying. With Phillipa gone on a cruise, it was the perfect setting for such a moment.

But okay, the garage where they'd spent the better part of almost nine months would be Just. Fine.

Maybe it was symbolic. The start of their life together on the steps of Flo, their—no, Jack's—1970s-era mint-green city bus, restored to be a home on wheels. But she'd expended enough sanding, painting, and general sweat equity in the monster to call it hers too.

Besides, when Jack had first shown it to her, he'd said . . . well, he'd said magic words to her. *"Someday, Harper Malone, I'm hoping you'll be my wife."*

Not a proposal, of course. Because that would come with a real question, but . . .

Except he hadn't brought it up again. Not once during all the hours they'd overhauled the engine (although she had learned the difference between a carburetor and a fuel injector and how to adjust the valve clearances). Not when they'd installed the kitchen cupboards and redone the plumbing (although she had learned how to install a new kitchen faucet). And not once when they'd run all-new electrical through the bus and he'd asked her opinion on where to hang the flatscreen television. He'd even taken her suggestion on adding shiplap to the kitchen walls, installing a retro lime-green Frigidaire refrigerator, and adding a bench with a hidden tabletop that converted into a queen bed.

He'd installed the queen bed, painted the walls her suggested hazy mint green, and even added a laundry area—also her idea—behind the wet room while she'd been in New York City meeting her new publisher, so that felt promising.

Still. Not a word. Maybe he'd wanted to surprise her.

"Okay, careful now." He guided her, his strong hands on her shoulders, into the garage, rich with the scent of sawdust, diesel from a rest test of the engine, and even burnt coffee, a hazard of Jack's tendency to overfocus on a project.

"I won't trip. I know this place by heart," Harper said. The workbench along the long wall with all his woodworking tools, not to mention the bench mechanic's box on wheels. And on the other side of the bus, almost a living area, with a couple of worn floral-patterned overstuffed chairs he'd gotten from a discard pile at an estate sale. He spent hours in the garage after work at the King's Inn, reading, planning, sketching. Thinking.

No one would have the faintest idea that Jack possessed a portfolio in the seven digits, a beachside home, and lived off his investments.

Then again, he'd landed a bestseller years ago, back when he'd wanted to be a lawyer, and had cracked the case of a Minnesota girl gone missing. It had ignited the remodel of his first bus and too many years on the road, searching for lost souls.

And running from her.

But he'd returned and was building them a second chance.

She'd probably been too absent recently, finishing her second book and helping Penelope, a.k.a. Penny Pepper, on research for her murder podcast. A cold case, now solved, of a serial killer in Alaska.

"Yes, but tonight is different." He moved her over to the bus—she knew that much—but then brought her all the way to the back. Strange backdrop for a proposal, but . . .

But she'd marry Jack regardless of where he proposed. Tropical beach, lakeside picnic, or in the metal garage, in front of an old city bus.

"Stay." He moved away from her, and she heard wood creaking.

"Okay. Take off your blindfold."

Admittedly, she'd expected him on one knee, in front of her, a ring box open, so when she took off the handkerchief and spotted him standing in front of a folded ladder that led to the top of the bus . . .

Okay, her shocked expression felt justified.

Jack grinned at her. "I made a rooftop verandah."

Oh. But she conjured up a smile. "Nice."

"Yeah. So, the stairs are strapped to the back, and they simply fold down, and then you access the verandah from the rear. C'mon." He held out his hand.

Okay, so maybe this was the moment. He certainly grinned at her, his beautiful blue eyes shining, as if he had a secret. And he did seem a little gussied up tonight—a clean flannel shirt, his hair just a little long and curly, wet from being freshly washed. And oh, he smelled good, a little bit of cologne lifting from his skin.

Truth—she'd do just about anything for this man.

So she took his hand and climbed the stairs—probably silly of her to have put on a dress, but . . . *engagement, right?*

He stood back as if to protect her modesty, and she climbed up and found a small deck platform secured to the top, and on it, a thick foam cushion, a bucket of ice, and a bottle of champagne.

Bam. *See?*

And sure, no stars sparkled overhead, just the girders of the garage, but maybe he feared it would rain?

Whatever.

He climbed up and sat next to her on the cushion. "What do you think?"

"It's . . . fun."

"Yeah, it is. Imagine lying up here at night, watching the stars." He reached for the champagne, the top already popped. "It's nonalcoholic. I know you don't love the real stuff."

Sweet. She lifted the two plastic stem glasses, and he poured out the bubbly. Felt like maybe they should wait until after the proposal, but . . .

He set the bottle back in the ice and took a glass. Turned to her.

Sometimes she felt like she was back in high school, falling hard for Big Jack, the eldest of the Kingston family. Swept up by his intensity, the sense of bold adventure that emanated from him. And sure, he'd broken her heart once upon a time, but a girl never forgot her first love.

And Jack would always and forever be her first and only love.

He lifted his glass. "Bee. I never would have finished this project without your help. Your insights, your opinions, so many hours helping me overhaul the engine and fix the brakes and wire the bus, adding cabinetry and benches, painting . . . It's better than I could have imagined."

He was talking about them, not the bus, right?

"And I want to thank you."

Oh. "Absolutely, Jack. I mean . . . Flo is . . . she's something special."

"Yes, she is." His gaze held hers. "Just like you."

Okay, that was a little romantic. Sappy, but he'd never been a poet. A wannabe lawyer, maybe, which translated to him knowing what to say at the right time. She'd take it. "Thanks."

He tapped her glass with his, then leaned forward and kissed her. Sweetly, lingering. Then he leaned back and took a sip. Set his glass on the rooftop deck.

Looked at her, his blue eyes twinkling. "Okay. So I need to ask you a question."

Her heart thumped. She set down her glass too. He took her hand.

"It's important. It's permanent and it's . . . well, I feel like it's a decision we need to make together."

Well, clearly. But she just smiled.

He blew out another breath. *C'mon,* it wasn't *that* scary. She'd been an all-in *yes* and *about time, Jack* for a few months now.

Maybe a few years.

"Would you consider . . ."

She held her breath.

"Naming the bus?"

She blinked at him. "What?"

"I mean, I know that we've been calling her Flo and that I nixed the Power Flowers, but you never really liked Flo and . . . well, I need to get new license plates, and I wanted to buy custom plates. But, you know, it's a big decision. Permanent registration and . . ." He was still grinning. "And I was thinking we could come up with a new name together."

What?

Seriously?

She looked away, hating the terrible fist in her chest, and what— now her eyes burned? *C'mon, Jack—*

He still had hold of her hand. And she didn't want to be a jerk, but . . . *whatever.*

Her breath hitched. "I think Flo is . . . fine."

"Really?" He released her hand. "I got the distinct impression that you weren't a fan of Flo."

"Flo is a great name. I mean . . . why not?" She needed to leave, but she didn't want to take off in an all-out run.

Okay, maybe she did, but she needed a ride home and . . .

"I think Flo is perfect." She forced a smile. "You know, I need to get back home. I'm on the last couple scenes of my book, and my deadline is this weekend."

"What about the state fair?"

The fair. Right. "I don't know, Jack, I—"

"Please? Austen is coming home, and the whole family is going. And I thought I'd take Flo for a test drive this weekend."

She found herself nodding. Glancing past him to the steps. "Sure. Fine."

"I need to make sure she's running well before she hits the road." He took another sip of their fake champagne. Just like their fake future.

She didn't know what to think, really. And suddenly, it just felt so . . . raw. And maybe desperate to ask him . . . *Am I going with you?*

Nope. She wasn't the lovestruck high schooler who'd sorta, maybe, a little, tricked him into kissing her so many summers ago. Paved a road of regrets.

She refused to force his hand. Because then, well, how would she know if she was truly the one?

So . . . "Jack, I really need to get back to work. With Mom gone, the house is quiet and—"

He frowned. "Sure."

He got up and helped her as she climbed down the ladder. Landed beside her. No blindfold needed as she headed back outside to his Geo.

She got in, grateful for the darkness. *Don't cry. Don't—*

"You okay?" He pulled out of the lot, heading toward the King's Inn and her mom's cottage, located next door.

"Yep." Oh, she sounded strained. She swallowed. "Just . . . thinking about my next scene."

"It must be romantic. I know how you get when you're working on a romantic scene."

He looked over at her, and she caught his wink. "Need to act it out?"

A spear in her heart, despite the humor in his voice.

"No. I think I got this. They're breaking up, so . . . you know. No kissing."

"Sad." He reached over, squeezed her hand. "I'm sure you'll figure it out."

Yeah, she would, thanks. He let her go.

But when he pulled into her driveway, he said, "You sure you're okay?"

Nope. But she just couldn't . . .

She reached for the door handle.

"Harper?"

She turned back, her throat tight. His smile had vanished, concern in his eyes now, a frown. "I love you."

Oh. She found a smile. "I love you too."

Then she got out and closed the door. He waited until she went inside before he pulled out, his headlights disappearing in the night.

Then she grabbed a blanket and the envelope from the top of the trash, went outside, and sat on the round cobblestone patio, the twinkle lights splashing around her. She pulled out the contract inside and stared at it one more time.

A job offer from *PopMuse* magazine in Nashville, in-house editor of their "Hot News and Hot Stars" section. Straight from Clarice, her manager, who'd had lunch with the publisher and two weeks later, landed her a second chance and a contract for a job . . .

One she hadn't wanted.

Until today.

Now, Harper stared at the blurry stars.

Clearly, the answer was yes.

FOUR

EMBERLY'S STORY BOTHERED HIM MORE THAN Stein wanted to admit, even after they'd turned on the television and embarked on a short *West Wing* marathon.

She'd helped him clean out the junk-food supply in the galley, and when the copilot came over the speakers and told them to buckle in for landing, he found her snoozing.

Emberly was impossibly pretty, and he had to catch himself because she was most likely right— *"This is going to end badly."*

Maybe. Probably. And he might be a fool for thinking anything else. Because he didn't trust her.

But he wanted to.

Shoot. A smart man would put a tracker on her, because deep in Stein's gut, he knew that at the first—or best—chance she got, Phoenix would ditch him. He should probably let her.

Emberly, however, the girl who'd tried to care for her sister, who longed for a family . . . That girl spoke to the guy inside who'd grown up with that exact family.

They were cut from the same double-sided cloth. And four days ago he'd been desperately trying not to think about their kiss—okay, all the kisses between them.

Then she'd launched herself into his arms in Sintra, and something had shifted inside him. *"Don't make that bet quite yet . . ."*

Aw. Maybe he just needed to help her with this one thing, get her—and this mission—out of his system. Walk away, back to a life without thieves and Russians chasing him.

No more danger and trouble and waiting for her to betray him.

However, now as she sat in the rental beside him, driving from the airport the hour-plus to Duck Lake, their life felt almost pedestrian. Just a couple of . . . spies? Not thieves, but maybe . . . operatives? Heading to his parents' home.

Okay, maybe not so pedestrian.

"You okay?"

She stared out the window, the early autumn sun casting upon the red silos and barns that sat amidst fields of corn and soybeans on this stretch of highway between Minneapolis and Duck Lake.

"Last time I was at your house, I snuck in like a thief."

"Not *like* a thief. You *were* a thief."

She glanced at him. "A dancing thief. You had nice moves there, Travolta, if I remember correctly."

"I should have realized you were just using me for my jacket." But yes, he remembered that dance with a stranger, the one that had lingered with him.

Maybe because, deep inside, he'd *known*.

Phoenix, the girl he'd tried to forget, somehow, impossibly, in his arms.

"Listen. No one knows why you were there. Not even Austen. Calm down—for all they know, you're my secret girlfriend."

Her eyes widened.

He glanced at her. "There's that panic again. Listen. Just for the next twenty-four hours, until we track down Declan, maybe just . . . take a breath. Loosen up. Let your inner Emberly out."

"You do remember that Emberly was a little unhinged."

"I think Emberly just wanted to be safe."

She stared at him. "Listen, Dr. Phil, I don't need to be fixed, or even pandered to. We're here for one reason—to find Stone. And get Axiom. I'm not here to be your 'girlfriend.'" She finger quoted the word. "Or even some project."

"Project?"

"Like, the broken girl who needs a family . . ."

"What?"

"Yeah. Ever since I told you my story on the plane, you've been acting all . . . weird. Nice. Sweet." She made a face.

"Baby, I promise you, I'm not sweet."

"You are—you put a freakin' blanket over me when I fell asleep!"

"Wow. Okay. You're right. Next time, you can freeze to death. You don't even get a roll of newspaper."

Her mouth opened. Then she shook her head and looked away.

He smiled. "I hope my mom made cinnamon rolls."

"You can't bribe me with food either."

"You've never had my mom's cinnamon rolls."

"For the love, this is not *The Family Stone*."

"The what?"

"You know, that Christmas movie about the family who gets together one last time before their mom dies, and they all bring their crazy spouses or girlfriends, and one of the girlfriends falls for the brother and—"

"Please do not fall for any of my brothers."

"I won't—what—no. I mean, okay, just . . . I'm . . . Could you just book me a hotel?"

"Sure. At the King's Inn. We have plenty of rooms."

She huffed. "Fine. But you'd better deliver on that promise of cinnamon rolls."

He held up three fingers. "Scout's honor."

Silence. Then, "Oh no, you *were* a Boy Scout, weren't you?"

"All the way to Eagle, just like my brother Jack."

"Beautiful. The Boy Scout and the thief. This is like a bad rom-com."

"What?"

"Yeah, it's *Silver Linings Playbook*."

"That was an award-winning movie."

"About *mental health issues*. It wasn't a rom-com; it was a drama. You can't just call something a rom-com if it has no comedy. Therefore, bad rom-com."

"It had funny moments."

"See, another reason I can't trust you—your taste in movies."

"Me?" He looked at her. "You can't trust me? This from the woman who spent two hours trying to convince me that *The Last Jedi* was a terrible movie."

"It was. Luke Skywalker was supposed to be this superhero Jedi. Instead, he was a broken hobo on some forgotten planet. And no way would he try to kill Ben Solo—never buying it. And I really wanted him to be Rey's dad."

"But he looked into Ben's mind and saw who he'd become."

"And that was justification for trying to kill him?" Her voice had risen, and weirdly, for a second, they were back in the safe house in Krakow, her sitting on the sofa finishing off her ramen, him leaning against the doorjamb, wondering how he'd gotten there, too invested in a story in a galaxy far, far away.

And then, just like that, he got it.

"You wanted Luke to be a hero and believe in Ben . . . because if he did, maybe it would have changed him."

She blinked at him. Looked away. "It's just a movie."

His throat thickened. *Yeah.*

After a bit, "You do seem rich in your movie lore."

"My mom found a slew of movies in a dumpster, and we had this little television that had a DVD player attached to it. Nim and I wore them out. We have our own language of movie quotes."

"Our family had movie nights, but usually we were outside on the lake or helping at the inn."

"Sounds like you had the perfect childhood."

He glanced at her, but she hadn't sounded bitter, the tone not a barb. And besides, maybe he had.

Silence deepened as they drove into the outskirts of Duck Lake, past the Lumberjack's Table, which used to be an old bowling joint, and Echoes Vinyl Café—which served a decent cup of coffee— and the Tipsy Canoe, a craft brewery. The town's facelift after the tornado had upscaled the place.

He finally glanced at her. Again, his voice soft, "You're not a project, Emberly."

She glanced at him. Nodded. "If calling me your girlfriend stops questions, I can handle it. Just don't . . . be sweet."

"Nothing but full-on Grinch."

He got a smile.

"For the record, it's a cute town."

He turned north, toward the King's Inn, situated on the lake. "Thanks?"

"I mean, I would have loved to grow up in a town like Duck Lake."

"It's hard to escape your past in a small town." He didn't know why that sneaked out, but maybe . . . Well, she'd told him about her life.

Not that he had much to tell. "We were sort of big shots in town. My brother Jack was this all-around athlete. People called him Big Jack. And Conrad has always been the hockey star. Austen and I were the Wonder Twins."

"Seriously? I didn't realize you were twins."

"Well, fraternal. I'm older and much wiser by two minutes."

"Your poor mother." She'd turned, leaning against the door to watch him. After the plane ride, she'd changed into leggings, white tennis shoes, and an oversized sweatshirt. With her tousled red hair, she looked like a coed, the weekend "girlfriend."

Aw. He had to stop thinking that way. Really.

"Yeah, then she had Doyle and Brontë, so we had a wild, full house. My grandparents ran the inn until they retired. We grew up in the carriage house with my dad running maintenance and my mom helping Grandma."

"Sounds perfect."

"Probably was. At the time, I couldn't wait to leave."

"Why?"

"I don't know. I felt . . . in the middle, I guess. And maybe tried too hard to bust out of that."

"Eagle Scout?"

"Oh, that was my grandpa—he pushed me into that with Jack. And my dad pushed me into hockey until he realized King Con was the superstar."

"King Con?"

"That's his nickname. But when we were kids, he wasn't near as tough as he is now." He turned onto King's Inn Drive. "I saved his hide from being checked more than once."

Words rose up, fingers in his chest tightening. "Except once."

"Once?"

"Yeah, we were in a game. He was about eight, and we were playing on the same team, and the kids weren't allowed to check, but that didn't stop some of the kids—anyway, Conrad was playing center, and I was down at defenseman, and I still remember it like yesterday. He had the puck, was taking it down the ice, and this one Goliath of a kid just rushed him from all the way across the ice. I saw it before it happened and took off, but no way was I going to get there in time. Con got slammed into the board, lost his helmet, broke his nose, blood everywhere. Total chaos."

"You got the kid, didn't you?"

He looked at her. "I got thrown out of the game. Sat out for three more games." He raised a shoulder. "Sometimes, when I'm really tired, I think—I dream that I'm nine years old again and racing across the ice, trying to get to him. And I can't. And bam, he's hit and bleeding, and I wake up in a cold sweat."

Silence.

Wait. Aw. He hadn't meant to—

"Thank you."

He glanced at her as they pulled into the driveway. There were only a few cars in the lot, but it was Tuesday, so a shoulder day for guests. "What?"

"Suddenly it all makes sense."

He parked. "What makes sense?"

She unbuckled. "All of it." Then she smiled. "Okay, Thor, I'm ready to meet the family Stone."

"The . . . Kingston family."

"Whatever."

"Thor?"

She winked and got out.

He had nothing. But he got out, and the smell of the lake, the stirring of the leaves in the trees, and the beauty of the King's Inn in the early fall with the wide apron porch, the hanging baskets of flowers, and the serenity just caught him up.

This *wasn't* going to end badly. He'd find Declan. They'd get Axiom. And somehow, they'd figure out how to save the world.

Then he'd disentangle himself from Miss Movie Quotes, and his life would go back to normal.

Stein walked up the steps, and the fragrance of something baking—maybe cookies this late in the day—filtered out through the screen door of the kitchen. Opening the door, he walked through the service entrance, into the pantry area, and followed the smells into the kitchen.

His mother wore a King's Inn apron, a pair of yoga pants, and a

T-shirt, her short blonde hair caught in a bandanna as she plated cookies.

And of all people, his sister Boo, back from Alaska, stood at the kitchen sink, elbows deep in suds. She looked over, grinned. "Seriously?" She shook out her hands, grabbed a towel.

His mother also looked up. "Stein. You're back. Did you have a nice trip?"

And right then, Jack walked into the kitchen from the other door. "We finished washing the porch—hey, Stein." But his gaze landed on the woman behind Stein, who walked in to stand beside him.

Jack grinned.

Boo's gaze passed over Emberly too.

And his mother smiled, came over. "And who is this beautiful woman?"

He had nothing. Just . . . no words—the lie, the truth all snarled up together. *Friend? Foe? Partner? Teammate? Spy? Thief?*

But she slid her hand into his, wove her fingers through his, and said, "I'm Emberly, Stein's girlfriend."

She didn't belong here.

In this convivial, embracive family.

Run.

She squelched the urge as she met his family, as Mama Em introduced herself, gave her a hug, scooped her up into preparations for dinner.

To her memory, Emberly had only experienced a family dinner like the Kingston family dinner once in her life. The entire family sat at the twelve-foot table located on the back porch of one of the stately Victorian homes—Stein called it the Norbert.

Twinkle lights hung from the porch ceiling, and a chandelier dropped golden puddles of light onto the dinner. Orange candles flickered in the center, and so much food—homemade rolls and a tossed salad and tiny smashed golden potatoes and a tomato salad and wild rice and glistening, buttery steaks.

Beyond the deck, the sun had started to slide past the horizon, casting rose gold through the trees and turning the lake a deep amber. A scant wind caught the scent of fresh-cut grass and the fragrance of the blooming chrysanthemums along the porch.

"So then, there I was, in my prom dress, Harper with me, trying to change the tire on the old Bronco . . ." Stein's sister Boo talked with her hands, glancing across the table at her friend Harper.

Laughter.

Emberly sat in the midst of it, flanked on one side by Stein. His older brother, Jack, sat next to him. He'd given her a strange look back in the kitchen when she shook his hand. Jack's girlfriend, Harper, sat beside him, a cute blonde with a pixie cut, wearing a pair of wide-leg pants and a cropped tee, a sort of curious intensity about her when she met Emberly. Now, she was finishing Boo's story.

Across from Harper sat Conrad, Stein's hockey-star brother, and his girlfriend, Penny, her long dark hair cascading down her back, bearing a tan and wearing a diamond necklace with her casual pink sundress.

And next to them, Boo. Of course Emberly recognized the bride from the wedding she'd crashed eight months ago. Boo sat next to her country-superstar husband, Oaken, as she segued into a story about some recent rescue by their Air One team.

Their father sat at one end, a big guy, so that's probably where the Kingston boys had gotten their height and impressive shoulders. Salt-and-pepper hair, a smile on his face, the king at the gate, listening.

Mama Em carried a pitcher of lemonade to the table. She set it down and Con got up to push in his mother's chair at the other end.

The entire thing felt . . . provincial. And sweet. And what was she doing here?

Stein glanced over at her as Boo finished her story, smiled.

Oh yes. Girlfriend.

She could do this.

Today, Emberly was her disguise.

"We're so glad you could make it for dinner, Emberly," Stein's dad—Grover, she remembered from the introduction—said. "Stein is usually pretty tight-lipped about his, um, girlfriends."

"I knew about her," Jack said, raising his hand. He glanced at Stein with a smile and a wink.

Who knew what that meant?

"Well, he's never brought home a girl before, so this is a celebration," said Mama Em, who reached out and patted Emberly's hand.

What? The gesture left an unfamiliar warmth.

"And just in time to catch Boo and Oaken." She cast a look at her daughter and the sandy-haired singer at the end.

"Let's pray," said Grover and held out his hand.

Really? But Emberly put her hand into Stein's and then Mama Em's and listened as Grover thanked God for blessings and favor and prayed for the family who wasn't present—she guessed that meant Austen and their son Doyle, back in Mariposa—and something about his low, humble voice unwound the coil in her gut.

Everything would be fine. She'd have a nice dinner, and then she and Stein would sneak out and find Declan.

And she'd leave, AI program in hand. Without Steinbeck, because he was a good man. The kind of man who showed up, protected, even if it got him hurt.

Suddenly it all makes sense.

He wasn't a guy who stood on the sidelines. And his story about his brother only confirmed that.

Despite his former-SEAL skills, her world would eventually get him killed.

And she simply didn't belong in his. Even in the guise of Emberly.

But for now, she'd laden her plate with potatoes and a gourmet steak off the grill and salad and she would enjoy her lemonade and her walkabout in the world of . . . normal.

"When did you get here, Boo?" This from Stein, who held out the basket of fluffy rolls to Emberly.

Yes, and amen. She took one and slathered it with creamy butter.

"A couple days ago. Oaken spent the day at the fairgrounds, rehearsing for tomorrow night's show."

"You're performing at the fair?" This from Conrad. "How did I not know that?"

"You're too busy with hockey camps," Penny said. "He's done four youth camps this summer for EmPowerPlay. The kids are crazy about him."

By her grin at Conrad, Emberly guessed that the kids weren't the only ones.

Conrad rolled his eyes. "Yeah, whatever. Besides, what was I going to do, say no after I signed a three-year deal with the Blue Ox?"

"Oh please," Penny said. "You love it."

He smiled down at her, and oh, the sap was heavy on that side of the table. Their laughter made it easy to fall into this family's ambiance.

"I guess we're going to have to go to the fair tomorrow," said Conrad. "Do we get free tickets?"

Emberly hadn't ever listened to an Oaken Fox album, but he definitely had rugged country star appeal, with his slow smile, the tenor of his voice. "Absolutely. I'll leave them at will call."

"The fair?" Emberly said. "You're playing at a county fair?"

"The Minnesota State Fair. It's the second largest fair in the country," Stein said. "We go every year. This is the last weekend."

"What, you go and check out the pigs?"

"And the cows and chickens and horses, and all the exhibits, and especially the cool food." This from Penny. "I heard this year they have deep-fried Twinkies."

"They've had those for years," said Grover. "I'm interested in the chocolate-covered bacon."

"And the bucket of cookies and fresh milk," said Jack. "No offense, Mom."

"None taken. I love the new Amish donut stand." She wiped her mouth. "Although, I did bake up a batch of cookies, as a reminder before you decide to defect."

"Never," Conrad said, grinning.

"Oh please. I know you love that cookie place near your house," his mother said.

"Ironclad Desserts? Poor substitute for the real thing." He winked.

His mother smiled, clearly touched.

Emberly was in an episode of *The Waltons*. And that memory stirred up, bloomed through her.

"What are you smiling about?" Stein said, and she hadn't realized she had settled into the past.

"Just . . . 'The family is a haven in a heartless world.'"

He raised an eyebrow.

"John-Boy Walton."

"You watched *The Waltons*?"

"We had a DVD set that someone gave us. Some of the episodes were scratched, but my sister and I watched them endlessly."

At one end of the table, Oaken talked with Grover and Jack about his summer tour, the state fair being one of the finale events.

At her end, Penny explained the latest crime in her podcast, a hunt for a serial killer in Alaska, who had committed crimes that spanned a decade.

Emberly ate her steak, listening, and the urge to run slowly diminished, the night turning easy.

Until Mama Em turned to her. "And what do you do, Emberly?"

She stared at the woman, all words leaving her. *What*—"Um..."

And just like that, she didn't want to lie. Didn't want to fabricate something that she'd have to perpetuate, building a layer of falsehoods—

"She's a procurer of all things rare and valuable."

Stein. Emberly looked at him, frowned. He had taken her hand on the table and now squeezed.

What was happening?

"So, rare art?"

"Um. In . . . some cases," Emberly said. She let go of Stein's grip and reached for her lemonade.

"That's cool," Penny said. "What kind of things?"

"I once found the Scepter of Charles V of Spain," she said. "It had gone missing from the royal palace of Madrid."

Never mind that she'd been the one to steal it.

"So, artifacts and treasures—our sister Austen is a treasure hunter," said Conrad. "Only, she's a diver. Lives in the Keys."

Yes, she knew Austen, but Emberly just nodded, gave a smile.

"Jack searches for missing people," Harper said.

"Not right now," Jack said. "Currently, I'm on the hunt for Grandpa's spokeshave." He looked at his father. "Are you sure he had one?"

"He made all the curved legs on the living-room chairs. I remember him carving them out."

"What are you working on?" Stein asked.

"Piano-bench legs," Jack said.

And just like that the inquisition was over. She'd passed, and without completely lying, and maybe even earning an unfamiliar sense of respect.

They finished dinner, and she helped carry plates into the kitchen. The Norbert, a smaller version of the main house that had hosted Boo's wedding reception, still possessed the vintage charm of the rest of the Kingston homes, all Victorians built during a time of grandeur and wealth.

This home, however, wasn't outfitted with the circular conversation sofas or cigar and wingback chairs of the main house. Instead, a leather Chesterfield sofa sat in front of the grand marble fireplace over a gleaming parquet floor, the scent of lemon hinting at a recent oiling of the oak banister that wound up to the second floor.

She set the dishes on the quartz countertop in the remodeled kitchen. Boo stood at the sink, rinsing and loading them into the dishwasher.

Penny came in with another load of plates. "Did you see that moon outside? It's gorgeous." She glanced at Emberly and winked.

Emberly just stood there.

Penny smiled warmly. "Do I need to be clearer?"

Maybe. "I can help clean up."

Boo shut off the water. Turned. "Steinbeck has never brought a girl home before. You definitely mean something to him. Don't waste the moonlight."

Oh.

Harper had also come inside, holding the leftover salad and bun basket. "It's a gorgeous night."

"Fine. Okay." And she laughed. Mostly because they were smiling, but maybe a part of her wished . . .

Nope. This was just a show. Nothing real here—

Steinbeck had left the porch, helping his brothers carry firewood out to what looked like a firepit area on the beach. She toed off her shoes and stepped out onto the freshly clipped grass, letting the coolness soak into her.

An old memory rose—laughter, she and Nimue running through a park, playing a game. Hide-and-seek with their mother.

She shook it away and walked out to the beach. The waves whispered against the shoreline, the lake tranquil, the moonlight dragging a lazy finger across the ripples in the water.

Conrad and Jack built a teepee of wood while their dad unloaded the firewood from Steinbeck's arms onto a wood cradle.

Oaken sat on a rough-hewn wooden bench with his guitar, tuning it, the sounds soft in the air.

Distant in her head stirred the word *Run*, but she dismissed it. Nothing to fear here. She'd made it through the worst of it.

Now she just had to survive the romance of a moonlit night.

The fire lit with Jack blowing on newspaper, and Conrad fed in kindling. The crackle grew, and the flame caught the logs, started to snap, shooting tiny embers into the night.

Steinbeck smacked woodchips from his hands, and Conrad nodded toward Emberly. Grinned.

Stein turned, and in the glow of the fire, he stood looking strong and safe. The man who'd opened her cage in the darkness and caught her as she shook off her fear. His burnished hair flickered gold, an unreadable emotion in his fathomless blue eyes. *Desire?*

No. It couldn't be. Except a forbidden spark flamed when he stepped over to her. He smelled of the soap from his earlier shower (she'd taken her own shower in her gorgeous guest room at the Norbert) and maybe a little of the cotton of his shirt, and not a little redolence of Steinbeck—determination, might, and an unyielding sense of sanctuary.

Oh brother. Now she was in a Hallmark movie.

He held out his hand. "Want a tour of the grounds?"

He played his part well.

She took his hand, and he tugged her away toward the darkness, along the grass and lakeshore.

"The estate was built by my great-great-grandfather Bing Kingston. He was a newspaper baron and built a home for each of his sons back in the Gilded Era. I grew up in the carriage house, which my dad remodeled. Grandma and Grandpa lived in the Rudolph—one of our rentals." He pointed to a darkened Victorian across the lawn. "I think probably they'll rent out the Norbert when Jack leaves."

"He's leaving?"

"Probably. He's working on his travel bus, although he has a home in Florida. I think he's probably going to propose to Harper first."

"This is an amazing place."

"Someday my parents are hoping to leave it to one of us, although I'm not sure who. Doyle, maybe. He worked as caretaker for the last few years."

"What about you?"

He still had hold of her hand, as if keeping up the ruse, but she didn't hate it. Nor the way his fingers wove through hers.

"I'm not . . . I'm not an innkeeper. My mom loves people. My dad is a fixture in this town. I . . ." He drew in a breath.

She stilled, turned to him. "You still feel stuck in the middle."

He frowned at her.

"You're not the oldest. You're not the hockey star. You're not Doyle. You're . . ."

"Just fine, Emberly. Not a project."

"Thor."

He raised an eyebrow.

"Just the guy trying to look after his brothers, trying to fix everything."

"I'm not trying to fix everything."

"Me. You're trying to fix me."

"No." He stepped up to her then. "I'm not trying to fix you."

She didn't move away from him, and he stood so close she could put her hands on his chest. Maybe lift herself up and . . . "I'm not kissing you." But her gaze went to his mouth.

"It looks like you want to." And his stupid mouth smirked.

The wind stirred around them, a reminder of summer in the night air.

"This is just a . . . game," she said softly.

"You're the one who started it," he said, his own gaze roaming her face. "Calling yourself my girlfriend."

"It's just a cover."

He made a sound, deep in his chest. "They might be watching." Then he dipped his head and kissed her. Soft lips, but strong against hers, his hands cupping her face, his fingers in her hair, kissing her with the taste of desire and longing, and so what if it was a game?

She kissed him back, losing herself to the fairy tale. To this pocket of make-believe and what-ifs and even . . . a different life.

She wrapped her arms around his waist, stepped closer, hanging on to this man who seemed so inextricably entwined in her life.

I'm just not built for anything real, Stein.

But this wasn't real. And for now, it felt exactly right.

And in his arms, as he wound them around her and deepened his kiss, the sense of her other life, of Phoenix, faded, leaving behind . . .

Emberly.

Eager, hopeful.

Oh no—

Her breath caught and he lifted his head.

"You okay?"

Her stupid eyes burned, her throat tightening. "Yeah."

He studied her for a moment, frowned, then let her go. From down the lakeshore, the fire had bloomed into a bonfire, the cinders alight in the darkness. The family had gathered, and Oaken's deep tones carried down the beach.

"My family likes you."

"I don't like lying to them."

He took her hand again and led her back toward the fire. "Maybe you're not."

What? She glanced at him.

"At the very least, I think our cover is intact." He looked down at her and winked.

"Really? That's why you kissed me?"

"Mission first," he said, his voice holding a laugh, but he tightened his hold on her hand as they entered the ring of firelight.

Boo sat beside Oaken, clearly caught up in her husband's music.

Jack sat next to Harper, eating a chocolate chip cookie. She stared into the flames as if thinking, lost somewhere else.

Penny lounged with her back against Conrad, who straddled a bench, looking up at the stars.

Grover stood, hands on his hips, contemplating the fire. Mama Em perched on a nearby bench, holding a roasting stick, the firelight on her face as she smiled at her oldest son. "Those are supposed to be for the s'mores."

"It's your fault for being such a good cook, Mom," Jack said.

Mama Em rolled her eyes.

"You two have a nice walk?" Penny asked.

"It's quite the place you have here," Emberly said. "Why aren't you full right now?"

"We will be this weekend. It's the last weekend before school starts. And we have a wedding scheduled next week," Mama Em said. "So it's a nice breather. Grover and I are going to the fair tomorrow to listen to Oaken." She looked at Stein. "You two should join us. The fair is a great date."

"They're not dating."

The voice stilled Emberly, silenced the group, and she looked over to see—

Austen. Her auburn hair down, wearing a pair of shorts and a

T-shirt, looking tan and strong and not at all frayed and on the run—the last clear memory Emberly possessed of Steinbeck's twin sister.

And Austen probably possessed the same memory, because her gaze landed hard on Emberly as she walked into the family circle.

"Austen! I didn't know you were back in town." Her mother got up.

"What do you mean they're not dating?" Conrad said. Penny sat up, frowning.

Austen met her mother's hug, her gaze on Stein, something accusatory in it.

Stein tightened his grip on Emberly's hand, as if he heard the little voice inside her saying *Run*. "Austen—"

"This is Phoenix. She's a thief and a spy, and the last time I saw her, she was running from Cuban authorities after setting a truck on fire."

Oh. Right. She'd forgotten the fire-and-bullets part of their history.

Austen turned, her hands on her hips, her face steel. "She's dangerous and trouble, and what in the world are you doing with her, Stein?"

FIVE

IS SHE YOUR GIRLFRIEND OR NOT?"

Steinbeck didn't have an answer for Jack. Frankly, he didn't even have an answer for himself and his out-of-body behavior out on the lawn. He could have kept kissing her until . . . well, until he forgot himself, his mission, why she drove him crazy.

"Listen, I didn't exactly lie, but the truth felt too complicated."

"Because you knew we'd all freak out!" This from Conrad, who sat on one of the single beds, shaking his head.

They had bunkered up in one of the upstairs bedrooms of the Norbert after the showdown at the campfire.

She's dangerous and trouble, and what in the world are you doing with her, Stein?

He couldn't argue the first two. And with the taste of her kiss still inside him, he went right to, "Reasons, Austen. You don't have to rubber-stamp my every move."

Which probably hadn't been the right thing to say, because Austen's mouth had opened and she'd then turned to Emberly, her voice tight. "I'm glad you're alive."

To which Emberly had nodded. "You too." She'd twisted out

of his hand despite his grip and said, "I'm sorry, but I think this game is over."

And then she'd stalked toward the house.

He'd nearly run after her—should have—but he'd been pinned into place by the expressions of his family. They'd stared at him, his mother stricken, his father frowning, Jack with his hands in his pockets, shaking his head, and Penny and Conrad sitting up, mouths agape.

"It's complicated," he'd said and headed toward the house. He'd gone to Emberly's room on the second floor at the end of the hall. Knocked.

And knocked.

And knocked.

Until finally Jack and Conrad had followed him and dragged him down to another guest room.

Now Jack stood at the window, arms folded, that big-brother look of disapproval on his face. "You should have trusted us. I mean, I knew who she was, but . . . c'mon, bro. This is me. And Con. We *know* you."

"What's that supposed to mean?"

"You can't help but get involved," Conrad said. "Of course you're going to dive into something completely crazy—and that's what this is, right? Something crazy?"

Steinbeck hung his hands behind his neck, folding them there, which felt like a better alternative than using them to strangle his sister.

Thanks, Austen.

At least now he knew Declan's whereabouts, so that was something. Austen told him that she'd caught a flight back to Minnesota with her new beau.

"I can't get into it, but yes. Emberly—"

"Phoenix?"

"Emberly is her real name. Phoenix is her—"

"Spy name?" Conrad raised an eyebrow.

"Cover name. And you might consider cutting her some slack. She was trying to protect you all."

"Please," Jack said. "She was trying to protect herself. And maybe you. But from what? It's not like we're not used to you living a clandestine life. You spent years not telling us where you were going, where you'd been. You didn't have to lie." Jack leaned forward, quirked a brow. "I want to know what went down in Portugal."

Stein sank down onto the edge of one of the twin beds. "What do you mean?"

Jack just stared at him. "A week ago you could barely admit that you might be more than friends. Now she's your *girlfriend*?"

"I think we made it clear that was a cover story."

"No. You don't lie that well." Jack glanced at Conrad as if for confirmation, and the traitor nodded.

"You *are* a terrible liar," Conrad said. "Which is why I totally bought the girlfriend act."

"Because it's not an act," Jack said quietly. "Not to our boy Stein."

Stein stared at him. "Jack—"

"Like I said before you took off for Portugal, you care about this woman. Although I don't know why, or how she fits into your life."

"She doesn't. I told you. I met her on an op a few years ago, the one that ended my career. I blamed her for a long time for what went south, but we ran into each other again in Barcelona and then on Mariposa and I got her side of the story."

"And that changed things?"

He shrugged. "Maybe. And then we got trapped on Declan's boat together, and she helped me rescue Austen and Dec from the Cuban police and . . . well, maybe I misjudged her."

Silence as his brothers considered him. As *he* considered his own words. "Then I found her in Portugal, captive, on her way to Russia and . . . I don't know. She seemed grateful."

Jack's eyebrow went up.

Conrad's mouth lifted on one side. "Grateful?"

He nodded. "Grateful."

"As in full-kiss-on-the-mouth, Steinbeck-I-love-you grateful?"

"Less PG-13, but something like that."

"And there went Steinbeck, stepping off the sidelines into whatever game she was playing," Jack said.

"It's not a game. There is a real threat to our national security, and she's a part of neutralizing it."

"And now so are you."

Steinbeck shoved his hands into his pockets. "So I am. So shoot me."

Jack nodded, sighed.

Conrad leaned back, bracing his hands on the bed. "And what part of that brought you guys back to the King's Inn for a family dinner?"

"The part that included him thinking that maybe there's a happily ever after waiting at the end of this gig." Jack's blue eyes turned hard on him.

"For the love, Jack, let's not get carried—"

"Stop. You're always the levelheaded, sensible one in the crowd," Jack said. "You don't do anything without thinking it through, so . . . you think you have a future with this woman?"

The question hit him, a blow across his chest. "No. I—I don't know."

"That's the first honest thing you've said," Jack said quietly.

Stein narrowed his eyes, then leaned forward, his face in his hands. "This woman makes me crazy. The first time I met her, she derailed my entire life. And yet I'm like a moth to a flame. She's funny and brave, and—"

"She stands up to you."

Stein looked at Conrad.

"Hey, I'm just saying I get it," Con said. "Penny is exactly like that. Smart and maybe a little impulsive, and it drives me to my last nerve, and yet I can't look away. Or stop myself from wanting to protect her. She makes me feel invincible." He made a wry face. "Okay, that was a little much."

"No. It's perfectly stated," Jack said. "Harper looks at me like I could find her in the dark with my hands tied behind my back. It makes me want to be everything I see in her eyes." He lifted a shoulder. "Please do not tell her that."

Conrad let out a huff, shook his head, gave him a wry smile.

Stein stared at them.

"Is that panic on your face?" Jack raised an eyebrow.

Steinbeck ran his hand across his mouth. "I just know that nothing had felt right for three years, and something just . . . clicked when I found her in Portugal. And maybe before that, in Cuba, when we were trying to survive."

"Maybe we can figure out how to get past survival together?"

"I think maybe I've been in survival mode for the past three years. Survive my injury, get back on my feet. Find my way. And now I have a chance to do something . . . patriotic—"

"With the woman who makes you feel—"

"Necessary," Conrad said.

Stein stilled.

"And, goal," Conrad said, raising an eyebrow.

Aw. Stein looked away.

"Bro," Jack said quietly. "You've never been *not* necessary."

"I don't need a hug."

"But you *do* need truth. Running from one high-adrenaline mission to the next is not going to heal you from the loss of being a SEAL."

"I'm fine."

"We see you, Stein. You've always been the One Most Likely to Get It Done. And then you got blown up and sidelined, and you've put on a tough face, but . . . we get it."

"Being a SEAL is just a job," Stein said.

"Right. As if the warrior ethos wasn't scrubbed into your DNA," Jack said.

Stein lifted a shoulder.

"But you're not on the teams anymore. So there has to be something more—otherwise God would not have brought you here."

The words were a knife, and for a second, Stein couldn't breathe. "You're saying God derailed my life?"

"Not derailed. Redirected. I'm saying that nothing happens to us that doesn't pass through the hands of the Lord. And he is good. And not to quote my little brother or anything, but eight months ago, you said that God has a plan for my life. And that even I can't screw it up."

"You remember that."

"I do. And you should too."

Steinbeck sighed. "Listen, I'm not worried about screwing it up. I'm worried that . . . I'll end up chopping wood for family campfires for the rest of my life. No offense."

Jack shook his head. "None taken. Mostly because chopping all that wood means I'm in better shape than you."

Even Conrad smiled.

"Listen, little bro," Jack said, "Dad always says a person's steps are directed by the Lord. How, then, can anyone understand their own way?"

"That's a proverb, Jack. Not Dad," Conrad said.

Jack rolled his eyes. "Seriously?" He headed toward the door, dropping a hand on Stein's shoulder as he stopped beside him. "God did not make you to sit on the sidelines, Steinbeck. We all know that. And we have your back. Whatever it is you need to do to save the world, we're in. But don't pursue this woman with the hope that she's going to give you some sort of purpose. Only God can do that."

He slapped his shoulder. "So be smart, and don't let this girl run away with your heart."

Jack left.

Stein lay on the bed, his hands behind his head. "When did he get all wise and knowing?"

"Feeling a little usurped?" Conrad got up, pulled off his shirt.

"What?"

Conrad threw the shirt into his open suitcase. "For years, all I got was you telling me how I should live my life."

"Not true."

"You were always so confident, like you knew exactly what step to take. Especially after you became a SEAL." Conrad turned, hands on his hips. "But I didn't care because you were my big brother, and I knew you were watching my back. So it's your turn to listen." He stood at the door to the bathroom. "You don't always have to save the day."

He went in and shut the door.

Stein stared at the rotating ceiling fan. Yes, actually, he did.

But even as he stripped down and climbed into bed, as he lay there in the darkness listening to Conrad snore, he heard Jack circling his brain. *But don't pursue this woman with the hope that she's going to give you some sort of purpose. Only God can do that.*

He closed his eyes. The only problem was, he'd never felt more as if he was *supposed* to be right here, doing this one thing, with this particular woman.

But Jack was right. There was no happily ever after waiting for him at the end of this mission. Phoenix was . . . messy. Dangerous. Frustrating. Never mind that she ran alone—she'd made that clear. No room for him, or for that matter God, in her life.

And maybe he had been, deep inside, trying to figure out how to help her. So yes, a *project. Shoot.*

The truth was, it wasn't a question of if but rather *when* she was going to ditch him. And the last thing he needed was the spy he couldn't forget running away with his heart.

•————————•

She refused to be the villain in this story. Which was why Emberly hadn't packed her bags. Hadn't run.

Had even endured a showdown with Austen, who'd come to her room later to deliver an apology.

Which Emberly listened to through the closed door.

Then she'd lain in bed, rehearing Steinbeck's pounding on the door, over and over, driving sleep far into the corners of the night.

Fine.

She threw back the comforter and got up, pulled on a pair of yoga pants and an oversized T-shirt, and headed downstairs and through the dark house to get a glass of water.

Then she slipped outside onto the porch, sat on the steps, and listened to the wind call her a fool.

She should have never let Steinbeck come along for this ride.

She was so engrossed in her thoughts, she didn't hear the door open and close, or the footfalls on the porch.

She sensed a presence beside her. Looked up.

Austen. Steinbeck's twin stood in a pair of long pajama bottoms, a T-shirt, and a cardigan, her auburn hair long and in tangles. "Can I sit with you?"

Emberly bit back an "Are you sure it's safe?" and nodded instead. Scooted over on the top step.

Austen lowered herself next to her. "I'm sorry. Again."

"It's okay. Again." She glanced over at her. "You're not wrong."

"I was wrong to call you trouble. You aren't trouble. From what I recall, you got us *out* of trouble."

Emberly gave a harsh laugh. "Now you're the one lying."

Austen gaped at her. Then smiled. "Fine. I guess it's complicated. So, Emberly is your real name?"

"I prefer Phoenix." At least, right now.

"Because?"

She looked over at the woman. "Emberly is . . . someone Stein wishes was real, I think."

"She's not?"

"She can't be. But . . ." She looked out at the lawn, the moonlight on the water, spotted the place where Stein had kissed her. "It was a nice fairy tale for a moment. The Boy Scout and the thief."

"Stein was hardly a Boy Scout."

"He said he was an Eagle Scout."

"He was. And sure, he'd help an old lady across the road—probably would lay down in traffic for her. But he's not Clark Kent—mild mannered by day, superhero by night. The guy has never backed down from a fight. Which I guess is why you two seem to ignite like fireworks."

That was the second time someone had used that description about them. Emberly didn't correct it. Mostly because she'd definitely felt like fireworks out there on the lawn, *thank you very much*.

"Don't worry, Austen. I'm not going to let him get hurt." A promise to herself as much as to Austen.

"Have you met him?" Austen gave the tiniest of laughs. "I don't think that's in your control."

Emberly smiled.

"What happened to you in Cuba?" Austen asked softly. "He was really worried."

That was probably the last thing Emberly needed to hear. She told Austen the story, ending with "I couldn't believe it was him speaking to me in the darkness. Just . . . a voice. But . . . it was everything."

Maybe that was too much information, because Austen said quietly, "Are you in love with my brother, Phoenix?"

She glanced at Austen. Swallowed. "No. I . . . I don't have room in my life for love."

"That's not what I asked."

"But it's the answer. Sure. Steinbeck is . . . he's . . ." She sighed. "Just, like I said . . . everything."

"Yes, he is," Austen said, and nudged her. "He's the all-in guy."

"But you don't want him to get hurt."

"Of course not." She glanced at her. "Although I do know that Steinbeck is a big boy. He can figure out what he wants on his own. And he's been destroyed before. I have no doubt he can come back from a broken heart."

Emberly's chest tightened. So Austen *expected* Emberly to break his heart.

Well, in truth, she did too. Except, what if . . .

"I like your family."

Austen smiled. "They're okay."

"I had this sort of pseudo-family for a very short time. A foster family. I ran away and screwed that up. But . . ." She shook her head. "It was just a nice dinner, is all."

The wind stirred the chrysanthemums, the scent mingling with the night.

"You could stick around."

"Here?"

"Here. There. Wherever Stein is. Maybe figure it out together."

"Is that what you and Declan are doing?"

Austen glanced at her. "Um—"

"Please. Like Declan isn't crazy about you. And Stein says he's not a terrorist, so . . ."

"He's not, Phoenix. I promise. And yes . . . we're together. He's busy, though. He's got an exhibit at the state fair tomorrow. Some

AI tech he's developed and is using to help train service-animal robots."

"And you're along for the ride?"

"I did snag a free ticket from Florida on his Gulfstream, but I've never been interested in his money. I have everything I need. It's the man inside that intrigues me."

"His outside isn't so terrible either."

Austen laughed, and it sounded so much like Steinbeck that it closed Emberly's throat. *Oh no,* she just *might* be in love with the guy.

Or as far in love as she could allow herself to go.

"We're figuring it out together," Austen finally said. "I think that's all you can do. We don't know what tomorrow will bring. We just have to walk one day at a time. And it's nice to do it hand in hand with someone." She leaned back against the pillows.

Emberly stared out at the dark lake, the rippling of the moonlight upon the waves. "I've been a Black Swan for the better part of a decade. I've always had a mission. A plan. An objective. I'm not sure I can do one day at a time."

"Just start with one day," Austen said, and shivered. "I'm going in. But apparently, we're all going to the fair tomorrow."

"Yay. Cows."

"You might be surprised." She got up. "My guess is that you've never had cheese-curd tacos." She winked. "Glad you're here, um, *Emberly.* You've told yourself that you are one type of person for a long time. You might consider that you could be another, even for a day. Don't give up on that name quite so quickly."

She went inside.

And Emberly sat on the porch for a long time, hearing *"What kind of different life?"*

Six hours later, she piled out of an SUV with Steinbeck and his family. The deep-fried, farm-animal, cotton-candy smells of the fair, the heat of the crowds, and the screams of children on rides just might convince her of that different life.

"Welcome to the Great Minnesota Get-Together," Stein said as he handed her a ticket.

"The what?" She glanced at Conrad, walking hand in hand with Penny. Turned back to Stein. "Where do we start?"

"The Peg for an egg sandwich, and then down to the cattle barns for milk."

The what? But Steinbeck grabbed her hand—as if they were continuing with the charade—and pulled her toward a tall space tower. He pointed to a restaurant with a red sign and matching umbrellas shading square picnic tables. "Save room. This is stop one."

The family took up two tables, and she shared an egg muffin with Stein.

"I promise, I'm saving you," he said when she eyed his half.

From there, they walked down to a cattle barn. Inside, fat cows lounged in tufts of straw, eating hay, the smell earthy.

"It looks like people are camping out between the stalls," she said.

"They are. There are competitions every day, and people—mostly kids—earn prizes for the best cows, and in other barns, sheep and goats and pigs and horses . . . We usually watch at least one judging. My mom loves the horse shows."

"Really?"

He bent to pet the hide of a fat tawny-colored cow. "Yeah. Salt-of-the-earth people."

Grover and Mama Em, holding hands, had stopped to talk to a farmer.

So that's what happily ever after looked like. Emily, dressed in a pair of leggings and tennis shoes, wearing an oversized T-shirt with the King's Inn emblem, her blonde hair tucked into a baseball cap. Grover, in jeans and a T-shirt, also in a ball cap. *Sheesh,* those two even matched.

They moved on to a milking demonstration. "I've never seen such a thing in real life," she said, watching the milk run through the tubing into metal canisters.

"We're just getting started," Boo said. She grinned at Emberly as if . . .

As if Austen *hadn't* outed her last night. As if they still saw her as Emberly. Stein's *girlfriend*.

Apparently he did too, as he kept his hand around hers, tight.

No. Wait. He was most likely just trying to keep her from running away.

They visited the sheep barn, where she dug her fingers into the thick wool of a sheep, then went to the goats, and finally to the big-pig stall, where a huge boar named Gerald lay on its side.

"He's eaten a lot of milkshakes," said Conrad.

Emberly laughed.

They headed outside and stopped at—yes—a milkshake stand. Jack and Harper shared a strawberry shake; Stein grabbed a chocolate shake.

"Again, halfsies?"

"Trust me."

They bought Scotch eggs and cinnamon rolls, and then they stopped at a minidonuts stand.

"I had these once, at a street fair in Bozeman."

He reached into her bag and she let him. "I love minidonuts."

"You're going to roll out of here like Gerald."

"The day is young. We have miles of walking ahead of us. I gotta keep up my strength." He kept his hand on her shoulder as they wove along the street, working their way to something called Machinery Hill.

The men parked themselves in front of the combustion engines, Conrad and Jack and Stein listening to their father explain something about pistons.

"I'm going to sit with your sisters," Emberly said to Stein, who glanced over at a picnic bench.

Only the slightest hint of worry flashed in his blue eyes. "Okay."

"Declan's exhibition doesn't start until late this afternoon. I promise, I'm not going anywhere."

He blinked at her, his mouth opened, and then, "I know."

Oh, he was a wretched liar.

She didn't know why the truth pinched as she walked over to the picnic table, sat on the bench.

"Every year," said Mama Em. "They have to study every engine, as if he's never seen them before."

"You do this *every* year?" Emberly asked.

"Family tradition," Austen said. "We'll hit the horticulture barn next, and then the dairy barn—check out the butter girls—"

"The butter girls?"

Boo had joined them, carrying a bag. She reached in and handed her mother a disfigured donut dripping in glaze. "Amish donuts."

"The butter girls are local pageant winners whose likenesses are carved into slabs of butter, and even as I say that it sounds creepy." Austen laughed.

"We usually get ice cream at the dairy barn," Mama Em said. "That's a tradition on Grover's side."

Boo had ripped a donut in half and handed a piece to Emberly. "Try this and tell me you haven't died and gone to heaven."

The words hit her, burrowed in. "How long has the state fair been running?" She took a bite. "Oh, this is good."

"Right?" Boo said, grinning.

"Since 1859," Mama Em said. "It closed down six times—during the Civil War, the US-Dakota war, during the Chicago World's Fair, of course, World War Two, and then twice for epidemics—polio and Covid. It's one hundred and sixty-six years old. And I believe the Kingston family has attended every year since the early 1900s."

She leaned over to Emberly. "At some point I'm going to park myself in the bandshell and listen to the polka bands." She winked.

Yes, Emberly had walked into a different life.

The sun started to bake the day, seasoning the streets with the smells of fried food, beer, cotton candy. The crowds thickened.

They got newspaper hats, wandered through the horticulture barn, bought apples, then went to the dairy barn, ate more ice cream, visited something called Heritage Square. Then Austen grabbed cheese curds, and they shared as they watched a parade with marching bands and fire engines and baton twirlers and rescue dogs in need of adoption.

And finally, they indeed parked on a bench, watching polka.

Steinbeck came over and handed her a root beer float.

"I swear to you, I drink that and I'll explode. Bam. Human shrapnel everywhere."

"That's disgusting. And I'm sorry, but you have to have at least one sip. It's a state-fair rule. I'll let you opt out of the deep-fried Twinkies—but after we talk to Declan, you have to leave room for a turkey leg. And the finale—cookies and milk." He sat down next to her as someone played an accordion on stage, women in red hoopskirts dancing.

"They clearly have not eaten their way through the fair." She took a sip of root beer. "Oh my, this is good."

"Right?" He took a sip from the other straw. "Everything is more amazing at the fair."

She looked at him. The sun had kissed his face, and he hadn't shaved this morning, burnished whiskers on his chin. He wore a black T-shirt and a pair of cargo shorts, loafers. A normal man enjoying a normal day.

Admittedly, she didn't hate the way his arm fell naturally around her, or the way that Boo, like a normal sister, handed her a big piece of her funnel cake, the powdered sugar dusting over her pants. Or how Penny leaned up from behind her and pointed out a couple of kids, a boy and girl around five years old, dancing the polka, a perfectly normal gesture.

She could survive normal.

"It's almost time for Dec's exhibit," said Austen, and she got up. "You coming?"

Stein held out his hand. And of course Emberly took it. *Why not?*

"We'll meet you guys at Oaken's show," Stein said.

"He has backstage passes for us," Boo said.

"So what will your parents do after the polka?" Emberly said as they walked away with Austen.

"Oh, they'll head over to the natural resources building and Dad will watch the muskies, and then they'll grab some sweet corn and eat it near the WCCO building. Maybe read a paper. Then they'll tour the grandstand and Dad will buy something random, like a waffle maker or homemade caramel sauce or some other fair special. And then they'll mosey back to grab a turkey leg, and maybe end watching a horse show."

"And eating cookies."

"And eating cookies." He grinned down at her. "You like the fair."

"I like"—she shrugged—"this day."

He made a soft hum, deep inside, and nodded.

They walked past Kidway, with its amusement-park rides and a giant Ferris wheel, and overhead, a skyride carried yellow and red cars along a cable.

"What is this exhibit Declan is doing?" Stein asked Austen as they passed a giant karaoke area.

"He's been working with a robotics department at a local college on a project aimed at meeting the need for service animals for the vision impaired. The students are trying to earn a grant to develop the program."

"Using Declan's AI program, Axiom?"

"A version of it designed for this project."

They entered a building on the far side of the fairgrounds, more of a warehouse, but with booths hosting various college-led technology projects. Emberly spotted Declan standing off to the side as a handful of students set up animal prototypes—two dogs and a monkey.

The tech billionaire was dressed in a T-shirt and jeans, like just a guy hangin' out at the fair.

Austen walked up and took his hand, rose on her toes, and whispered into his ear.

Probably something along the lines of *Don't panic, but Phoenix is here.*

It didn't work. He turned, and his mouth gaped a second before he sighed and then . . . smiled?

What?

They walked up and he held out his hand. "Stein. Phoenix."

Stein shook it. "We need to talk to you when this is over."

He nodded as the exhibition started. A small crowd had gathered in the space, industrial fans whirring to keep everyone cool. Emberly noticed a display not far away that advertised robotic fish. A few kids stood around a small pool, watching and pointing, others directing the fish on tablets.

She was missing the presentation and turned back to it just as a big dog, built to look like a friendly Labrador, navigated an adult through an obstacle course. The students reset it, and the AI dog went again.

"The dog can be trained to respond to voice commands, of course, but the best part is that it can predict danger, like a real trained service dog."

They'd set up a racecourse with battery-operated cars circling around the dog. The man urged the animal to move, but it waited, pressing against the trainer's legs in warning, then walked the subject through the maze of objects.

Applause. And then the dog barked.

It sounded so real, the crowd stilled.

Then it turned, *growled*, and launched itself at its trainer.

Screams as the man went down and the dog, toothless but still powerful, locked onto his arm.

The man howled, and Emberly probably just imagined hearing a bone snap with the chaos erupting from the crowd.

Steinbeck bolted, plowed into the middle of the mess, and launched himself onto the animal.

Man against dog machine? Emberly sprinted into the fray even as the dog turned on Steinbeck, obviously *thinking, reacting*, and clamped down on his knee.

Stein grabbed its throat, trying to tear it free, and Emberly kicked the robot's head.

A grunt from Stein as the clamp dislodged, and then Emberly seized the dog by the neck, the robot writhing in her double-fisted grip. "Help!"

Stein scrambled up, nabbed the robot's tail.

Declan showed up, threw his arm around the dog's neck, clamping it to his body.

"The pool!" Emberly shouted.

"Make a hole!" Stein's shout, but it was unnecessary since the onlookers had already fled.

They dropped the dog into the water, Steinbeck jumping in to hold it down. Declan too, right beside him, shoving the college project under water, the robot jerking.

Dying.

Steinbeck looked up, breathing hard. Met Emberly's gaze.

Declan wore a look of horror.

"Well," Austen said, standing at the edge, her hands on her hips. "I've never seen that at the fair before."

SIX

T HE GAME WAS OVER. WHATEVER MAGIC THEIR day at the fair had stirred up, it had died in the cool water of the fish pond, in the horrific aftermath as Stein watched Declan and his college students root around the program of the deactivated service robots.

Stein's arm throbbed and a bone bruise was probably forming on his shin. At least maybe his artificial knee had kept the joint from being crushed.

Unexpected graces.

He and Emberly, along with Declan and Austen, stood in the security offices inside the grandstand, in a private conference room that somehow Declan had commandeered to investigate the accident.

Declan leaned over the chair of one of his college techs, the deactivated monkey lying on the long table.

Outside, Oaken and his band had taken the stage, Stein's brother-in-law working his country-music magic on the crowd.

Steinbeck might have enjoyed singing along, maybe catching

Emberly in a dance—*aw*. He'd let this day get to him. Let her words find soil. *"I promise, I'm not going anywhere."*

And she'd been right there beside him, taking down the rogue animal, so . . .

"It's not a glitch. Someone logged into this code and changed it," Declan said, pointing to the screen. He stood up, folded his arms. "How'd this happen?"

"I don't know, sir," said the tech. Early twenties, maybe, the guy was a reed, wore glasses, and with his curly mop, seemed like a modern-day version of the tech geek Zuckerberg.

The other two students—a female with blue hair and glasses and a short man with Asian-American features—seemed just as computer savvy, the way they burst into a conversation about the code.

But Stein got the gist.

"So you wrote the code, parked it in the cloud, then downloaded an update to the animals last night," Declan said.

"Yes, sir," said the man at the computer.

"Thank you, Elliot." Declan glanced at the other two. "Remove the hard drive from both animals and bring them to me. You can take the robots back to the lab."

He walked over to Steinbeck as they left, his mouth tight. "Now what?"

"We need access to Axiom," Emberly said. She'd stood away, her arms folded, for much of the debrief, but now stepped up to him. Stein might be reading too much into her accusatory expression. "Imagine what this glitch could do in the wrong hands. We need a way to shut it down. What if that water hadn't been there—or hadn't worked? Any military application would include a waterproof design—"

"Okay, calm down, Phoenix," Declan said. "I agree."

And that shut her down.

Steinbeck fought a grin.

"I'm not opposed to the idea of a controlled virus, the kind that could ensure that any system could be shut down. In fact, I've been working on something."

"In between hijacking ships and sailing the high seas?"

"Calm down, Emberly," Steinbeck said.

Declan's eyebrow rose.

"My name is Phoenix, and I will *not* be calm." She rounded on him. "This is exactly why I was trying for the last eight months to get my hands on Axiom." She turned back. "We can't wait. The Russians who were chasing us in Cuba might already have a copy of the program."

She stared at Declan then, her chest rising and falling.

And in case Steinbeck wondered, yes, *Emberly* had vanished.

Phoenix stood in her place, in her skin.

"Wait—you don't think I gave it to them?" Declan.

"I think you've been doing some kind of dance with them for years, Dark Horse. Who knows what you've told them?"

Declan's expression morphed right then into the operative he'd been so many years ago.

Steinbeck stepped between them. "Everybody take a breath."

"We need that program, Stone." Phoenix.

"I don't carry it in my back pocket, Phoenix." Declan.

"Okay, listen." Steinbeck turned to Declan. "Where can we get access?"

He met Steinbeck's eyes. "In my vault."

"In Mariposa?"

"Montelena. I reactivated a bio-key and parked it back in the crypto vault."

"Perfect. All I need is your phrase, your thumbprint, a sample of your DNA, and your eyeball. Happy to retrieve any of those—"

"Phoenix!" Stein turned, put his hands on her shoulders. "He said yes." He glanced at Declan. "Right?"

"Yes," Declan said. "Except I have to be in New York City tomorrow to prepare for a military conference, and—"

"I think saving the world from the Terminator *might* be more important," Phoenix snapped.

"Hokay . . ." Steinbeck turned, put his back to her. "How do we get it, then?"

"I'll meet you in Montelena. Give me two days."

"In Montelena."

"You want to create a virus that actually works—you'll need the source code. And probably a roomful of programmers."

"I'll take care of that," Phoenix said. "Don't stand us up."

Declan glanced at her, back at Stein. "Not sure whose side you're on here."

The words stung. "The world's side," Steinbeck said.

Declan nodded, his eyes hard, then he glanced at Austen. "Sorry you're missing the concert."

"Seriously? And miss all this?" She walked over to him, slid her hand into his, looked at Steinbeck. Then Phoenix. "You can trust him."

Declan offered a grim smile. "Two days. See you there." Then he walked out with Austen.

Steinbeck rounded on Phoenix, but she put up her hands. "Sorry. He's still a terrorist to me."

"And you're still a thief to him. So the fact he's trusting you—"

She flinched at that, and *shoot,* he hadn't meant to hurt her. "Sorry—"

"No. You're right. I am a thief. It's time you remembered that." She pushed past him.

Great. Whatever. He followed her out to the hallway, where she stood near the entrance to the stands, the music carrying into the night.

He stood by her, arms akimbo, watching, listening as Oaken

sang, standing at the mic, his band behind him, the people in the stands cheering, singing along.

"You're the missin' piece, the melody to my song.
With you, I've found where I truly belong."

Stein glanced at Emberly, and she was listening, bobbing her head to the music. And he nearly turned to her, the last twenty-four hours stirring inside him, but she shook her head and walked away, back down the hallway, pulling out her phone.

"Underneath the stars, hand in hand, side by side,
In your embrace, I'm living a blessed, forgiven life."

He listened a moment longer, sighed, then joined her.

She'd walked all the way outside, to a small bridge that overlooked the crowds, the night starting to fall, drops of twilight on the horizon. She held the phone to her ear, pacing.

"Yes, we found him. And yes, he's going to help. Axiom is back in the vault in Montelena."

Probably a call to her boss.

"Right. Yes, I agree, we need him—oh."

She glanced at Steinbeck, her mouth tight.

What? She turned away.

"Yes, of course. I'll be there."

He stilled. *Oh no she wasn't.*

"No, I think—listen. He knows me. It's enough—"

Another long pause. Then, "I can handle it!" She drew in a breath. And now walked away from him.

Sorry, honey. Not happening. He caught up.

"Just . . . Fine. Yes. I'll be there." She hung up. Turned and nearly slammed right into him. "What?"

"You're not going anywhere without me."

She stared up at him. "Apparently not. Apparently you're my new teammate."

"I've been your teammate for a while now."

She narrowed her eyes at him. Sighed. Closed her eyes, and he might have imagined it, but some of the fight seemed to release from her. "I know. That's the problem, isn't it?"

Her words clung, seeped in, tangled inside him. "I don't—"

"Today was amazing." She opened her eyes, her beautiful green-eyed gaze on him. "Normal. One perfect day."

"Yes—"

"But we don't live in normal. We live on the edges. Trying to save normal for the world. And . . . maybe it's dangerous to"—she offered a smile—"to enjoy it too much."

He had no words, Jack's, instead, in his head. *"You think you have a future with this woman?"*

Today, yes, maybe.

Right now?

He too had liked today. Liked *normal.*

"When I was training to be a SEAL, one of the greatest fears of the Navy was for the guys who didn't make it through BUD/S. They had three suicides in the classes ahead of mine—guys who failed out, walked away, and . . . quit their lives. So the trainers came up with a new policy. As soon as a recruit rang out, they sent him home for a week. Made him see his people, eat his mother's cookies, pet his dog—whatever made him reset, realize that this one thing didn't have to define his life. Change him, yes. But tattoo failure on him? No." He put his hands on her shoulders. "Normal helps you get a view of your life. Of the things you love, the things that matter."

He hadn't meant to go there, not really, but . . . he let the words reel out. Let them sit there. And held on to her gaze.

She sighed then, nodded. "Yeah. Maybe. But time-out is over." She pulled away from him. "Apparently Luis was being held in a

Russian safe house in Porto. I'm not sure how, but he got away and sent an SOS through the dark web. He's in hiding, and he won't come in without . . . me."

"And London doesn't want you going in to get him without *me*."

"Apparently." She sighed. "We're supposed to meet them there . . . Okay, maybe it's not a terrible idea."

"Scared you might like me sticking around?"

Her eyes widened. "She's arranged a flight back to Portugal in two hours."

"Shoot. I would have liked to stay for the fireworks."

"Keep up the whining and I'll lock you in the bathroom the entire flight."

Maybe he wouldn't miss the fireworks after all. "You could try."

She rolled her eyes. "Let's say goodbye to your family and catch an Uber to the airport. We'll have to pick up some clothes on the way."

He turned as she headed toward the grandstand. "Why does it feel like we're going to check on our kid?"

"Seriously?"

"We did fight over him."

She shook her head. "Am I ever going to be rid of you?"

He didn't know how to answer. Instead, "What, you still think I'm slow and annoying?"

She stopped just outside the side entrance. "Maybe just annoying."

But she smiled.

And he didn't need normal anyway.

●————————————————●

"Something's up with Harper." Jack didn't know why he let those words out to Conrad as they stood in line for french fries, the stars arching overhead, sprinkling magic down upon the fairgrounds. But the words had been soaking for the better part of the past day. Maybe he was imagining the chill from his girlfriend. She'd been normal. Nice. Just . . . something felt not quite *right*.

Behind him, in the grandstand, a mid-concert band stoked up the crowd, country music twanging into the night during the break between Oaken's sets.

"Well, I think everyone is a little weirded out about Steinbeck. I mean, who is this girl, really? A spy, like Austen said, or a regular girlfriend? I mean, he's been holding her hand all day. And now, what, they're leaving, just like that?"

"That was weird, but you know Stein. He can't just . . . be normal."

Conrad laughed. "Yes. *Normal* is not the word I'd use for him. He's been so restless for the past few months."

"It's the girl. She makes him crazy."

Conrad looked at him. "So, yes to the girlfriend."

"Yes to something. And I get it. Harper has always been . . . I don't know. Under my skin, I guess."

"In a good way."

"In a makes-me-crazy kind of way. Except for today. She's acting . . . weird."

Conrad stood beside him, hands in his pockets, reading the menu board. "She seems fine to me."

"That's because you're not dating her."

"She's holding your hand, laughing at your jokes." He glanced at Jack. "You're overthinking this."

"Maybe. I mean . . . Okay, so a couple nights ago, I had this whole romantic thing planned. I was . . ." He sighed. "I was going to ask her to marry me."

Conrad looked at him, a smile cresting across his face. "About time."

"I know. I was sort of . . . Maybe I did it wrong, but I told her I needed her help naming Flo."

Conrad frowned. "That doesn't sound like a proposal."

"I know—but see, I was going to say it was like naming our first child, and then suddenly it sounded stupid in my head—"

"That is stupid."

"And I just thought . . . *nope.* I sort of blew it, and before I could regroup, she asked me to take her home so she could keep working on her book."

"Penny says she's close to finishing it." Conrad turned back to the menu board. "So, you take another shot."

"That's the thing. I feel like . . ." He sighed. "I have the ring and everything, and it all suddenly feels wrong."

Conrad moved up in line. A popcorn machine bulleted fresh corn into a glass case. Behind that, nacho cheese baked in a hot pot and fresh pretzels spun in a warmer.

The server asked for Conrad's order. Popcorn for Penny. Nothing for him. Conrad glanced at Jack.

"I'm not sure I know what she wants."

Con glanced at him. "Um, she said a giant pretzel and cheese."

Right. Actually, "No, that was Austen. Harper wants nachos. Although I'm so full I could . . . Okay, I'll have a long dog, with onions."

The server punched in his order and Conrad paid with his phone.

"Thanks, bro."

Conrad moved over to the receiving line.

Jack shoved his hands into his pockets. Outside, the band sang a Ben King cover.

> *"When you need a friend . . . a shoulder you can cry on,*
> *someone who understands what you're going through,*
> *Just look over here, see me standing closer . . ."*

Conrad folded his arms.

"What?"

"So, propose already." He smiled. "Because if you don't, I'm going to."

"Propose to Harper?"

"No, idiot. To Penny. I wanted to propose before I left for training camp, and you're mucking it all up. I don't want to steal your limelight, but your window is dimming there, Big Jack."

"That's the thing. I don't know what she wants."

Conrad's mouth opened. Closed. "Okay. I think she's always made that pretty clear."

"Right." He hung a hand behind his neck, moved out of the way as an order was called.

A teenager picked up nachos and cheese. Maybe Harper had wanted the pretzel . . . He couldn't remember, suddenly.

"Stop panicking, Jack. Harper loves you."

He nodded. "Except she also loves Duck Lake, and the King's Inn, and our family—I mean, last night at the bonfire, there was just something in her eyes. Sadness, maybe."

"She was quiet."

"Maybe she doesn't want to go out on the road."

"And live in a school bus? No. That can't be right." Conrad grinned.

"A city bus, and it's pretty sick. We have satellite Internet and an upper deck and—"

"And it's a *bus*. No offense, but, dude, you have a home in Florida. A nice home. With a boat. Just sayin' . . ."

Jack drew in a breath. Another order was called, this time pizza in a box. "That smells good."

"There's clearly something wrong with you. All we've done is eat today. I can't imagine that anything smells good right now."

"You'd be wrong." Although maybe not about Flo. In fact . . . "What if I stayed?"

Conrad lifted a shoulder just as a nearby teen said, "Hey, are you King Con?"

A selfie, a short conversation, and a small gaggle of fans cut off their conversation. Jack retrieved their bags of food, stepped away, and stood at the entrance to the grandstand listening to the band play.

"I never knew a love like this . . ."

"Sorry about that." Conrad came over. "A couple kids from the recent hockey game showed up too."

Jack passed him the bag of popcorn. Conrad stopped him from descending to their front-row seats with a hand to his arm. "What do you mean *stayed*?"

"I just . . . I did something crazy and I took the bar exam in July."

Conrad stole some popcorn. "Interesting."

"I just, you know . . . hate not finishing something."

More popcorn.

"I thought it might be useful as a tracker too. In case anyone gets into legal trouble."

"Anyone meaning *you*."

He lifted a shoulder. "It helps to know the law when you're staring down a sheriff. But now I'm thinking . . . what if she wants to stay? And that's why . . . I mean, maybe that's why she's being weird."

"Still don't think she's being weird, but she is your girlfriend. You know her best."

The words hit him, and he drew them in as the band finished up their song.

"I never knew a love like this . . . 'til there was you."

He *did* know her. And the Harper he loved was adventurous and smart and brave and . . .

A homebody, the girl next door, a woman who wanted a family. A home.

Yeah, that was it.

Applause, and it felt like he'd landed on the right answer. He'd find out the results of the bar, and then . . . and then he'd figure out the right moment to propose.

And they'd live happily ever after.

Alone, it might be simple. Sneak in, grab Luis, sneak out—

But with Steinbeck in the game, they might actually all live too, so there was that.

"I have to admit, Phoenix, you know how to pick a view." Steinbeck perched on a clay-tiled roof next to her, having climbed out onto the seven-story building via the Airbnb she'd rented—conveniently close to the safe house.

In fact, maybe she'd consider moving it, since from here it was a simple jump from one building to the next—if one ignored the gap of sure death—and a scramble across a clutter of buildings all the way to the stone balcony built into the roof of the one-room apartment-slash-safe-house.

For a brief time, she'd lived here, back when she was trying to shake off the terror of Krakow, so yes, the view was etched in her memory.

An orange-rose sunset blushed the Douro River, turning the red roofs flanking each shore a deep copper, and on the water, boats stacked up, one against the other, along the harbor. Spanning the river, the impressive Dom Luís I Bridge, created by the architect of the Statue of Liberty, cast a golden glow across the water.

From the wharf and the long stone boardwalk, cobbled streets wound uphill to the district of Ribeira, the historic buildings bathed in soft light, the sound of fado music drifting up from the street cafés.

Across the river, in the Vila Nova de Gaia, the terraced restaurants and hotels sparkled against the deepening light, and perched on a tall cliff, the arched entrances of the old Serra do Filar monastery glowed like eyes over the river. The Taylor's Port winery building anchored the other end of the boardwalk.

And overlooking it all, the Baroque Paço Episcopal, shining like a light on a hill.

"I take you to all the best places," she said, glancing over at Steinbeck.

He wore a black shirt and a pair of dark cargo pants, and frankly, he looked like a thief. But he grinned at her, those blue eyes sparking, a smile on his face, and *oh, focus.*

Because it was one thing to play a role in a game of normal. Completely another to have this man in her real life, shoulder to shoulder . . .

"Am I ever going to be rid of you?"

She shook the question away and focused on the route. "Listen. There's cameras. And a wire all around the balcony, just like at my place. You trip it, an alarm sounds. He'll know we're coming."

"So?"

"He might shoot us."

He glanced at her. "You go first."

"Coward."

"Brawk, brawk, baby. I've already been shot once hanging out with you."

Oh. Right.

He drew in a breath. "Hey. Kidding. You also saved my life. So—I'll go first—"

"You're right. He might not recognize you." She put a hand on his arm. Muscles. *Hello.* "But I go first. Let's go."

She scrambled down the roof, careful not to dislodge any tiles, and made the leap to the next building. Flatter roof, so nothing fell, and she crawled up to the peak as he followed her. Across the ridgeline, and there below, another short drop and they'd land right on the stone-covered balcony. A light burned inside.

She glanced at Steinbeck. "On the off chance that the Russians have found him—"

"I got you—"

"Save Luis."

He cocked his head at her. "No one dies on my watch. Just go."

Her mouth tightened and she gauged the drop—seven stories down. Six-foot gap. She motioned him back and he complied.

"You sure you can—"

She took off at a run, sailed off the edge, landed on the stone balcony.

The alarm screeched, and she hustled over to the security box and punched in the code just as the sliding door opened.

Luis Sousa appeared at the door, holding a weapon, and within a second, Steinbeck had snatched it away, disarming him.

She hadn't even seen him land behind her. Now he pushed Luis back into the room, his gun out.

"Clear."

She followed him in, her hands up. "Luis, it's me, Phoenix."

The poor man had his own hands up, his eyes wide as he stared between her and Steinbeck, his breath catching. Then, "Phoenix?"

Stein lowered his gun. "You okay?"

Luis looked at him, and it took a second, but, "Steinbeck?"

"Yep, it's me."

Luis had been in his late twenties when they'd scooped him out of the Ukrainian embassy, had liberated him from Russian hands. A genius hacker who'd made an enemy of the Russian government by hacking into their servers and leaking troop movements during the war.

He'd put on weight in the year since she'd last seen him, filled out, and bore the appearance of someone accustomed to trouble. He put his hands down. "What are you—" He glanced at Phoenix. Then, "Are you two working together?"

Steinbeck let out a breath. "Yes."

Luis grinned. "I knew it. Even then, I knew you two were partners—"

"Stop," Phoenix said. "We need to get you out of here."

"Finally," he said and walked over to the round table where his laptop sat. She glimpsed the photo on the lock screen a moment before he closed the lid. So Luis had found a girlfriend. Or maybe his sister?

It didn't matter. She walked over to the kitchen and looked at the security screen, the same system she'd set up in her apartment. "Hallway looks clear."

"I created a false trail," Luis said, tucking his computer into his backpack. "I hacked into their system and left breadcrumbs. A plane ticket to Barcelona. Another to New York City. Hotel accommodations in Manhattan."

"How'd you do that?" Stein asked, closing the balcony doors, locking them.

"I logged in via their smart TV."

Phoenix stopped near the door. "How?"

"It's connected to the Internet—they're like a welcome mat for hackers. I'm hungry."

"We'll eat on the plane," she said. Looked at Stein. "Ready?"

He nodded, got behind Luis, grabbed his backpack.

"What plane?"

"The one to Montelena." She opened the door.

Darkness bathed the hallway, and she eased out, then nodded to Steinbeck. He pushed Luis out right behind her as she hurried down the stairs. Seven flights, no problem, and when she hit the bottom, she waited for them at the entrance to the alleyway that overlooked a cobblestone street leading down to the boardwalk.

She met Stein's eyes in the semidarkness.

"He gets to the plane, no matter what."

Stein rolled his eyes. "Now you're annoying *me*."

"Keep up." She opened the door.

Outside, shadows darkened the narrow alleyway. Streetlights and tourists cluttered one side; the other ran up to a dead end.

She edged out and took off, quick-walking to the end. Holstered her Glock as she reached the corner.

Luis stepped up behind her.

"Any reason to think they know you're here?"

Luis shook his head.

She peeked back out at the street. A riverboat cruise ship had let off passengers who now wandered the shops and ate at the cafés along the boardwalk.

Music filtered up from the wharf.

Their rented car waited three blocks up, parked near the bridge on Rua da Ribeira.

"Let's take the wharf. We'll blend into the crowd."

Stein nodded, and she rolled out of their corridor, into the twilit night. Stein walked behind her, Luis between them. She quick-walked down the gray cobblestones toward a plaza with streetlamps and an expansive restaurant with tables topped with red umbrellas, glittering with twinkle lights.

The romance of the city sparkled on the water in multicolored lights and long dinner-style ferryboats with music lilting into the velvety night. Couples walked hand in hand, some with dogs on leashes, others stopping to look at the wares in one of the many kiosks that lined the boardwalk. Art, jewelry, cork purses, sardines in colored tins, scarves, and food—so much food. Her stomach growled.

She glanced over at Stein. He wore his Krakow expression, all business, scanning the area, and it struck a sense of camaraderie inside her.

No, he far from annoyed her.

Stairs to her left led to a long elevated boardwalk with more tables and chairs. It overlooked the wharf like a promenade deck. Shops below it offered more souvenirs.

A ferry's horn bellowed from the pier ahead of them. She glanced again at Stein, whose gaze scrutinized the pier. But out of the corner of her eye—

Someone was following them on the upper deck. She spotted him—dark jacket, bulky form.

Boris.

What—

"They're onto us."

Steinbeck glanced at her. "How?"

"I don't know!"

Stein put a hand on Luis's bag. "Where?"

"Upper deck. Could be more behind us."

A short nod, then, "Take Luis. Get on the ferry. I'll be right behind you."

Her mouth tightened. Exactly what she'd said to him in Cuba. But—"Fine." She grabbed Luis's shoulder strap. "With me."

Stein peeled off, headed toward one of the stores under the archway. She didn't look at him, but she guessed he'd find a shadowed alcove, wait to see who they chose.

Probably her. And Luis—

"I don't know how they found me!" Luis said, and she glanced at him.

"They might have known where you were all this time. Probably, you were bait." And it hit her then, right in the chest. They'd been *waiting* for her. And the voice of Tomas, the Bratva leader, ran through her head: *"We'll see."*

It *had* been ridiculously easy for them to escape Sintra. "Let's go," she said and picked up her pace, bumping into a couple tourists. "Sorry." The ferry's horn blew again, and she urged Luis into a run.

Screams erupted behind them, but she didn't look back as they cut down the pier, headed for the ferry, pulled up broadside to the dock.

A man stood at the gangway.

"Tickets on board?"

He nodded, and she shoved Luis through the gated entry. Followed, and then turned.

On the boardwalk, Steinbeck had overturned a couple tables and was now grappling with a man. People shouted, backed away from the violence.

The horn blew one last time. *C'mon, Stein.*

The struggle turned the twinkle lights garish, the music now dying as more people screamed.

Phoenix scanned for the man's backup.

Yes, there—Boris, running along the upper deck.

Run, Stein!

Except, the Russian Steinbeck grappled with—she wanted to guess Igor, but really, she couldn't see his face—grabbed Stein around the neck, a sleeper hold.

Don't—

Stein stepped back, and she knew the move—chin tuck, grab, a knee bend, and the man flew over him. Crashed into more tables and slid to the cobblestones.

"Stein!"

She couldn't help it. And he probably couldn't hear her, but he took off running.

So not slow. She'd been wrong about all of it.

The ferry started to pull away just as he rounded the pier, the gangway already up.

"Run!"

She left Luis, ran over to the edge of the ferry, near the pier, and held out her hand. "Jump!"

Steinbeck leaped out over the water. Slammed against the railing.

She got a hand on his shirt and reached for his belt, but he was already scrambling up, working his feet onto the side, hooking a foot into the railing.

Winding an arm around his torso, she pulled him over.

He landed right on top of her on the deck, her arms around him, holding on as he breathed hard, his back to her.

"Welcome aboard," she said.

He rolled onto his hands and searched for Luis. Then his eyes landed back on her and he grinned.

What?

"I hope this is a dinner cruise. I'm starved."

SEVEN

STEIN REFUSED TO BELIEVE THIS WAS THE END. Mission accomplished, and *thank you so much—you can go home, Steinbeck.* He was no longer necessary.

He sat in a Learjet, across from Phoenix and the empty box of some kind of Portuguese hamburger she'd picked up on the way to the airport. And a Snickers bar, of course.

Good thing Portugal kept European late-night hours.

Luis lay across a sofa in the back, probably getting his first decent sleep since he'd escaped from the Russians two days ago. Or had he really escaped?

The entire event nagged at Steinbeck. *Something . . .*

Or maybe he could blame his grumpy mood on his aching knee. The area around his artificial joint had swollen, burning, a deep bruise forming, maybe from the dog, maybe from the leap onto the ferryboat.

Probably the all-out sprint. Because while he could run, his lack of speed and stamina had disqualified him from returning to active duty status with the teams.

Really, it had not been a bad showing for Mr. Slow and Annoying.

Still. He should have seen the guy following them from the upper deck. He was losing his touch. At least he'd caught the guy on his six.

"Stop."

He looked over to where Emberly—no, *Phoenix*—sat, under a blanket, her legs stretched out onto the seat next to her. "What?"

"You're pacing."

"I'm sitting here."

"In your head. I know that look."

He arched an eyebrow.

"Krakow. Trying to figure out what went south. And what to do next."

She leaned up. "For the record, me too. I keep rounding back to the idea that they had to have been tracking us."

"Or him." He glanced at Luis, then back at her. "But yeah, I keep going back to Sintra. How they didn't guard you . . . You just walked out."

She nodded, sighed. "I can't help but think they've been one step ahead of us the entire time."

"Us." He didn't correct her.

Maybe this wasn't over. And *shoot,* his chest filled with hope at that thought.

"What's in Montelena?" he asked. "I looked. It's a landlocked country in the middle of nowhere."

"It's in a valley in the middle of the Dolomites. It's about as big as Liechtenstein, with only one city—Luciella. It's in a valley, stays green most of the year despite the snowcapped mountains. And it's ruled by a king, a whole royal family."

She sat back, folded her legs. She'd purchased a sweatshirt at the airport. Deep green that matched her beautiful eyes and . . . *Stop.* This kind of thinking wouldn't help . . . well, him, at the very least.

She was describing Luciella. "Gorgeous old city, it was nearly destroyed twenty years ago. Meticulously rebuilt. Underneath the facade of the cobblestone streets and the Baroque and Renaissance architecture, you'll find state-of-the-art technology. And . . . the world's most secure cybervault."

"A cybervault?"

"Montelena is the world's bank for all things crypto. Has its own cryptocurrency, and its own dedicated, unhackable satellite. Countries use their system for international trading because they have impenetrable security. They're the Switzerland of digital currency. And virtually anything digital that needs protecting."

"Now I understand why Declan parked Axiom there."

"They also have a secure lab where Luis and Declan can create the virus." She glanced at the hacker. "He's brilliant. And with Declan's help, he'll figure it out."

She turned back to Stein, considering him. "But that's not what you're worried about."

"I just want to deliver the package."

She quirked an eyebrow. "And go home?"

He met her eyes, held her gaze. "I—"

The pilot came over the speaker and announced their descent into Montelena.

She looked away, and his response died.

I don't know. I . . . don't want to.

Except, there was Jack again, in his head. *"Don't pursue this woman with the hope that she's going to give you some sort of purpose. Only God can do that."*

Stein looked out the window. Below, an azure-blue river curved through the city with jewel-crowned trees—ruby, amber, emerald—tufted along the banks. Hugging the shoreline on either side, the city was a clutter of red-roofed apartments and whitewashed stone buildings. A drawbridge connected the city, with an Oxford-looking university on one side, an old town on the other, and a row of stately embassies at the foot of a palace on a cliff. On the old-town side, the buildings circled a central cathedral with tall Gothic spires.

He half expected a dragon to appear, swish its tail along the cobbled square.

They touched down. A trio of SUVs waited for them on the tarmac.

Declan had kept his promise. He stood in front of one wearing a suit jacket and a pair of Ray-Ban sunglasses, his expression pensive, alongside another man with a military bearing and short brown hair, wearing wraparound sunglasses, also in a suit coat. And with them, a petite woman with short dark hair, wearing black pants, a Blue Ox sweatshirt, and a computer satchel over her shoulder.

He recognized London, her blonde hair tied back in a sleek ponytail, wearing a leather jacket, black pants, and aviator glasses, but not the man next to her. He'd expected Roy, maybe, and this man was about his size, solid, with brown hair and a solemn expression on his face.

Steinbeck grabbed his backpack, disembarked, and walked over to them. He threw a glance at Luis, who had followed him down the stairs, and held out his hand. "London."

"Steinbeck." She turned to the man next to her. "This is my fiancé, Shep Watson."

Interesting. He shook Shep's hand as London hugged Phoenix.

"Emberly. Good job." She turned to Luis with her hand outstretched. "Luis. So glad you're safe."

Steinbeck approached Declan and shook his hand. Declan gestured to his companion. "Logan Thorne, head of the Caleb Group."

Right. He'd heard of him through his cousin Colt. "I heard you were on Team 5."

"A long time ago," Logan said. "This is Coco Marshall." He smiled at the woman beside him.

"Your husband plays goalie for the Blue Ox," Steinbeck said.

"With your brother Conrad." She had a strong grip, held his gaze without flinching.

"So you're the hacker that saved us on the high seas?"

"Glad you weren't shark bait." She hitched up the satchel and glanced at Luis. "Excuse me."

Declan and Logan went with her, which left Stein standing beside Shep.

"You hungry?" Shep asked.

"What do you have in mind?"

He nodded toward the others. "We'll need a debrief, and then my guess is that they'll all huddle up in the bunker. Can I introduce you to a pig's knuckle?"

"A what?"

Shep clapped him on the shoulder, smiled, and directed him to one of the SUVs. Steinbeck turned at the open door, searching for Phoenix.

In the middle of a conversation with London, she glanced at him and smiled.

Warmth exploded in his chest, a crazy wash of longing and desire. He stupidly lifted his hand to her.

She nodded and turned back to London.

He got in the car, Shep at the wheel. They pulled out of the airport onto a road toward town.

And just like that, it was over. He was dismissed.

No longer needed.

Stein leaned his head back against the seat, closed his eyes.

"Declan said you were his bodyguard for a while?"

"Mm-hmm."

"And Thorne mentioned a stint with the SEALs."

He looked over at Shep. "Yep. You?"

"I'm on an SAR team in Alaska. But I was a medic with the Tenth Mountain Division before that."

"And now?"

"Today I'm here for London."

"Phoenix also calls her Mystique."

They drove through the countryside outside Luciella, along the road that traced the river. The grand palace seemed even more ominous as they drew closer.

"Yeah, that's her Swan name. She took over leadership after her handler was . . . injured." His mouth tightened around the corners.

"Injured?"

"Taken by the Bratva. Interrogated." He shook his head. "She disappeared from the hospital in Luciella and we haven't heard from her since."

"You think they took her?"

"No," he said, and glanced at Stein. "I think she's in the wind. And the only person who might know—a guy named Roy—"

"I know Roy."

"Then you know he's not giving her up even if she wants to stay gone."

"So London—Mystique—is now head of the Black Swans?"

They entered town, slowing as they drove through neighborhoods that looked very much like Old Town Krakow, with twists and turns and opulent Renaissance-, Romanesque-, and even Baroque-style buildings, most with tall windows and grand balconies with ornate balustrades, the building numbers carved into decorative plaques. A representation of centuries of architecture all in one small footprint, although recently built. All part of the deception to keep their cybersecurity safe, probably.

"Yes," Shep said. "I'm not thrilled, but it's in her blood. She can't let go until she finds someone else to take over." They drove past the square, along the row of embassies, and pulled up to a creamy-white five-story hotel that hugged the base of the mountain. Over the door, a blue-and-gold flag adorned with a royal crest rippled in the wind, and a crest with a crown at the apex was imprinted over the ornate entrance.

"The Royal Guardhouse," Shep said as he took a parking ticket and drove down, under the mountain. "It's connected to the palace via an underground tunnel. They converted it after the earthquake. It has a few surprises."

He parked in what seemed to be a cavern, half concrete, half mountain, and they got out. "The Swans lease the top floor." Shep pushed the elevator button. "Prince Luka has a soft spot for London."

They got on, Shep keyed in a code, and the lift rose to the penthouse suites.

They entered a small domed foyer with deep-blue carpet and a gold chandelier. "This used to be full of prison cells where they kept people waiting for execution. It survived the earthquake, as did the palace."

"Thanks for the history lesson. I'm not going to be haunted by the voices of old prisoners, am I?"

"The view from the cells is worth it." Shep smiled and opened the double oak door. They entered another room, this one expansive, with plush white carpet, two dark-blue velvet sofas, and a polished-stone coffee table. Along one wall ran a dark mahogany table with chairs for twelve, and a built-in buffet stocked with white china. The other wall held a number of television flatscreens.

But the view ahead caught Steinbeck—the oversized French doors leading to a balcony that overlooked the town, the river, and the snowcapped mountains.

"Offices are to the right, guest rooms to the left." Shep pointed down a hallway. "You're in the first on the right, facing the view."

"Is Emberly staying here too?"

"Last door on the end, facing town."

"I'm grabbing a shower."

"I have a better idea. Drop your gear—I'll meet you here in five."

"As long as it involves food."

"Trust me."

Stein dropped his backpack on the bed of a room that rivaled the King's Inn and headed back to the lobby.

Shep waited with a couple towels and tossed him one.

They took the elevator back down and got off one level above the garage, a tunnel burrowed through the stone. Electric lanterns lit a pathway, splashing luminescence on the rock, an eerie walk back in time.

It felt like Stein was back in the dungeon in Portugal. Which only made him think about Emberly. Maybe he shouldn't have left her on the tarmac.

"Welcome to the private hot springs of the royal family," Shep said. They strolled along the corridor until it opened to a cavern, more lights bathing a series of steamy pools.

"There's also a cold plunge—" Shep pointed to a man-made grotto. "And a sauna." A glass-walled room with wooden planks was built into the side of the mountain.

"This is . . ."

"A perk of being one of the Cobs."

"Cobs?"

"They're male swans. I'm not a fan of the term either." Shep opened a wooden door and entered a dressing room. Handed Stein a bathrobe. "It's coed, but I reserved it for us for an hour."

Stein showered, then donned the robe and found Shep in the sauna, already sweating.

The hot air caught his breath, filled his lungs. He climbed onto the wooden bench. "So . . . what—you're arm candy?"

Shep laughed. "No." He picked up a ladle and splashed water on some rocks, bathing them in steam. "London is the most amazing woman I've ever met. But more than that, she's got a lot on her shoulders. Unfinished business with the Petrov Bratva. And someone needs to watch her back."

"That's you?"

"I'm not . . . I wasn't a SEAL. But I do know how to spot an oncoming avalanche." He glanced over at Stein. "There's a Bible passage that says 'Two are better than one . . . If either of them falls down, one can help the other up . . . Though one may be overpowered, two can defend themselves.'"

"'A cord of three strands is not easily broken,'" said Stein. "I know those verses."

"London is one. God is the second. I'm the third."

"You don't mind sitting on the sidelines?"

"Someone has to watch the field."

The door opened and a man walked in.

Shep started to get up, but the man held up a hand and Shep sat back down.

"I hope you don't mind the intrusion." The man bore a hint of a European accent, maybe a layer of Italian thrown in. "I heard you were back."

"Got in last night, sir," Shep said. He gestured to Stein. "This is Steinbeck Kingston. He came in with one of the Swans. Stein, meet His Royal Highness, the crown prince of the House of Ribaldi, Prince Luka of Montelena."

"Well done, Shep." The prince turned to Stein. "Luka will be fine."

"Do I . . . bow?"

"You're in your bathrobe. My thought is probably not." Luka grinned. Square chin with a cleft, blue eyes, confidence in his smile.

"I'm sorry, I don't know anything about the Montelena royal family."

"We're a small but sturdy lot," Luka said. "My father, King Max, is on the throne, and my mother, Queen Isabella, is from the royal family of Montenegro, a country in the Balkans."

"I've never heard of it."

"It's located across from Italy, on the Adriatic Sea, part of Serbia-Croatia for many years. Beautiful country. We vacation there."

Right. To get away from the big city of Luciella.

Luka might have read his mind because—"We're really quite normal. My youngest brother, Alrick, is at uni, twenty-one, still figuring out that a major in medieval studies has no practical future. My youngest sister, Madeline, is our fiery redhead and is fighting tradition by joining the military. She's completely obsessed with Hannibal and his march over the Alps with war elephants. We're a part of NATO, but we have a small but fierce security force. I think she wants to be a commander."

He shrugged. "We'll see. My father is fairly open-minded. There are no arranged marriages anymore, although we still have to marry inside royal circles." He sighed. "Hard to do when everyone is a cousin." He glanced at Shep.

They exchanged a look that Steinbeck couldn't read.

"I have a brother, Rillian, who is a chopper pilot a couple of years older than Maddy. He's testing my father's patience regarding the aforementioned law." He smiled.

Shep chuckled.

"The one with her head on her shoulders and most likely to change the world is my oldest little sister, Victoria. She's next in line after me, and just finished her surgical residency in Paris. She's headed back to Queen Grace Hospital to join the staff here."

He leaned back, his head against the wall. "And then there's me. Just . . . the crown prince. Standing at the ready."

"Cry me a river," Shep said. He glanced over at Stein. "Prince Luka is heavily involved in the running of Montelena."

Luka glanced at Shep, grinned. "Indeed. Just because my life's purpose is to wait doesn't mean my days aren't filled with duty."

He looked at Steinbeck. "What do you do?"

"He's working with one of our Swans."

"I see. Well, good luck to you, mate. Not a job for the faint of heart." He laughed, glanced at Shep. "Although enviable, perhaps." He slid off the bench. "The cold plunge is calling."

It was calling Steinbeck too. He followed the prince out and waited in the clammy cave as the man dropped into the cold bath, came out with a growl.

Stein did the same, and the chill flushed away the fatigue in his bones.

"Ready for a pig's knuckle?" Shep said, rising from the dunk.

"Promises, promises," Stein said.

Another shower and an hour later and he sat in a restaurant in the hotel, a red votive candle flickering on the table, the scent of roasting pork and frothy beer embedding the stone walls and wooden floor. He could imagine knights of the realm eating under the wrought-iron chandeliers that hung from ceiling timbers.

He groaned as he set down the thick roasted pork knuckle.

"Told you," Shep said. He pushed the glistening thick-cut fries in a basket toward Stein. "And these are the real deal."

"I have them brought to the palace sometimes," Prince Luka said, sitting across from them in an oxford and a pair of dress pants. He'd rolled up his sleeves.

Stein had changed into a pullover and pants that he'd picked up at the airport in Porto.

"So, what's next for you, Stein?" Luka swam his fry through the ketchup—homemade, Stein guessed, because it was thick and dark and spicy.

"He's working the Petrov op," said Shep. "Helped bring in the Axiom program. They're working on a virus."

Stein glanced at Shep, then at Luka.

"In trade for the Swans parking their HQ here, I'm briefed regularly by London's mother, Ambassador Brooks, and especially her father, Mitch." He took a drink of his craft beer. "What's our next move?"

"Nothing," Stein said. "It's over. We found Axiom. They're creating the virus." He lifted a shoulder. "I guess I'm going home."

Silence. He hadn't meant for that to sound so pitiful.

Luka raised an eyebrow, glanced at Shep, back at Stein. "What about your Swan?"

Stein frowned. "What about . . . my Swan?"

"Swans work alone. Until they don't." Luka glanced again at Shep. "He doesn't know?"

"Know what?"

"Swans mate for life," Shep said quietly.

A beat. "What?"

"Yeah. Clearly you know more than you should, so . . ."

"So it's either stay or I'm shot at high noon?"

"We like to schedule our executions early. Say, dawn," Prince Luka said.

Another beat. "You're kidding."

Shep nodded and Luka made a face. "We had him. You can't fold that easily, mate."

Stein shook his head. Except, for a second, a terrible, burning second—

"But we're also serious."

"About the execution?"

"About . . . well, Phoenix has never had a partner. Until now."

"We're not partners."

Shep looked at him.

"We're . . . we . . ." Stein reached for a fry. "She's just, you know, a force to be reckoned with. And gets in over her head. And I'm not even sure how I got here—"

"You're in love with her, mate." Prince Luka, staring at him over his golden beer.

Stein met his gaze. Opened his mouth. Closed it. "She doesn't have room for me in her life. She's made that pretty clear. And she's not leaving this life either."

"Have you told her how you feel?"

In the silence, he heard his own pitiful voice. *"Maybe we can figure out how to get past survival together?"*

"I think, by the look on his face," Shep said, "he's just figuring that out."

Stein sighed. "It's not so much how I feel, but . . . like I said—"

"There's no room for you in her life." Prince Luka finished his drink. Pushed away his basket of bones. "I don't think that's the real problem here, mate."

Stein folded his arms.

"Hear me out. I used to think my time was empty, a waste. Just a guy waiting to be king. But then I realized that standing in the shadows gave me a view that others didn't have. I saw the stress, the threats, even the sacrifices my father made. And that gave me insight into how to protect him. Help him. Like Aaron did for Moses. You might consider that you're the *only one* she'd make room for. And perhaps that's why you're here."

"Eating a pig's knuckle?"

"Talking to a prince who understands that it's not my title that matters but my everyday obedience and value to the King." He got up. "And I'm not talking about my father. Good to see you, Shep. Dinner is on the house."

He walked away, and only then did Steinbeck see a couple of security guards peel from the shadows. *Huh.*

"So," Shep said, picking up his knuckle. "I'm going to ask you the same thing my future father-in-law asked me when I was where you are. Are you still on mission?"

Steinbeck stared at him. But deep inside, he knew the answer.

"There's no use waiting up. Go back to the hotel; get some sleep." Mystique stood outside the glass doors of the secure lab under the mountain in the Cybertex vault. She sipped coffee, having just made another pot for the geniuses inside working on the Axiom program.

"Nim would love this." Emberly had lost all track of time while debriefing Mystique on the last month, and especially the haywire hack of the service robot, along with the snatch of Luis in Porto.

All the while, Coco, Declan, and Luis talked computer geek.

And Steinbeck's strange wave as he left with Shep rattled around her brain. Like . . .

Was he leaving?

But maybe that was the only right answer. Let him go before . . .

Before her worst nightmare materialized before her eyes. She'd slept briefly on the plane, had woken with a start, the memory of Steinbeck fighting on the pier searing through her.

She worked better alone.

Really.

"You did well," Mystique was saying. "Eight months. We would have never gotten here if you hadn't stayed the course."

"Yeah, well, mission failure on getting the program."

"You'll do better next time." Mystique took a sip of coffee.

And the words simply swelled up, through her, and out. "What if there is no next time?"

Mystique froze, and Emberly did too because . . . *Really?* She swallowed.

Blue eyes considered her. "How long have you been thinking of leaving?"

"About thirty-two seconds."

A half-hidden smile.

"I'm not sure I'm even considering it. It's just . . ." She rubbed her arms. "I've been doing this for so long, I've forgotten what normal feels like." She gave a wry sort of chuckle. "Maybe I don't even know."

"Emberly. This is your normal."

She met Mystique's eyes. "Maybe I want a different normal. A different life."

Mystique nodded. "Okay. This is not one of the three-letter organizations. You can walk away, no looking over your shoulder." She took another sip of her coffee. "But is that what you want?"

Emberly stared at the group of hackers through the glass. "I don't know. Maybe I'm fooling myself. Maybe this is all I am."

"It's not all you are, Emberly. What you *do* is not who you *are*. Let's get that straight."

She shook her head. "Forget I said—"

"Okay. Let's just dial it back here. You need a vacation—there's no doubt about that. Take some time off. Go see your sister. Spend some time with Mr. Minnesota. Listen to your heart and maybe . . . God."

Emberly cocked her head. "I don't think God is interested in me, or what I do."

"I think He's *extremely* interested in you and what you do. He made you, after all. Gave you your life experiences, your skills. It's not for nothing." She took a sip of coffee. "I know you believe in God, Emberly. You told me about what happened—"

Emberly held up a hand. "That was a long time ago, and I was—"

"Scared, desperate, and overwhelmed. Exactly where we all are when we finally realize we're in over our heads. And that's when God shows up in our life."

"You have a painfully good memory."

"I'm just saying. You're very, very good at what you do. But God knows you better than you know yourself, and maybe you should ask Him what your next step is."

Emberly sighed.

Mystique cocked her head, raised an eyebrow. "I tried to walk away more than a few times, and this life always pulled me back. And God was generous to give me a man who considers it his mission to walk this journey with me."

She took another sip of her coffee, the dim light of the foyer casting over her. "But you are not me, Emberly. Life is a journey of choices. I believe everything happens for a reason, one step leading to the next. I think every step, whether good or bad, is meant to bring us closer to God."

She finished her coffee, tossed the cup into a nearby trash can. "God loves you. Every move you've ever made has been under His watchful eye. He has a plan, and it's a good one. So . . . maybe take a minute or two and ask Him what he thinks. And remember, His answer is good. Even if it's confusing. Faith is the only way out of the chaos of this world. Get some sleep." She pushed into the lab.

Emberly watched as she walked up and stood, arms akimbo, surveying Luis's work, and his words back in Porto filtered back, softly, a nudge. *I knew it. Even then, I knew you two were partners.*

Maybe she had known it too.

She turned and headed down the hall. *Please let Steinbeck not have left—he wouldn't have, right?*

Except, their mission was over.

And he'd . . . waved. *Goodbye?*

The vault led to a tunnel that ended at a gated entrance and an elevator. She hit the button and it opened.

She took it up a level, to another tunnel connecting the vault to a passageway that led through the mountain. Finally she stepped out onto a stone walkway, the night glittering above, a thousand tiny lights peering down from the sky.

"Faith is the only way out of the chaos of this world."

She didn't know why that lingered inside her more than any of Mystique's other words, but she wanted to believe it—that God did care.

That maybe she hadn't been alone after all.

And perhaps not anymore either. The thought caught her up as she entered the Guardhouse Hotel, keyed in the code to the penthouse apartment, and took the lift up.

The light from the foyer splashed into the hallway, and she stood at the door, took a breath.

Then she pushed in her door code. The door opened.

Darkness bathed the big living room, just starlight pushing in through the shades. *Oh.* She didn't know what time it was, but certainly it wasn't so late that he'd gone to bed?

"He's not here."

She turned, and Shep stood in the hallway. He was barefoot, wore a button-down shirt, and came out into the dimly lit room. "Steinbeck. He left about an hour ago."

"He . . . what?"

Shep sighed. "We came back from dinner, and I was in the office when I heard the front door close. I saw him on the monitor taking the elevator down. He had his backpack."

She stilled, her mouth opening. "I don't . . . I thought . . ." She wrapped her arms around herself. "Okay."

"I'm sorry, Emberly."

"Phoenix. I know Mystique calls me Emberly, but . . ." Her eyes burned. "I'm Phoenix, really."

Shep nodded, shoved his hands into his pockets. "How's London?"

"She's still at it. With the others."

"I set up a room for you. Last one at the end of the hall."

"Okay."

She headed down the hallway, let herself into her room. Didn't bother to turn on the light, but sank down on the bed.

So he'd left. He *had* waved goodbye. Her stupid words burned in her head. *"Am I ever going to be rid of you?"*

Swans didn't cry. She'd chosen this life. He hadn't. He'd been, at best, voluntold, roped into being her teammate.

Boyfriend.

Whatever.

She got up, went over to the window to pull the curtains, and caught her scream between her teeth.

Movement on her balcony. A man leaning against her railing, arms crossed, a stalwart figure in the darkness.

She wrenched open the doors, her heart hammering. "What are you doing out here?"

He'd dropped his backpack at his feet and now leaned up, took a step toward her. "I left. On a mission. And got locked out. I think Shep must have fallen asleep, so I climbed up the outside, and your room was the only balcony I could reach."

She stared at him. "You . . . climbed up the outside? What kind of ridiculous person are you?"

"It's not hard, which is something your team might want to consider. So much for a secure location—"

"You're nuts! That was three flights."

"Actually, no. It was a walk up to the rooftop dining area of the restaurant and then a scramble up to the balcony." He nodded to the jutting terrace just a story below.

She leaned over. Twinkle lights edged the eating area, a few patrons at tables, enjoying the balmy early September night.

"Besides, I wanted to bring you this." He leaned down and picked up his bag, opened it. Pulled out—

"A . . . a Snickers bar?"

He shrugged. "Felt like the right thing."

"The right thing."

"I thought you . . . I thought you left." *Oh,* the wavering in her voice didn't help at all.

He stepped toward her, frowned. "I was going to. And then I realized—" He took a breath. "The mission's not over."

"We got Axiom."

He took a step closer, his blue eyes holding hers. "That's not my mission, Emberly."

Oh.

"I don't know what's next for me, but I do know I don't want to leave you." He swallowed. "I don't know why, because you're unpredictable, and dangerous—"

"And trouble?" But she stepped up to him. From somewhere on the street, music rose, along with laughter, the night crowd eating.

"Maybe a little trouble," he said softly.

Her heart thumped, the richness of the autumn night in the air, the stars blinking overhead, the scent of adventure and even mystery on his skin. "I don't mean to be trouble. But this . . . this is me." She gestured to herself, her dark pants, the green sweatshirt. "This is me. Or I thought so until you . . . you . . . you . . . showed up. And you totally—"

"Messed up your world," he said, dropped the candy bar back into his pack, then closed the gap between them. His hand went around her neck, his eyes held hers, just for a moment; then his mouth took hers, as if it belonged to him.

As if she was his.

And maybe she was. Maybe she had been for a long time, like Luis had said—*"I knew you two . . ."*

She wrapped her arms around his waist, holding on, lifting herself on her toes so she could have more of him.

And him, more of her.

He tasted salty and yet sweet, his kiss deepening as his strong arms curled around her. He took another step, and her back touched the cool stone wall of the ancient building. She made a noise and he lifted his head, met her eyes.

"You okay?"

"I have no idea what I am."

He smiled. "You're beautiful. And smart. And brave. And crazy—"

"The first thing that actually sounds like me." She laughed.

He cut her off with another kiss, this time slower, taking his time, although his arms tightened around her.

As if he couldn't bear to let her go.

She'd kissed him before—stolen kisses, really—and the one in the yard might have been for show. But this . . . this one bore the sense of something real. As if he was giving over a piece of himself. His heart? His future—

She closed her eyes. *"Are you in love with my brother, Phoenix?"* *Oh no.*

He lifted his head again. Met her eyes. "I—"

The lights to her room glared on, and her balcony door slammed open. "Get away from her!"

He stepped back, hands up, just as Shep and Logan pushed out to the balcony, weapons up.

"It's just me!" This from Steinbeck, and just in case, Emberly stepped in front of him.

"Stop!"

Mystique barreled in behind them, breathing hard. She stared at the two, then at Shep. "The alarm went off."

"Logan pulled it—"

"Because security called and said they saw a man climbing the side of the building," Logan growled.

"Again, just me," said Steinbeck. "Sorry. I lost my key."

Shep gaped at him.

Logan lowered his weapon, his jaw tight. "Thank you very much. I was asleep."

"You shouldn't sleep. It's bad for your jet lag," Emberly said.

He looked at her.

She lowered her hands. "Just saying. I travel a lot. I know these things."

Shep shook his head, headed out of the room, Logan behind him.

"You need better security!" shouted Steinbeck after them.

Mystique had remained on the balcony. Gave them both a long look, then shook her head. "Okay, then."

"Okay, what?" Emberly said, her entire body still a little flushed.

"Okay, you're on a plane tomorrow back to the States. We got this. And you two"—she pointed at them—"need to figure out what you really want."

She turned and walked off the balcony.

Steinbeck drew in a breath. Took a step back. "That's probably a good idea."

"What? Figuring out what we want?"

He smiled then, something soft, even sweet. "Oh, sweetheart, I know what I want. Which is why I'm following London out of your room." He leaned into her, however, his mouth close to hers. "But I'll be just down the hall, so don't even think of leaving without me."

She grabbed his collar. "Leave the Snickers bar."

He laughed, kissed her again, and just as she was about to slide her arms around his neck, he stepped back and walked across her room.

"I want—"

He turned and tossed her the candy bar. "I know." Then he winked and was gone.

You.

"He is one hot man."

Harper glanced at Penny, dressed in an oversized Blue Ox jersey, custom-made, with *King Con* and his number embroidered on the back. She wore a pair of jeans, her long hair back in a messy bun, barely any makeup on her tanned face.

"I know you're talking about Con, but . . . you're right." Harper turned back to watching Jack and Conrad slap around a puck in a Sunday afternoon Duck Lake community scrimmage at the North Star Arena. Conrad had roped Jack into helping out with a handful of youngsters from the Ice Hawks, a team put together by the Pepper charity foundation, EmPowerPlay.

Conrad had the moves of a professional center, but Jack knew his way around the ice and could still skate circles around these kids, earning both their respect and frustration as he stole passes and inspired footwork.

"You two okay?" Penny looked over at her.

Harper should have worn more than a sweatshirt over her leggings, because she had to pull the sleeves down over her fisted hands, her breath catching in the frigid air of the arena. Outside, the sun hovered over a perfect, nearly cloudless September day, and frankly, she would have rather been home, watching the lake lap the shoreline, editing her book, but . . .

No, not true. She'd rather have been looking at wedding-dress catalogues or even asking Penny to be her maid of honor.

Apparently, that wasn't in her future.

She wouldn't have even agreed to show up today, except . . . well, she had to tell Penny her big news in person. Never mind Jack.

She had to stop dodging the future.

Step one, level with her best friend about quitting the podcast.

Step two would be breaking up with Jack.

"We're fine." But maybe her sigh gave her away, because Penny looked over and raised an eyebrow.

"That sounds like trouble in paradise. I thought . . . well, Conrad says that the bus is finished."

"It is. And Jack invited me over to see it—I mean, I knew it was nearly done, but I admit I've been head down in my computer for the last couple weeks."

"You finished the book?"

Harper made a face. "I'm stuck on the ending. I got them to the breakup, but I can't see to get them all the way to the happy ending."

"You need that big grand gesture," Penny said. "Like John Cusack in *Say Anything*, showing up with his boom box."

"You're doing Cusack marathons now, are you?"

"Just the romantic comedies. Especially *Serendipity*. I love that one."

"You're just cold. And it has ice skating."

"He's an unsung hero. But maybe you need a refresher." Penny looked back out onto the ice, where Jack and Conrad were facing off for the kids. They laughed, even as Jack checked Conrad, fighting for the puck. "That over there is a happy ending. Jack, the wanderer, back home, Conrad laughing. I think our work here is a grand success." She lifted her fist.

Harper met it.

"Well, that was wimpy. Seriously. What's going on?"

Here went nothing. "Penny, I was offered a job with *PopMuse* magazine."

Penny turned to her. "That's fantastic. I figured they'd come crawling back to you after you landed Boo's exclusive, not to mention your two-book deal."

"It's in Nashville."

"Oh."

"I could ask them if I could work remotely, but the contract specifically says I need to be in office—"

"Why? I mean . . ." She pointed to Jack. Wore pain on her face. "I thought . . . And what about the podcast?"

"Oh, Pen, you know you can do the research without me. I think you were just being kind when you hired me."

"Hardly. You're my secret weapon."

"You're your own secret weapon. All I do is fact-check, and even that . . . well, you have a way with sources. You always get to the truth."

Penny sighed. "I wondered if something had happened." She frowned. "He didn't propose, did he?"

"No." The admission bored into her, a splinter into her already raw heart. "I thought . . . Anyway, I don't know. He's taking Flo up to Little Falls tomorrow, a test run before he leaves town."

Penny frowned. "I don't think he's leaving. He took the bar."

She stilled. "What?"

"Yeah. Jack told Conrad at the fair that he took the bar exam in July. He's waiting for the results."

Harper looked at him, racing after Conrad, who was just toying with them all now. No wonder he'd landed that fresh contract with the Blue Ox.

"He didn't say anything to me."

"Maybe he wanted to surprise you."

"Or maybe . . . he didn't think I'd want to go out on the road with him."

"Do you?"

She tucked her arms around her. "I don't know. Maybe. I guess I really hadn't thought . . . I mean, that's been the plan. Or . . . not."

"Does he know *you're* leaving?"

"I don't know how he . . ." She stilled. "Maybe. I had the contract on the counter when he came to pick me up. I went upstairs to change into a dress. Came back down and he was already outside, on the patio, waiting for me, looking at the lake." Her eyes widened. "You think he didn't propose because he thought I was leaving?"

Penny lifted a shoulder.

"But why would he take the bar?" She sighed.

"You know what could solve this?"

Harper lifted a shoulder.

"A *conversation*." Penny bumped her. "It's something that two people who love each other do sometimes."

"Thanks, Dr. Phil. Except how is that supposed to go, exactly? Hey, Jack, so were you going to propose the other night? Because if you were and then didn't because you thought I was leaving, um, feel free to get on one knee, because I'll stay if you want me to. How desperate and sad does that sound?"

"You are not desperate and sad. But you do want to marry him."

Her mouth tightened. "I also don't want to force the guy to propose. I feel like if he wanted to pop the question, he would."

"Jack is not going to stand in the way of your dreams."

"*He* is my dream. And even as I say that, it sounds . . . Aw, see—I need to be on the first plane to Nashville, never look back."

"And end up alone? Please, have a conversation with the man. It goes like this: Jack, I got an offer to go to Nashville. Penny hates it. Do you hate it too? Do you have any reason I should stay?"

She raised an eyebrow.

"Still sounds needy."

"Yeah, well, love is about putting it out there. Being vulnerable. Saying the hard things. Do you believe you two are meant for each other?"

Of course, old words, the ones that had skulked about her heart for the last week, dragged up. *"You were the one, always."*

Jack's words to her, but, "Yes. And always."

"Then maybe it's time to step up and write your own happy ending. Tear up the contract. Stay. And not for me but for you." Penny took her hand, warm against her cold fingers, her golden-brown eyes holding Harper's. "What do you really want?"

Harper turned, her gaze following him on the ice—strong, capable Big Jack.

"That's what I thought. Now sit back and can we please just enjoy the view?

EIGHT

H E'S AMAZING, EM."

Emberly looked up at Nimue, who sat with her legs folded on her wide daybed swing under the front porch of her beachside cottage. White porch, sky-blue house, not even twelve-hundred square feet, but perfect for Emberly's little sister. It had been remodeled inside and out by Nimue, who'd gutted the kitchen, the bathroom, and the two bedrooms and even renovated the back patio to include a small round hot tub.

Never mind her upstairs office that overlooked the ocean. Teched out with the latest gear, Nimue freelanced out her hacking skills, under contract with security companies to test their systems.

Now, they both watched Steinbeck in the yard, building a gazebo over the stone patio in Nimue's quaint yard.

Indeed, the man exuded amazing, stripped down to his shorts, a layer of sweat sheening his body, the sun glistening on his skin. He wore a pair of wraparound sunglasses, a baseball hat backward over his dark golden hair, and talked to himself as he read the printed instructions for the build.

The scent of sawdust mingled in the salty breeze, and the crash of the ocean on the beach hummed in the air.

Four days and she'd finally started to unwind. She'd eaten pizza. Watched movies. Played chess with Steinbeck.

It felt like Phoenix had dropped away, lost somewhere over the ocean.

"I never thought you'd find someone who could—"

"Put up with me?"

"No. *Keep* up with you."

Emberly smiled. "I wasn't sure bringing him here was the right move." She wore a pair of cutoff jeans and a tank top, sipped lemonade. "But..." She glanced at Nimue. "What if I left the Swans?"

Nim raised an eyebrow. "Really?"

"You're smiling."

"I just...I worry." She lifted a shoulder. "So do Boz and Anna."

"Boz got me into this."

"Doesn't mean he doesn't worry about you. His sixtieth birthday is coming up. You should come."

She met Nimue's golden eyes. "That's your family, not mine."

Nim sighed. "You're always welcome. Your picture is still on the wall—"

Emberly held up a hand.

Nimue drew in a breath and took a sip of her lemonade. "All right. For the record, I'm a fan of you leaving the Swans. But..." She glanced out at Steinbeck. "What does he think?"

"I haven't told him yet. I've barely told myself."

Nimue laughed.

"Truth is, I can't seem to break away from the idea that this isn't over. Somehow the Bratva found Luis in Porto, and..."

Nimue's mouth opened. "You came to check on me."

"Of course I did." She met Nim's eyes.

"You can stop taking care of me, sis. I can take care of myself."

Emberly watched as Steinbeck raised one of the poles and fitted it into a concrete anchor he'd built.

"Maybe you should be more concerned with yourself and making sure you're not in for heartbreak."

Emberly glanced back at her sister. "What?"

"I'm not talking about him—I'm talking about you. Leaving *him.*"

"What would I—"

Nimue gave her a look.

"Listen. I'm not the same person I was back then."

"Mm-hmm."

"I just know when I'm not wanted."

"You are your own worst enemy, sis. Maybe stop projecting all of your greatest fears onto someone and then reacting as if you're right." She unwound herself. "Maybe give the guy a chance before you ditch him."

"I brought him here, didn't I?"

"So far, so good. I just don't want you to suffer from the same ailment our mother had and abandon a good thing when it gets scary."

Emberly glanced out at Steinbeck, who'd set the other pole in place.

"You're almost all the way to happily ever after," Nimue said softly. "Don't spook now."

Emberly breathed in the words. Turned back to Nimue. The wind stirred the nearby planter of geraniums. "We'll see who spooks first."

"He's a former SEAL. My guess is that you're in for a fight."

His words on the balcony filtered back to her. *"That's not my mission, Emberly."*

Oh no. Was she still a project?

Nimue leaned forward. "So, I dug through the dark web, and

Tomas has gone silent. I know you're still worried about what the Bratva is up to."

"I just can't figure out how they corrupted that service animal at the fair—or if it was even them. We could be dealing with a global threat."

"One day at a time," Nimue said. "Let's start with tracking down Tomas and his ilk and figuring out their agenda. And that means sleuthing out how they found you in Porto. All I can think is that they picked up Luis's 911 call to your boss."

"But how? We have the safe house on its own encrypted server. I updated the entire place a year ago. New server, new equipment. Besides, Luis said he'd created a false trail."

"How?"

"He logged into their smart TV—"

Nim sat back. "And left a footprint."

"He's smarter than that."

"Yes. Maybe. Technology is changing all the time. Although . . . maybe . . ." She got up. "Give me your server information. I have an idea."

Emberly followed Nimue into the house, where she opened her computer and pointed Nimue to her stored information.

"Can I take this upstairs?"

"To your lair?"

"To the hub." Nimue winked. Emberly shooed her away.

She filled a water pitcher and made more lemonade, was turning to bring it outside when Stein came in, covered in sweat and sawdust, his blond hair peeking out of his hat.

"I'll give you everything I own for a glass of that."

She smiled. "Wow. That's quite an offer." She pulled down a glass and filled it.

"Not really. My bank account is nearly deflated. I'm going to have to cash in some index funds."

He'd pulled on his shirt and now stood at the counter, drinking.

Admittedly, Emberly didn't think Steinbeck could fit into this world. Not her world, really, but . . .

"I should have the gazebo done by tonight," he said. "I guess all those months helping Doyle and Jack at the inn finally paid off. Your sister did a great job on the remodel."

He was probably noticing the white wood-tiled floors, the granite island, the clean shiplap walls, the way her house seemed at once simple and yet relaxing.

"I love it here. Nim was always way more creative than me."

"Hardly." He slid onto a high-top chair. "You're plenty creative. You've tricked me more than once with your disguises." He smiled, so much tease in it that it only added to his devastating charm. "*Ashley*. And I keep thinking about the wedding. You were a server at the family dinner, weren't you?"

Her mouth opened. Closed. "You remember that?"

"I remember a waitress who nearly ran me down."

"I thought for sure you'd recognize me."

He took a drink, his blue eyes on her. "I should have. You're not easy to forget."

"Were you trying?"

"Maybe." He held her eyes. "Not successfully." He got up. "And not anymore."

And her words from Lisbon just over a week ago stirred inside her, when he'd asked her what kind of different life they might work in.

"A life where . . . when I look at you, I don't see my mistakes. The things I've done. And where you don't look at me and see . . . regret. And anger."

Maybe he remembered them too, because he stepped over to her. "That was then. This is now." He set down his lemonade. "I don't regret anything, Emberly."

"Even Krakow?"

"Especially Krakow." His fingers traced her cheek. "Truth is,

Krakow changed my life. I learned more about God, and myself, after that than I ever had . . ."

She couldn't think with the heat that tremored under her skin at his touch, so she caught his hand. "Like what?"

His gaze landed on her mouth for a moment before he stepped back. "Like in my darkest moment, God showed up. I woke up in the hospital in Germany, doped up on morphine, the world hazy, and the first thing I saw was my parents, hanging out beside my bed. And through the glass, the entire rest of my family, who'd boarded planes to make sure I was okay. Ironically, it was one of my happiest moments." He sat on the stool. "Because I knew that despite the trauma, and whatever would happen ahead of me, I had . . . my team."

Her throat tightened. She exhaled and leaned on the island. "I guess I never had that kind of team. It was always just Nim and me. My mom loved her dad. He was this professor from Nigeria. My mom always said he was a prince." She laughed. "She was happy with him. I remember that."

"And your dad?"

"A rogue Scot."

He grinned. "Of course."

"But Nim and I, we just . . . we were always glue. Especially after her dad died and Mom sort of . . . lost it. Nim was my responsibility."

"Which is why you went back for her."

She nodded. "And then we ended up at the Davidsons' and everything changed." She looked up at him. "It was really good for a while. The Davidsons were good people. They'd cultivated a sort of camaraderie with the other kids. Boz was—"

"Why do you call him Boz?"

"Some of the kids called him Dad, but I . . . well, he suggested Boz—his real name was Boaz—and Anna. And everybody loved them. And I started to also."

She stood up, turned to the fridge. "Want a sandwich?"

"Why did you leave, Emberly? What really happened?"

His soft voice could unravel her. She stood, gripping the fridge handle. "I got saved."

Silence.

She turned and he wore a frown. "And that's bad?"

"No. Yes. I mean—Boz was involved in this summer tent-revival thing. He was there every night for a week, and so . . ." She sighed. "I just . . . I wanted it, all right? I sat there with the other kids and listened to this message of forgiveness and I saw who I was, and I wanted what they had. So . . . I went forward."

He said nothing.

"Boz and Anna were—they were so excited. And for a long minute there, I thought everything would be . . . better. That I'd have a family and maybe I didn't have to be who I was . . ." She scrubbed her hands down her face. "Anyway, about two days later, one of the kids claimed that they had twenty dollars taken from their bedside stash, and Boz and Anna asked if anyone had taken it. I hadn't . . . and even now I realize it was a just a question, but at the time, I thought they were blaming me. I looked at Boz and laughed when he asked me if I knew where it was, when he said that he wasn't going to allow stealing. And he said, 'It's not funny, Emberly. You can't live your old life and call yourself a new creation.'" *Shoot.* Her eyes filled. "I realized I was never going to really be . . . different. Or new or whatever. So I left."

"Self-sabotage."

"Survival."

He raised an eyebrow. "*Yeah.* You said that Boz tracked you down . . ."

"*Yeah.* I called Nimue and she told him where I was. I guess introducing me to Pike was his way of trying to fix the situation."

"But in doing so, it sent a message that he was right. That you were a thief." He slid off the chair and came toward her.

"I *am* a thief, Steinbeck."

"In your eyes. Not in the eyes of your Savior. In his eyes, you're forgiven."

Her eyes stung.

She took a step back. "I don't need a hug."

"Yeah, whatever."

But he didn't advance, just held out his hand.

And heaven help her, she took it. And let him pull her to himself. She leaned her face against his chest.

"Emberly, the one Jesus loves."

She stilled in his arms. He put his cheek against her head. "My mother used to say that to us. There is this disciple, John, in the Bible, who only identified himself as the one Jesus loved. She always said, what might it look like if we did the same?"

Emberly, the one . . .

No. It felt too . . . "That's not me, Stein."

"That's all of us, Em." He leaned back. "That's how we go from survival to . . . saved. To a different life. To the life we were created to live."

He seemed to be taking his own words in, nodding, almost to himself.

And maybe that's why she said it, letting the words spill out. "What if everything was different? What if . . . I left the Swans?"

He pulled away, his blue eyes on hers. "What? Really?"

Except, of course, Nimue chose right then to enter the kitchen. She stopped, her golden-brown eyes wide. "Sorry."

Stein's mouth tightened, and he sighed.

"Nothing to be sorry about," Emberly said and stepped back.

He considered her a moment, as if trying to salvage their conversation. She looked away.

"I need to get back to work," he finally said quietly. He picked up his lemonade and walked out the door.

"I have mentioned he's amazing, right?" Nimue stood, hands on her hips. "Yum."

"He's taken, Nim."

She turned, grinned. "Finally."

Emberly met her smile.

"So, good news. I got into your server and found the trace of Luis's hack into the Russian compound. He's good, but I'm better." She winked. "Because it led me into their cloud storage. I'm downloading it now. Maybe, just maybe, we'll figure out what Tomas is up to."

Emberly turned, looked back outside at Mr. Handy, putting up another pillar. "He's right. The mission isn't over. But it will be. And then . . . then this life is over."

•———————•

Steinbeck hadn't originally hoped he could stay here forever, but frankly, after a week, and now, with the morning sun just tipping the far horizon, the warmth of the day eating at the dissipating velvety night, and the sense of doing something with his hands—building the gazebo—he'd started to wonder.

That's how we go from survival to . . . saved. To a different life. To the life we were created to live.

His own words stuck in his head, along with *Steinbeck, the one Jesus loves.*

Those words could change his life if he let them dig into the soil of his heart. But he couldn't escape the sense of purpose. The sense that maybe God had put him right here, right now and . . .

Well, he had no other moves on his horizon.

Which didn't seem tragic as he stood, his feet mortared in the sand, the ocean waves soft, the sea almost tranquil. The scant wind off the ocean was just enough to cool the thin layer of sweat that coated his skin, thanks to his morning calisthenics, and it stirred the scents of salt and brine and seaweed into the air.

He'd need a walk on the beach this morning, especially after Declan's phone call. Clearly the man had forgotten the time change, because a glance at the clock had registered 4:00 a.m.

"Fun and games are over. I need you to come back and work for me."

Not the call Stein had expected after walking away from his job as Declan's private security. But he'd sat up in bed in the guest room, the sky still dark, all ears.

"We finished the virus. And now I'm taking it to New York City."

He'd grunted, surprised when Declan said something about an exhibition at the upcoming UN General Assembly.

And then he said, "I need you, Stein."

And *shoot*. The words had the power of bait. He hadn't said yes . . . but the urge stirred inside him.

Except, *"What if . . . I left the Swans?"*

Stein hadn't had a chance to circle back to Emberly's words that night, not with dinner out with her and Nim at a cute Mexican place by the sea, followed by another *West-Wing*-a-thon.

And they'd all spent the next day at the beach, and he'd gone to bed staring at the shiplapped ceiling, the words settling inside.

By the third day, he didn't know how to return to them or to face the terrible desire they raked up inside.

Except . . . what then?

Maybe it didn't matter, because Declan had roused him out of the what-ifs back to reality.

Hence the early-morning trek out to the beach.

Nimue's cute little cottage sat nestled in the dunes on a side road that extended from the beach, a tiny place with the barest view of the ocean. Two blocks away sat the quaint town of Melbourne Beach, just a strip of shops on a narrow spit of road.

He liked it here. Quiet. A place he could hear his thoughts.

Maybe the answer to Declan was *no*.

Maybe he wanted to go all in, building something different with Emberly. Over the past five days, she'd shaken off her Phoenix layer and settled into someone he'd gotten a glimpse of back in Minnesota. Relaxed. Laughing. Somehow, Emberly had gone from DEFCON 1 to all defenses down. The woman who beat him in a game of chess, letting her lemonade sweat in the sun.

In truth, she'd slid into his heart and taken up residence.

Stein closed his eyes and lifted his face to the sun, letting it soak into him. *"I will bless the Lord at all times; his praise shall continually be in my mouth."*

"Whoo-hoo!"

The shout lifted from down the beach, and he glanced toward it and spotted a man rising from a beach chair, reeling in his fishing line, fighting with something past the breaking waves. Behind him was a cart with a cooler, a couple chairs, another rod and reel.

Steinbeck wandered down to watch.

Long dark hair pulled back, a worn ball cap on his head, tanned, a hint of a beard. He wore a pair of cargo shorts, a shirt with the sleeves torn off. He had strong arms and stood barefoot in the sand, bracing himself against the bowing fishing rod.

"What do you have on there?" Stein stopped, stared out into the waves.

"Pompano, maybe," the man said. He pulled the rod back, then quickly took up the slack. "He's a fighter."

And right then, the fish lifted out of the water, struggling against the hook, a spray of water off the silvery body.

"It's a tarpon!" The shout from the man emerged just as the fish shook hard and—

Aw. The catch splashed into the water, and the man took a step back, the hook releasing.

"Well, briny." The man stepped back and reeled in his line.

Glanced at Steinbeck. "I have an extra pole if you want to throw in a line."

"I'm not much of a fisherman. That's my brother Jack. And mostly on lakes in Minnesota."

The man reached over, handed him a pole. "You don't know until you throw your hook in." He winked. Kind face, brown eyes. Steinbeck couldn't place his age.

He stepped away from the man, then cast the line into the ocean.

"The waves will carry it out. Let your line reel for a bit." The man had reeled in his own line. The hook dangled, empty.

He picked up a stool from his gear and handed it to Stein. "Fishing is God's great reminder to slow down long enough to think."

Right. Stein took the stool and settled into the sand, the line reeling out into the blue.

"Set it."

Steinbeck stopped the reel. When he looked up, the man had handed him a rod-holder tube. He set it in the sand and affixed his rod.

"Beautiful morning for catching fish."

"Any luck yet?"

"It's not luck. It's Providence. Whatever God decides to give me." He glanced over. "So far, just a couple near catches. We'll see what the day brings. You from around here?"

"On vacation. I think."

"You're not sure?"

"I guess it's more like a time-out."

"Name's Judah," the man said and held out his hand.

"Steinbeck."

"Really? Great author. I loved *The Grapes of Wrath*. A great story about the struggle to survive during the Great Depression. And man's need to find meaning in life. 'Muscles aching to work, minds aching to create beyond the single need—this is man.'"

"He's not wrong."

Judah grunted.

"You disagree?"

"I think meaning is inherent in our birth. It's the pride of man to think he has to carve it out himself. We surrender, and God carves it out." He fixed his line and set his rod into the tube. "It's like my hook. It's been set out there. The fish find it. It's not what it does but what it *is* that matters."

"Is this like in *The Matrix* when the boy tells Neo 'There is no spoon'?"

"Oh, there's a spoon. But perhaps the spoon puts too much meaning into being the spoon. It doesn't matter how beautiful the spoon is. Just that it's able to be used."

"I've met Socrates on the beach."

Judah laughed. "Ever hear the story of Jesus feeding the five thousand?"

"Sure. Five loaves and two fish? It's a great story of God's provision."

"And a story of how the disciples missed the point."

Steinbeck frowned.

"Right before this, Jesus had called them to ministry, given them power to drive out demons and heal the sick, and sent them out. They returned, and the next thing that happened was the miracle of the five and two. But that's not the point. Jesus had already equipped them to heal and drive out demons, and yet they come to Him and say, 'Hey, feed these people.' And Jesus turns to them and says, '*You* feed them.' And all they can think is, *With what?*"

Stein said nothing.

"See, they saw themselves as not enough. Even though they walked and talked with Jesus and had been called by Jesus, they didn't see themselves as empowered. And yet, they'd already been about the task of ministry. They'd already surrendered whatever life they'd had to be obedient to Jesus, and He'd equipped them, so they understood what it meant to walk into purpose and meaning, to fight evil and win."

Stein couldn't move.

Judah glanced at his line tugging against the waves. Stein's was tugging too, but nothing resembling a bite.

Judah kept talking. "Although the disciples had gone out and done the big, tough things, when they returned, they thought their mission had ended. But Jesus was still calling them to believe. To trust in His power to do great things. Even something as 'simple'" — he finger quoted the word—"as feeding people." He fixed his brown eyes on Stein. "The failure of the disciples was that they looked at themselves and said . . . 'Not enough.' But Jesus asks us to look at Him and hear . . . '*By my strength.*'"

Steinbeck's line jerked. Judah held out his hand. "Hold. Let's see what happens."

It jerked again.

"Okay, grab it up."

Stein took the pole, stood up, started to reel.

"Not too fast." Judah also stood. "Pull back, slack the line, then reel fast. Then do it again."

Steinbeck obeyed, pulling the line back, reeling hard, repeating. Sweat sheened his skin, his back aching.

The fish skipped across the waves.

"A nice-sized pompano," Judah said and ran toward the water. In a moment, he'd snagged the fish, brought it to shore. The pompano lay in the sand, still breathing, twisting.

"The thing about the fish and the loaves," said Judah as he knelt to unhook the creature, "is that the disciples in that moment said, 'This is all we have, Lord.' And they handed Him the fish. And He said, 'Okay then. Stand back and see what I will do.'" He held up the fish. "Dinner?"

"No. I don't have a license."

"I do, but maybe we'll let this guy live." He walked to the shore and tossed him back out to sea. "Be free. Live a long and happy life."

Steinbeck grinned.

Judah walked back to Steinbeck. "You never know what your hook will bring in if you put it in the water."

"I didn't know you fished, Steinbeck."

He turned, cupped a hand over his eyes, and spotted Nimue walking down the weathered steps to the beach. Dark hair, expressive golden-brown eyes, olive skin, so clearly not from the same father as Emberly, who'd been bequeathed beautiful green eyes, red hair, and fair skin.

Still, they laughed at the same crazy TV shows and shared the same love of ice cream.

Now, Nimue walked across the beach in her bare feet, wearing a pair of dark shorts and an oversized shirt, her hair pulled back with cornrow braids. "Early morning run?"

He got up and walked over to her. "Cals. My knee is still sore. I'm trying not to stress it." He'd developed a nearly blackened bruise on his leg, and the muscles still ached.

"Yeah, that looks painful." She lifted a hand to the fisherman. "Hey, Judah!"

He waved back.

"I got up and made coffee and saw your bedroom door open." She kept walking.

Stein nodded, his feet depressing the sand. The tide had started to come in, filling his footprints.

"You look like a man with something on his mind. Did they finish the virus?"

He nodded. "I guess Emberly would tell you anyway."

"Of course she would. I've been helping her on this mission since the beginning. It really rattled her when she walked back into your life."

He glanced at her.

"Mostly because it also tore her up to leave you. I think . . . well, you're good for her, Steinbeck. You make her more careful. Less impulsive. Thoughtful."

Huh. She did the opposite for him. Ignited a fire inside that he had thought had died.

"Did she tell you she's thinking of leaving the Swans?" Nimue asked.

"She did. I didn't realize she'd told *you.*"

"A few days ago. Before you walked in." She shoved her hands into her pockets. "I thought she was a lifer, so you must have a bigger effect on her than I thought."

He glanced at her. "This is because of me?"

"Not just you. But I think . . ." She sighed. "I think she might see a second chance at that thing she ran from."

The tide was coming in, splashing at his heels. "What thing?"

"Family." She glanced at him. "My sister saved my life. I know she told you about our mother. She was so broken. And tried everything to fill that broken place. Romance. Alcohol. Drugs. She desperately wanted to be loved, and she did everything she thought she could to find it. It was a hard life for her, and for us. We didn't always have money, so Emberly started to steal from the men our mom brought home to buy us food. Usually they didn't notice. And then one morning she got caught."

His entire body tightened.

"She'd already left, but this guy—he was some guy my mother had brought home—he was furious. And he thought I took the money. I was about nine. And he came after me."

He stopped walking, turned to her, heat in his chest.

"I was under my bed screaming, and Emberly just showed up, carrying a frying pan from the stove. She hit him with it."

Nimue stared out into the ocean, and he could see the aftermath in her eyes, the way they filled. "She nearly died. My mom somehow stopped him from beating her to death, but . . . I realized that Emberly would do anything—*anything*—for someone she loved. It scared me. That's when I decided that I'd have her back. No matter what she did." She looked at him. "But Emberly has never, not once, allowed a man in her life. She's so afraid of ending up like our mother—broken, betrayed, desperate—she's never considered . . . Well, like I said, she's always been a Swan. And now . . . you're here."

He was here.

And now, leaving.

"I got a call from Declan. He wants me in New York for some exhibition for the upcoming UN General Assembly."

She shoved her hands into her pockets. "And you're trying to figure out . . .?"

"I don't want her to go."

"And you're afraid of . . .?"

He looked at her. "I'm afraid of the same thing you are. Her getting in over her head."

"No, you're afraid of losing her."

His mouth tightened.

"It's okay, Steinbeck. I love her too."

Oh. But yes, the words felt right as they washed over him. And weirdly, Jack's words stirred inside him. *"Don't pursue this woman with the hope that she's going to give you some sort of purpose. Only God can do that."*

Maybe purpose wasn't about doing but about *being.*

"I have one request to make," Nim said.

"Yeah?"

"Don't hurt her. Or I promise, I'll hack into your life and leave you with nothing." She winked, then turned and headed back up the beach.

He didn't for a moment think she was kidding.

Steinbeck caught up with her at the top of the stairs, on the narrow beach road to her house.

The scent of burning hung in the air.

She must have seen the trail of smoke filtering into the sky at the same time he did, because she picked up her pace. Then started to run.

No, no—

The smoke poured from the kitchen window of Nimue's cute cottage beach house.

"Emberly!" Nimue shouted as Stein passed her. Already sirens shrieked through the air, so maybe a neighbor had called, but flames burst from the window.

"Emberly!" He pushed through the gate, onto the porch. Took a breath, reached for the door.

"Stop!" Emberly barreled up, already outside, and grabbed his arm. She wore pajama shorts and a T-shirt, her hair tousled, her eyes wide.

And he just scooped her up tight, his breathing hard as he carried her off the porch, away from the flames.

"Stein, I'm fine—I'm okay—"

He set her down on the street, hands on her shoulders, searching her green eyes, his breaths cascading over each other.

"I woke up to the fire alarm. Nim must have it wired to a 911 trigger—"

Her gaze broke away and she searched for Nim.

Stein found her too, standing back from her home, her arms around herself, tears casting down her face.

"Oh, Nim," Emberly said, going to her, wrapping her up in her arms.

Nimue held on, her expression stripped.

The fire engine turned onto their street. But as Stein watched, he spotted a black SUV pull away from the curb. And as the man drove by, even Steinbeck recognized him—dark hair, black eyes . . . The man he'd grappled with on the dock.

And his ilk beside him in the passenger seat.

Emberly slipped her hand into Stein's, tightening. She glanced up at him, her voice hard, changing, as she spoke. Phoenix was back when she said, "I don't know how, but they found us."

NINE

SO MUCH FOR EMBERLY'S ATTEMPTS TO FOR-get who she was.

"I am *absolutely* going with you." She paced the family room of the Airbnb Nim had gotten while the fire department assessed the damage to her house.

A.k.a. the entire thing.

Emberly still couldn't believe that Nim's beautiful cottage had burned, almost entirely, to the ground, just the shell remaining, her beautiful kitchen charred, her porch blackened, and her living room smoke-damaged.

How it started, the fire chief didn't say, but he'd found a broken bottle in the remains and suggested it might have been an improvised incendiary device.

She added the Russian part and came up with *Molotov cocktail,* lit and left burning while she slept.

Nim's tech room, however, had survived with remarkably little damage, so she'd reassembled her system in the main room of the rental. Now she sat in front of the array of screens, wearing her computer glasses, her pajama bottoms, and an oversized T-shirt she'd picked up on their shopping run.

Outside, the last of the day receded along the palmy horizon, the ocean outside darkened, the stars scattered overhead. A half-empty box of Oceanside pizza lay on the counter.

Steinbeck's mouth had been a tight, almost angry line for the better part of the day.

Yeah, well, Emberly was mad too. And it might have been worse if she hadn't stopped him from *charging*, without a thought, into a burning building.

After her.

It turned her a little weak, not to mention the way he'd held on to her.

Oh, Austen was probably right.

And he wasn't going anywhere without her. "I can't believe you thought you could just ditch me for Declan."

Steinbeck's eyebrow rose. "I wasn't exactly going to *ditch* you. But I didn't see you necessarily jumping to protect a guy who, just a couple months ago, you called a terrorist."

"The shoe seemed to fit at the time."

Nimue picked up a half cup of coffee, took a sip, and made a face. "Oh, that's bad."

"Because it was brewed two hours ago," Emberly said, taking the mug. "Should I nuke it? And your sad piece of pizza?" She picked up the plate.

"No. I can't eat when I'm chasing something through the dark web. Grab me an Arnold Palmer." She gestured to the fridge, where a case of her brain drink—a lemonade-sweet-tea mix—chilled.

"What are you doing?" Steinbeck asked.

"I got curious when you mentioned the UN General Assembly," Nim said. She turned her screen. "This is a list of the exhibitions. The UN General Assembly meets every year, with the goal of discussing and trying to solve a wide range of international issues. Like peace and security, economic growth, human rights, and sustainable development." She pointed to the screen. "Spectra Cybernetics is on the agenda. They're exhibiting a search-and-rescue android for use in earthquakes, as well as minesweepers equipped with Axiom."

Steinbeck nodded, his arms crossed. "How does that connect with someone trying to burn your house down?"

"Or kill Emberly." Nim glanced at Steinbeck. "They had to have set the fire after I left."

His mouth pinched, and he nodded.

"They've been after me since Portugal," Emberly said. "Tomas was sure that I had a copy of Axiom."

"Which is why they let you go," said Steinbeck. "I'm convinced they were hoping you'd flush out Declan. And maybe Luis."

"Why Luis?"

"We never got to the bottom of who hacked Declan's bots at the fair." He shook his head. "I'm worried it was a test."

"I think it was," Nim said. "I did some dark-web sleuthing, searching some forums known for cybercrime and mercenary services with a custom script to flag terms like *droids*, and *Axiom*, and *UNGA*."

Emberly sat down on the sofa.

"Then I created a fake user and joined the conversation. And I tapped a Russian hacker I know. He works for a security team in Europe. Artyom and I work together sometimes, and he created a different user and we started up a conversation. I posed as a buyer. And then this guy showed up." She pointed at the user: @ZeroSum42. "He claims he has a copy of Axiom and is ready to sell. I asked him for a demo, and he sent me this." She pointed at the message: *40.756870, -74.001762.*

"In case you're wondering, that's the lat and long of the Jacob K. Javits Convention Center, New York City. And where Declan's exhibition is in three days."

"You think they'll hack the droids?" Stein asked.

"Maybe," Emberly said. "We have the virus, though. So?" She lifted a shoulder. "Feels like a failed play."

"How is the virus delivered?" This from Nim.

"It's stored on a cloud and downloaded. The problem is, we can't infect the droids if they're not corrupted."

"Who is @ZeroSum42?" Steinbeck had gotten up, walked over to stare at the screen, as if he could use his X-ray vision to reach through the computer and strangle Mr. Zero Sum by the throat.

"Down, boy. You'll like this part. I told him I'd pay a deposit to secure it until the demonstration. He sent me his wallet information. I used a blockchain analysis to identify past transactions and other linked wallets. This guy has been paid by the Petrov Bratva."

"And Bob's your uncle," Emberly said.

Nim pointed at her.

"So, what—this guy developed the hack that infected Declan's security dog droids?"

"Maybe." She turned her screen back. "I was able to hack into the cloud storage of the Russian Bratva a few days ago, and I downloaded the contents into my cloud. I spent the last couple days going through it, ran some malware, and found this." She opened a file and clicked on an image.

A woman stood in the shadows, the light from the street just barely illuminating her and her backpack.

Emberly stilled. "That's me. In Lisbon."

"What are you doing?" Stein asked.

"I'm buying your dinner." And she was on the phone. "I was calling you, Nim."

"Maybe they tracked the cell call to me," Nimue said. "And when I hacked into their server a few days ago, they found the trace and put it together."

"So they *did* let you go," said Steinbeck.

Emberly scrubbed a hand down her face. "All this time, they were following me? Why?"

"You're the only one who knows what Tomas looks like."

"No—Mystique knows him too."

Steinbeck considered that.

Wait. She turned. "What if they followed me to Minnesota?"

"And meanwhile, they took Luis and forced him to create the virus."

"How'd they get Axiom?"

"I don't know!" He held up a hand. "I don't know. Did you make a copy of it?"

"No. Like I said—I was on an island without Internet. And then on Declan's boat . . . Oh no."

He stared at her, and just like that, she saw the same answer click in his blue eyes. "The captain."

"Yes. Captain Teresa. From *Portugal.* You don't think . . ." Her mouth opened. "I had it with me on the boat. Maybe she took it. Or copied it." She drew in a breath. "And sent it to Luis."

"How can you—"

"Luis's lock screen had a picture of her. I thought something about it seemed familiar."

"He's been working with the Bratva the entire time," Stein said.

Nimue glanced at Emberly. "There's more." She clicked on a photo. "Is this you petting a pig?"

Steinbeck folded his arms.

"And eating ice cream."

"I've seen enough," said Steinbeck. He pulled out his phone.

"Okay, but you'll want to see this." Nim clicked on another file. It opened to a grid of five levels.

Emberly leaned over her. "What is that?"

"That is a floor plan of the entire Javits Center. There's another file for each floor."

"This was in a file on the cloud."

"Okay, that's enough for me." Steinbeck stalked across the room, pulled open the sliding glass door, and stepped outside.

"He's a little scary when he's mad," Nim said.

"He's not mad. This is his operator persona." But Emberly watched him, an outline in the darkness, pacing the balcony. She turned back to Nim. "You can't stay here."

Nimue raised an eyebrow. "I certainly can."

"No. Nim. They didn't get me. And they'll be back, I know it."

"I'm in a hotel. What are they going to—"

"This is the Russian mob! Name it!"

Nimue held up her hands. "Calm down."

"I'm not in the least calm." Emberly pressed her hands to her head. "It could have easily been both of us sleeping in that cottage today. And what if they'd decided not to burn it down but just to walk in and drop us with a couple shots to the head?"

Nimue blinked at her.

"Sorry, but . . . I did mention the *mob*, right?" She pulled out her most recent burner phone. "I need to call Mystique and warn her. You need to burn your dark-web trail."

Nimue turned back to her computer.

Mystique's phone went to voicemail. Emberly pulled open the balcony door and stepped outside. Caught Stein on a call.

"Listen, Colt, you need to tell Logan. Luis can't be trusted. And Declan may have a tainted virus. I don't know—right. Yes. I'll be there."

He glanced at Emberly, drew in a breath. "No, she's safe." He stilled. "No way."

She raised an eyebrow.

He turned away. "No. They just tried to kill—I don't care!"

"Steinbeck." She touched his arm. It tensed under her grip.

"Over my dead—I know!"

"I'm going with you."

He glanced at her, his eyes narrowing. "Hold on, Colt." He pulled the phone away. "No. You're not."

She laughed, shook her head. "You've met me, right?"

His mouth tightened and he shook his head, turned back. "You still there?"

He sighed, listening, his mouth pulling.

"Tell him—and yourself—that Mystique isn't answering," Emberly said. "Which means I'm the only one who can identify Tomas."

Steinbeck turned, leaning against the balcony, a knot of frustration. "And you should check on Logan. Mystique isn't answering."

He met her eyes as he nodded to something Colt said. Then, "No, I'll call Declan. I'm going to need a plane anyway." He shut the phone almost violently.

She stood there in the darkness, just the light from the moon and the glow from inside illuminating his scowl. "You remind me of a very upset sailor I once met."

He pocketed the phone and reached out, pulling her to himself by her belt loops. Set her in front of him. "This very upset *former* sailor nearly lost pieces of himself today when I thought . . ." He looked away, shook his head. Sighed. Turned back to her. "I was really hoping you meant it when you said you'd quit the Swans."

She pressed her hands against his chest, her fingers at the nape of his neck. "And what are you doing to do, Jason Bourne? Sell real estate?"

He huffed, but let himself smile. Then, quietly, "What am I going to do with you?" He pulled her in, his arms around her waist, and she stepped close, her hands to his face, her thumbs running along his whiskers.

"Maybe . . . don't let go?" The words tumbled out, a risk, her breath catching.

But he nodded, his eyes shiny. "Nope. I've learned enough to hang on."

Then he kissed her, his mouth sweet and soft and gentle. She sank into his embrace, the waves shushing against the sand, the stars blinking down. She let him deepen his kiss, moved in closer until finally he raised his head, breathing a little hard.

"We need to go to New York. So here's the deal. We save the freakin' world from Skynet and then . . . we walk off into the sunset, hand in hand."

"And we're back in the romance movie." She smiled.

"It feels more like a thriller. *The Terminator*."

She laughed. "Which was a *romance*."

He smiled and put his hand to her face, his thumb against her cheek, caressing it. "The first time I met you, I think you said something like 'Come with me if you want to live.'"

"Good advice."

"Promise me. When this is over, you'll take it. 'Come with me if you want to live.'"

His eyes shone, and she could see all the way to his heart. Steady. Honest. Determined.

Aw, what else was she going to do? She put her forehead to his. "I promise."

• — •

"I'm not sure how this happened."

Steinbeck stood in front of a mirror, straightening his tie, and glanced at his cousin Colt across the shared bedroom of the penthouse accommodations that Logan had secured.

Colt wore a pair of suit pants and a white dress shirt, his jacket lying on the bed. He looked up from his phone. "Which part? The penthouse, tonight's gala, or maybe just the fact that you showed up with a spy?"

Steinbeck cinched the tie and turned to Colt. "She's on our side."

"She's a Swan. They're not affiliated with any side." He stood, pocketed the phone. "But if you think we can trust her . . ."

Steinbeck tugged on his shirtsleeves. It had been a hot minute since he'd worn any sort of monkey suit. Probably Boo's wedding, in truth. When he'd danced with a disguised Emberly. The memory, now that he knew whom he'd danced with, stirred heat inside him, the sense of needing her back in his arms.

Needing? Really?

"We can trust her," Stein said. "I'll be right out." He walked to the balcony doors, opened them, and stepped out to a small balcony with an arched portico that overlooked the expansive view of the Hudson waterfront. To the south, roughly three miles away, situated on the Hudson River, the glass of the Javits building glinted in the fading sunlight, reflecting the twilight onto the darkening water. The sounds of the city chaos below were muted this high up, leaving just the scent of the river, the loamy autumn breeze stirring the night air.

Stein drew in the smells, lifted his gaze to the horizon, past the jutting of lower buildings, the glistening river, and even the Jersey shoreline, to beyond. Emberly's soft *"I promise"* hung inside him, along with Judah's words: *"Jesus was still calling them to believe. To trust in His power to do great things."*

He gripped the railing. *I'm trusting You, Lord.*

Then he exhaled and headed back into the living room.

An oversized oil painting of a New-York-in-autumn street scene with a couple walking in the rain hung over a massive marble-faced fireplace. White bouclé sofas faced each other, and two-story gray-plaid drapes framed the expansive windows that overlooked the massive rooftop patio. Edison bulbs lit up the stone surface and stone planters that held boxwoods and hydrangeas and fruit trees. The doors hung open, stirring a fragrant breeze into the room.

The penthouse, from what he'd seen of it, could host a small army, or maybe just the cast of *The Avengers*. Which felt like an apt comparison when he walked into the room.

Steinbeck spotted Colt standing with a formally attired Director Logan Thorne, his brown hair almost military short. He also stood with another man whom Stein had met back during his overboard adventure in the Caribbean. Stein approached and held out a hand to the man with dark-blond hair, a little curly at the edges, the look of a warrior in his eyes—"Tate. How are you?"

"Good. I guess we're meeting Declan at the gala."

"He called," Steinbeck said. "The display is set up. We'll sneak away during the dinner and check security before tomorrow's exhibition. Any word from London and Shep?"

"The last I heard, they were planning on bringing Luis to a new location. Not sure where," Logan said. "They might just be off-grid at that location."

The entire thing had Stein's gut in a knot. "They need to be warned that Luis could be compromised. Emberly's sister is trying to confirm any financial transactions between the Bratva and Luis."

"Emberly?" Colt said. "You're talking about Phoenix?"

"Yes." Stein shoved his hands into his pockets. He probably needed to remember that they were back on the job. Even if tonight did feel like a party.

A smile crested over Colt's face as he looked past Steinbeck's shoulder. Stein turned to see a woman walk in. Her long blonde hair hung in waves around her face, and she wore a floor-length, pink, shimmery halter dress, her green-blue eyes fixed on Colt. He stepped out to meet her, holding out his hand.

"That's Taylor Price, his girlfriend," said Logan beside him. "She's a biochemist. Works loosely with the Caleb Group. Goes by Tae."

But Stein only had eyes for the woman who came in behind her. Her long dark hair parted in the middle and was tied back in a sleek French knot. She wore a stunning green silk dress with a draped plunging neckline and a three-strand pearl choker along with matching drop earrings. She was petite and elegant, and he had the sense that a panther, her beautiful green eyes latched on him, was stalking up to him.

"Um." He swallowed.

She smiled up at him. "*Um* back. My, my, someone looks good in a suit. But then again, I knew that." She winked.

Words caught in his throat until finally—"You were made for that dress."

She laughed, but her green eyes shone. Oh, this woman wound her way deeper inside him every moment.

"*I promise.*"

This mission couldn't get over fast enough. "Except, where are you going to wear your, uh . . . um . . ."

"Gun? Not bringing one. But I will have this." She held a small white purse and now pulled out an earwig.

"You won't need it. You're never leaving my sight."

She raised a dark eyebrow and inserted the earwig.

"I like the dark hair, but . . . why?"

"Because if Tomas is there, I don't want him to recognize me right off." She glanced at Logan and drew a breath. "Feels a little weird being on this side of the game."

Stein crooked his arm. "All we have to do is mingle and then run a scan on Declan's AI program to check for bugs. Is Nim ready?"

"I'm always ready," said a voice in his ear.

"Let's go. Our limo is here."

He held out his arm, Emberly took it, and they headed out. They were going to be just fine.

They passed through the soaring entryway with the dripping gold chandelier, and Emberly turned to Logan. "I could get used to your style of safe houses. Certainly an upgrade from the Swans."

"It doesn't belong to us," he said. "It's owned by the Taggert family. Jess Taggert Brooks and her husband are heavily involved in the Red Cross and work closely with our group and others. They've offered their home whenever we need it."

"They live here?"

"No. I believe this is a keen investment." Logan opened the tall wooden door. "Pete and Jess have a modest place in Chelsea." He stepped out into the hallway, where Tate had called the elevator.

Tate turned to Logan. "Glo really wanted to be here, but she's been under the weather with baby number two." He glanced at Taylor and Colt.

Clearly the man missed his wife. Steinbeck had asked Colt earlier, and apparently Glo was the daughter of the former VP-elect, who now sat in federal prison for her role in an assassination attempt on the sitting president.

President White had commuted her sentence to life, instead of execution for treason. Stein remembered the controversy from White's first presidential election.

He hadn't even been paying attention to White's reelection bid.

"Tessa also wanted to join us, but our two-year-old twins are a handful right now," said Logan. "She sends her regards."

Huh, Steinbeck hadn't even known that Logan was married. But maybe that's what it took to live this life—compartments and hidden identities.

The elevator opened and they got in, took it down to the lobby, and walked out past the concierge and security to a covered entry facing the street.

The wind raked up the scents of the flowers near the entrance, as if trying to mask the clutter of the city odor—garbage, gasoline, and from a distance, even the sickly sweet odor of marijuana.

But overhead, the stars glinted their diamond light and the air hung on to the day's heat. It would be a glorious night in Gotham.

A man stood near a stretch limo and opened the door for them.

"Thank you, Kais," said Logan as Taylor got in, followed by

Colt. Steinbeck helped Phoenix in—not that she needed it—and sat next to her.

Logan and Tate got in last.

Kais shut the door and Logan checked his watch. "Okay. The party is already in full swing. Dinner is in an hour. Once we get there, Tate and Colt will check the exhibition hall and set the CCTV feeds. Make sure you confirm with Coco that everything is online before you leave. Stein, you and Phoenix find Declan. You'll have to slip out during dinner or sometime, because he'll need to connect his bots—or whatever he's calling them—to the network so Nimue can access them remotely and check the digital hashes to verify the integrity of the program. According to Nimue, any mismatch of the encrypted signature could indicate tampering."

"Got it," Nim said in Steinbeck's ear. Beside him, Phoenix smiled.

"If she finds something, she'll follow the audit trail, see if she can confirm the source. More important, keep your eye out for Tomas, or any of the Petrov Bratva." Logan looked at Phoenix as he said this.

She nodded.

Steinbeck drew in a breath. "And if she sees him?"

"Alert us. We'll apprehend him—"

"On what warrant?" Tae asked.

Logan glanced at her. "For a friendly chat."

"Is that legal?"

Logan cocked his head at her. "My guess is that, at the very least, he is here illegally. No warrant needed for suspicion of a terrorist attack." He looked again at Phoenix. "You're the only one who can recognize him, so . . ."

"I got this."

"As far as the rest—just keep your head on a swivel. You see anything amiss, let me know. There are dignitaries from all over the world here. I don't want a ruckus, so stay under the radar."

They'd taken West End Avenue all the way south, then passed through the Lincoln Tunnel until they reached the massive glass building.

"This must be a bear to clean," said Colt.

Police cars lined the streets, officers in neon security jackets directing the traffic of a slew of limousines and SUVs, dropping off guests at the covered entrance.

White-gloved valets, security guards, and press congregated behind red ropes, and the glittering blue of the glass-encased lobby suggested an elegant evening.

Stein couldn't help slipping his hand into Phoenix's grip, just for a second. She didn't look at him, but a smile tipped her lips. It stirred inside him, an old pulse finding his veins.

Go time.

They pulled up and the door opened. He helped Phoenix out, and she took his arm again as they walked inside. Sheer glass walls arched over them as they entered, a spray of exotic flowers in massive urns flanking the entrance, a blue carpet directing them through double doors and up an escalator. At the top, another valet directed them to the next level, all the way up to the rooftop.

They got off, the murmur of the crowd greeting them as it spilled out of the River Pavilion. Security stood outside, scanning invitations, and Steinbeck glanced over at Logan, who'd pulled out his phone.

A woman scanned them in. They walked past a number of uniformed police who stood at the entrance.

They entered the pavilion, the size of the room easily gobbling the conversation, muting the sounds of the jazz orchestra that played at one end. Servers mingled amongst the evening-attired crowd, some offering glasses of champagne and house wines, others with hors d'oeuvres. At the far end, the terrace opened up to high-top tables, twinkle lights, and more guests.

"Dinner is upstairs, on the overview level. It overlooks the roof-top farm also," said Logan.

A security nightmare, no doubt, but a beautiful party.

"It's nice being on the approved guest list," Phoenix said and lifted a champagne flute. She glanced at Stein. "Don't get antsy. It's just for show."

She kept her grip on his arm, and he liked that show too.

Tate and Colt and Tae peeled off, mingling into the crowd, but Logan stayed with Steinbeck and Phoenix as they wove through the mix.

State leaders from nearly two hundred countries talked in conversation groups, security not-so-obscurely standing near their clients.

Music drifted, a Sinatra song. Maybe Stein would pull Phoenix into a dance later.

"Is that Prince William?" Phoenix nodded toward a tall man standing with—

"Yep," Logan said. He too had lifted a champagne flute. "And that's Princess Kate."

"What are they doing here?"

"It's not unusual for a country to send their royal representatives along with their delegates. It's a show for the world." He nodded toward another couple, and she startled to see—

"That's Prince Luka."

"And his sister, Princess Madeline. I see the house of Ribaldi is well represented."

Logan bowed his head with a smile of respect for the redhead in a deep-blue dress who had glanced at them. He raised a hand to Prince Luka, who'd followed his sister's glance. Luka smiled at them.

"Who are they talking to?" asked Phoenix, who'd been glancing around the room.

"That's Her Royal Highness Imani of Lauchtenland and her

escort, Creed Marshall. I hear they're contemplating engagement, but he has another year of college. She's taken on responsibilities for cultural exchange and development since her mother had a baby last year."

Logan raised his glass to a man standing not far away, clearly security for the couple. The man nodded, eyes stern. "Fraser Marshall. Creed's oldest brother. He works security for the princess, along with his girlfriend, Pippa. C'mon, I'll introduce you."

Funny, Fraser seemed familiar, and as Stein got closer—"Wait. He's from Chester. We played them in football."

Logan glanced at him. "Right. I'd forgotten you were from Duck Lake."

He walked over and Steinbeck followed. In his earwig, Stein heard Colt: "We're setting up the video feed now."

Logan was saying something about growing up in Duck Lake, but Steinbeck kept searching the room. Phoenix grabbed his arm. "I'm going to take a walk around, maybe head to the restroom."

"Phoenix—"

"I'll go with you."

He looked up as Princess Imani, her dark hair in braids decorated with diamonds and gold clips, her dress deep blue and gold, stepped up to Phoenix.

"Hi," she said and held out her hand. "I'm Imani."

"Your Highness," said Phoenix and—*wait, was that a curtsy?* Then again, she knew how to play a role.

A woman followed Imani, her dark hair in a sleek ponytail, wearing a pantsuit. She offered a grim smile. Her female security detail. Steinbeck released Phoenix's hand. Met her eyes.

She squeezed his arm. "Down, boy. I'll be fine." Then she adjusted her earring.

Right. He turned away, listening to her chat with Imani as they wound through the crowd.

Fraser held out his hand. Dark-blond hair cut short, wearing a blue suit. Solid. "I remember you. You played football and hockey for Duck Lake. I played against your brother Jack."

"I think I played against one of *your* brothers too. Maybe . . . Jonas?"

"That sounds right."

"Steinbeck was on SEAL Team 4," Logan said.

"Really? Are you still active duty?"

"No. Medical separation a few years ago."

Fraser nodded. "I get that." He nodded again, maybe at a word from his female counterpart, because Steinbeck also heard through his own earwig as Phoenix said, "I'm headed into the bathroom. Going offline."

Yes, well, that made sense.

"So, what are you doing these days?" Fraser asked.

"Um . . ." Stein glanced at Logan. "Just helping out."

Fraser nodded. "I see."

Logan clamped him on the shoulder. "Glad to see you, Fraser. I've been expecting a wedding."

"From Creed and Imani? Not yet—"

"From you and Pippa."

Fraser smiled. Then he held up his left hand—a ring. "A too-short getaway to Monaco."

And Steinbeck didn't even know the guy, but he couldn't help the slightest twinge of envy.

"Congratulations." Logan shook his hand. "How long is Imani in America?"

"She's attending the youth events of the General Assembly and speaking at a women's leadership summit, along with Britta White."

"The president's daughter?"

"Yes. She's pretty excited. And then she and Creed are taking a few days in Minnesota, at my parents' winery."

Muffled conversation came through the earwig. Logan was asking Fraser about his family—

Then, "I thought that was you."

A male voice, and Stein jerked. Glanced at Logan. Not even a flicker on his face as he listened to Fraser.

"Phoenix, are you okay?" Pippa's voice.

"Yes, I'll be right behind you." Phoenix.

No, no, she wouldn't. He'd been down this road. Stein kept his gaze on Logan, who was nodding. Logan gestured with his head. *Go.*

Yep. Stein turned, pushed through the crowd. Congress members, world leaders, diplomats, delegates, and security—he didn't care as he bumped past them, still listening.

The jazz behind their conversation had muted, so maybe she was out in the corridor. *Oh, Phoenix, don't leave—*

"It won't work, Tomas. Whatever you're—"

Stein banged against a table, righted it before all the china toppled off—wrong move, because she grunted.

Then, "Stop—"

Steinbeck took off in a half run, reached the back of the room. No bathrooms.

An exit sign lit up, and next to it, the restroom sign.

He pushed through the doors into the enclosed lobby.

Women emerged from the ladies' room, and he stood there, debating.

More grunting, and now what sounded distinctly like wind. "Tomas, I promise you, this will go badly for you!"

Yes, yes, it will. Stein turned—the doors led outside onto a flat surface—the *farm.* The ecological project, a full rooftop vegetable garden, bathed only by the lights of the city.

He scanned the darkness.

Nothing.

Maybe upstairs. He'd glimpsed a map on his way in and now

spotted an elevator. Thumbing the button, he waited, then—*forget it*—headed out into a hallway.

The escalator rose to the top floor, and he pushed past more security to see the party continuing on the overlook level.

He strode out onto the upper floor and glanced around the room. An ornate chandelier showered golden light over the acre of round tables topped with gold and blue flowers in glass vases.

No outside access. And yet he clearly heard wind.

And now fighting, the grunts of a struggle.

"Hang on, Emberly!" He turned and fled back down the escalator, pushed past security, and hit the door to the rooftop garden. Enclosed inside a gate, the garden edged up to a tall glass hothouse.

"Phoenix!" He shouted into the darkness and took off for the hothouse.

There, at the far edge, he spotted her, struggling, two forms in the shadows.

He shouted, but it didn't stop them. And then—

No!

The man lifted her up. And—

And *tossed* her over the edge.

Stein felt it in his gut, a punch that took out his breath, and he stumbled for a second. "No!"

Tomas turned, startled, then took off across the building's edge, toward another door.

"Steinbeck, where are you?" Thorne's voice in his ear, but he couldn't answer.

He lunged at the edge, caught himself on the railing, and looked down.

His knees nearly buckled again.

Phoenix hung from the robotic window-washing attachment ten feet down.

Even as he watched, she swung her bare foot up to the edge and rolled onto the platform, onto her back, breathing hard.

She looked up at him. And then smiled.

"What?" He glanced away, at shouting, then back at Tomas's retreat.

The man had disappeared.

Stein turned back to Phoenix, who now stood up and was trying to figure out the controls. The machine moved, ascending.

His entire body shook, along with his voice. He turned to Colt as he ran up. "Did you get him?"

Colt shook his head, and Phoenix breached the surface.

Steinbeck grabbed her arms, pulled her over the edge of the railing, and crushed her to himself.

"Okay, I'm okay." She was . . . *laughing*?

He pushed her away from himself. "Are you *drugged*? You could have died!"

She stared up at him, shorter now in her bare feet. "No. I'm not drugged." She was still grinning. Then she reached into her dress front and pulled out—

A cell phone.

"I pulled it off him while he was trying to throw me over the edge."

He stared at her, breathing hard. "Do you even hear yourself?"

She lowered the phone, her smile falling. "I don't . . . This is what I do, Stein."

Yes. Yes, it was.

What had he been *thinking*? He turned and walked away.

"Steinbeck."

He held up a hand to her voice.

"Stein! What's your problem?"

He rounded then, right there in the middle of a potato field, and he didn't care that Colt stood there—or actually had started to edge away. Steinbeck advanced one step, his entire body trembling. "You. Nearly. *Died.*"

"But I—"

"Because you didn't care. You went after Tomas on your own, not even a second to think 'Hey, I have backup. I have someone. I have . . .'" He lifted his hand, then turned it into a shaking fist. "Me. You had me. And you didn't . . ."

"Stein. He was right there in the lobby, and I . . . I didn't want to lose the opportunity to . . . Did you hear me? *I got his phone!*"

She'd taken another step, her hair falling out of the dark knot. The wind caught it, turned it wild around her face, the green dress shimmering in the light, matching the look in her eyes, and just like that, he knew.

Like another hit, dead center to the solar plexus.

She might want to live a different life, but even that was a lie. She lived for this—for the heist. For the danger. For the triumph.

To be a Black Swan.

And Swans worked alone, didn't they?

While the people who loved them stood on the sidelines.

So much for promises.

Stein drew in a breath filled with the rich scent of furrowed earth and the hint of autumn and shook his head. "Good job, Phoenix. Clearly you're the thief we all thought you were."

Then he turned and left her on the shadowed rooftop.

Logan stood by the door. "You okay?"

"Perfect. Miss Sticky Fingers got Tomas's phone." Then he headed back into the gala to find Declan.

The sooner he wrapped this up, the sooner he could walk away from the ongoing trauma of knowing the woman who just couldn't stop breaking his heart.

"How long are you and Tia in town?"

Jack glanced over at Doyle, who walked into the kitchen of the King's Inn, wearing KEENs, cargo pants, a collared T-shirt, and the look of a man who'd spent the last month on a Caribbean island.

"Just a couple weeks," Doyle said and walked over to his mother, who stood loading up a basket of cinnamon rolls for their newest guest: Nimue, Emberly's sister, who'd arrived just hours earlier, needing a place to stay after a house fire.

So Stein had sent her to Minnesota?

But Jack had learned long ago not to ask too many questions, and his mother seemed thrilled to give Nimue housing in the Grover with a handful of other guests while they cleaned the inn before this weekend's wedding.

For some stupid, unnamed reason, as he'd shown Nimue to her room, he'd suggested maybe she get a camper for long-term temporary housing. After all, nothing like a house fire to . . . ignite a desire to travel? *Oh brother.* Clearly he had Flo on his mind.

No, not Flo. Harper. And her tight smile last week after the hockey game, as if she were lost in her book again.

Or hiding something from him?

No. Everything was just fine.

"Any leftovers?" Doyle asked.

"There's always leftovers for you." His mother caught Doyle's wrist when he reached for a roll and eased it away. "But not these. Over on the counter."

The entire industrial kitchen smelled of fresh-baked cinnamon rolls, a batch of oatmeal scotchies, and biscotti in anticipation of the weekend guests. His mom put a tea cloth over a basket and handed it to Jack. "Heat them up when you get there. There's enough for everyone, a late-night treat."

He took the basket and glanced at Doyle, who'd grabbed a cinnamon roll and set it on a napkin. His brother pressed a kiss on his mother's cheek as he walked by.

"You keep making rolls, I'll keep coming home."

She laughed.

"You're such a schmooze," Jack said as they walked outside. The twilight had puddled over the far horizon, purples and oranges and reds washing through the evergreen and birch that surrounded the lake. On the beach, a fire popped and crackled, a few guests in Adirondack chairs watching the sparks wink out into the night. Warmth hung in the air, with just the slightest nip as the night deepened, a hint of autumn in the loamy wind.

It nudged a desire to take a walk to Harper's place, a cottage at the other end of the trail, invite her out to sit under the stars under a blanket, hopefully in his arms.

He missed her. He hadn't seen her since last week. She'd been trying to finish her book before her mother came home to invade the place, so he hadn't wanted to bother her.

"Tia and I are professional fundraisers," Doyle said as he got into the passenger's side of the King's Inn utility vehicle. "We know how to talk to people." He grinned at Jack. "The grounds look nice. How are the chickens? They hated me." He took a bite of the roll.

"It's all how you talk to them," Jack said. "You gotta say nice things."

"They hate you too, then."

"Pretty much." Jack looked over. "You look good. How are things on the island?"

"Calm. Or calm*er*. It's hard to be calm in a house with thirty kids, but you know . . ."

"And that group of pirates—"

"The S7 gang? Their leader was arrested, along with a few other principals, and since then, they've sort of disbanded. We're still rebuilding after the landslide."

They pulled up to the Grover and Jack got out, went inside. A few guests sat in front of a fire in the hearth. "My mother sent fresh rolls."

He set them on the counter. A woman walked in, mid-fifties, plump, blonde hair. "Those smell amazing."

"My mother suggested nuking them. I'll be by in an hour or so to bank the fire. However, if you want to sit outside, there's a campfire on the beach."

The woman had grabbed a napkin and a plate. "I love it here. My husband and I stay every year around this time. It's such a treasure."

He smiled at that, the words sinking in.

He liked it here too. Maybe too much, because weirdly, the idea of getting into a bus and tooling around the country . . .

Aw, anywhere he went with Harper would be home.

He returned outside to the UTV, where Doyle waited. "I'll drop you at the Norbert and then I'm headed over to Harper's place."

He put the vehicle in drive, started over to the magnificent Victorian, the long table he'd made still on the front porch, twinkle lights dangling above. The King's Inn estate at night could turn positively magical.

"So, you two are going to do the long-distance thing?"

He glanced over at Doyle as they bumped over the grass. "The . . . what?"

"I had lunch with Conrad on my way in from the airport. He said that Harper's got some new gig in Nashville. Editor of a magazine or something?"

His mouth opened. Closed. *Really.*

"Bro?"

"Yeah. I guess we're doing the long-distance thing."

Calm down.

He dropped Doyle off, then returned the UTV to the garage. He sat in the darkness, then grabbed the keys, hung them up on the key ring, and walked out under the stars. On shore, the fire still burned, guests now roasting s'mores.

Calm down.

He stared out at the trail between the two houses, and the ember inside just burned. *What?*

He was halfway to her house before he thought it again, and

this time took a breath of the cool early-autumn air, rich with the fragrance of the lake, slowed his step.

It couldn't be true.

Even before he emerged from the forest, he spotted the twinkle lights around the patio and a person sitting in an Adirondack chair, wrapped in a blanket.

Oops, not Harper, but her mother. Petite and blonde, just like Harper, except Phillipa possessed a straightforwardness about her that simply didn't feel Minnesotan.

She looked up from the tablet in her lap and smiled. "Jack. How are you?"

He shouldn't answer that. "Is Harper here?"

"Of course. She's inside packing."

Packing.

He blinked at Phillipa for a moment, and being the professional therapist that she was, maybe she read him.

She sighed. "It's a great opportunity, Jack. And I know that you'll both miss this place, but . . . things change, you know? And people need to find their own happiness."

Jack frowned. "I thought—"

She held up her hand. "I know. Me too. But sometimes things just happen, and you can't predict them or change the way you feel. And Harper knows this." She gave him a smile. "I'm sure you can understand, what with your love for adventure and the open road."

He stared at her. Is that what Harper thought? "I don't . . . I love . . . helping people."

"Of course you do. And it's so admirable. I know it's something that Harper loves about you." She picked up her tablet. "You two will get used to it. I know you will land on your feet. And of course, Duck Lake will always be home, right?"

Not without Harper. He looked at the house, back at Phillipa. And the urge to turn, to stalk back to the King's Inn and . . .

Nope. He wasn't that man anymore. And he loved Harper.

So yes, long-distance it was. Or maybe he'd follow her.

If she wanted him to.

His gut clenched as he walked up to the door, hesitated for a moment, and then . . . went in.

No Harper, but she was probably upstairs in her mother's office, a.k.a. the guest bedroom. "Harp?"

Music drifted from above. *"I've had the time of my life."*

Oh, she knew how to tear out his heart, didn't she?

"Harper?" He headed toward the stairs.

She came out and looked over the railing to the open living-room area below. "Jack. What are you doing here?"

And wasn't that a nice hello?

"I . . ." What *was* he doing here? "I . . . What's going on?"

She glanced behind herself, then sighed. "I'm packing. It's not a lot of stuff, but you know, it needs to be moved now that Mom's selling the house."

He raised an eyebrow. "She's selling the house?"

"Yeah. She got a job offer from this guy she met on her cruise. Back east. You know she's always wanted to move back to New York. And apartments are so expensive there, so . . ." She lifted a shoulder.

He just stared at her. "So . . . I don't understand. Are you leaving me, Harper?"

Her mouth opened, then closed, and she swallowed.

The gesture, her entire expression, exploded inside him. "It's true. You got a job in Nashville."

"I didn't ask for it—it was Clarice. And—"

He couldn't move. "When did you get it?"

Her voice fell. "A week or so ago. And I don't know why you're so surprised—"

Oh no. "I'm *not* surprised. Of course they want you. You're talented and smart and a fantastic writer—"

She was nodding, her eyes shiny.

"I just thought . . ." He sighed. "If that's what you want, Harper, I don't want to"—he ran a hand across his face—"stand in your way." *Wait.* What was he *saying*? Of course he wanted to stand in her way. But what kind of jerk would that make him?

And he should just say that, right? But then her voice softened. "Is there . . . any . . . I mean, I . . . why should I stay?"

Words simply left his brain. Why should she *stay*? His breath stopped and cut off a reply.

"I mean, my mom is leaving and . . . I don't have a home—"

"You . . . sure you do. I mean . . . you've always had a home here."

A beat. "No, I don't. My mom is leaving, and you know, it's an opportunity of a lifetime—"

What her mother had said. And yes, shoot—it was.

Compared to living in a bus . . . aw. He couldn't do that to her. Make her travel around with him, solving crimes, when she had this dazzling, amazing future in front of her.

He couldn't take that from her. His throat burned. "You're right." He'd finally found words. "Absolutely."

He was already backing toward the door. "And you know, Conrad's right. I mean, who wants to live in a *bus*?" A harsh laugh bubbled out of him.

She closed her mouth, her expression tightening. "Yeah. Exactly my thought. It's a good thing you didn't let me talk you into Power Flowers."

He stared at her, his entire body a fist, tightening, burning, choking off his words. Be strong. For her. Let her go. "Good luck in Nashville."

Then he turned and pushed out into the night. Not running. Simply stalking back down the path, every breath a razor until he reached the King's Inn property.

The fire had died, the families finished with their s'mores, the chairs vacated. The remains of the fire glowed, tiny red eyes blinking. He picked up a bucket of water, walked to the lake, filled it, and returned.

He doused the fire, and the charred wood sizzled, steam billowing up, mingling with the smoke and fading into the night.

Then he sank onto the edge of an Adirondack chair, put his head into his hands.

And let himself cry.

TEN

S TEIN DIDN'T DANCE WITH HER.

Not that Emberly thought he would—okay, she'd been hoping since the moment they walked into the gala. But when she'd followed him back into the event and tried to take his hand, he'd stuck it into his pocket.

Sure, he'd helped her track down Declan during dinner, and the man had given Nimue access to his SAR unit. So, mission accomplished.

But then not even a fist bump from her so-called teammate.

Emberly had no appetite for dinner as she passed off Tomas's phone to Logan. He at least asked her if she was okay.

Nope. Not even a little. Because by the end of dinner, she knew…

She'd finally driven Steinbeck away.

And finally, *okay, good.* Because he would've eventually left her anyway. *Aw,* the thought just choked her. Especially with the memory of his voice only two balmy nights earlier: *"Come with me if you want to live."*

He didn't sit with her on the ride home, and then he disappeared with Logan and Colt and Tae into an office. Closed the door.

So Emberly walked down to her magnificent bedroom overlooking the city, with the platform king-sized bed and curved bouclé sofa, the platinum silk drapes. She felt regal when she stepped into the room, a dress bag over her shoulder.

Shopping with Tae had been an event, something she hadn't expected when they'd arrived yesterday. Tae did most of the talking, telling her the story of meeting Colt—how she'd hidden her identity, how he'd chased her down after she'd run from him, his goal to protect her.

It sounded too much like Stein, and it stirred romance into Emberly's heart. Especially when she'd donned the dress and shoes, turning into a version of Cinderella.

Ha.

Emberly had lost her shoes, just like in the stupid fairy tale, but she and Steinbeck certainly weren't walking off into happily ever after together now.

She didn't turn on the light but went to the window, the night pressing in, the city outside sparkling with a kaleidoscope of colors. She really liked the green dress—for a hot moment there she'd actually felt like a princess, like beautiful Imani of Lauchtenland.

Except, no. She would always be a counterfeit.

The phone she'd left on her nightstand rang, and she picked it up.

"I'm working on the program now," Nim said without a greeting. "It seems uncorrupted, so that's good. But I've been thinking. . . What if it wasn't corrupted but remotely controlled? The AI commands superseded. There could be a back door—"

"It's over, Nim." She sank onto the bed, staring at the round chandelier that hung from the twenty-foot ceiling.

"What's over? Did you get Tomas?"

"Yes—no. I mean, yes, I saw him. Now that I think about it—I think he saw *me* first. And like an idiot, I took the bait. I think he was trying to kill me, and—"

"Wait—what happened?"

She put her arm over her eyes and told Nim the entire story, from the bathroom trek to the moment she landed on the window-cleaning platform.

"I don't quite know what I did, but . . . I think it's over, Nim. Stein is . . . so mad."

"He was scared, Emberly."

She closed her eyes, saw him looking over the edge of the roof. "Okay, maybe. But then he looked at me like I'd . . . I don't know."

"Take a breath, Em. Give the man a full minute to process the fact that he nearly lost you."

"I knew the window-washing unit was there—I saw it when we drove up. I purposely drove him to—"

"You shouldn't tell me these things."

"Sorry."

"So now what?"

"I gave the cell phone to Logan, and he gave it to his hacker, Coco. She's trying to trace the calls and see if we get any hits. Maybe figure out what's happening."

"Good. Meanwhile, I'm looking for vulnerabilities."

"You made it to the King's Inn?"

"Mama Em took me in like a long-lost daughter."

The words hit Emberly's chest, burned. "She's like that."

"She's very sweet—gave me a room in a house called the Grover. I have a window seat, and the room overlooks the lake, which is surrounded by trees that are already turning color. Reminds me of that place we stayed in Sturgis."

"You were seven. How could you remember that?"

"I remember way back, further than that, Em. I remember Ernesto. And his pizza."

Emberly sat on the bed, stared out into the darkness. "I liked him."

"I know. He liked us too. And he wanted to marry Mom and adopt us."

Emberly stilled. "No, he cheated on Mom."

"Em. He *proposed*. I saw it. You were asleep, and I'd gotten up to get a drink of water, and he was on one knee in the living room. And I heard her tell him no."

"She didn't."

"She did. She said that he'd leave her, just like everyone else, and that he'd break our hearts, and she cried and he left."

"She told me he cheated on her."

"Yeah, well, she probably thought he would. Or did. Who knows? Mom never saw herself as someone who could be loved. Sure, she longed to be loved, but in order to be truly loved, you have to be truly known, and she never wanted to trust anyone that much. That's the scary part, right?"

Emberly closed her eyes. Saw Stein's expression when he'd seen her in the dress.

Um.

But the sense of his maybe seeing her as someone who belonged in that dress had woven inside her. Made her believe the fairy tale.

"You should have heard him, Nim. He looked right at me and called me a thief."

"Well, you are a thief."

"No, I mean—he *meant* it. He made me feel . . ."

Silence.

"Like you were trash. Like you were . . . Mom."

Emberly nodded in the darkness. "He comes from this amazing family. He was a SEAL, for Pete's sake. A real-life hero. I don't know what I was thinking."

"You're thinking like a person who's been wearing a disguise for so long, you don't recognize who you truly are."

She wanted to roll her eyes. "And who is that, Nim?"

Nim's voice softened. "Emberly. The girl who asked Jesus to save her. To adopt her. The girl who still wants someone to love her and doesn't realize that love is already *right here*."

Emberly stilled. "No, that's . . ."

"Truth. I remember the day you went forward in that tent meeting. You were changed. You'd always been this tough little thing, and suddenly, I don't know. You laughed. And hoped. Fear seemed to fall off you. I wasn't the only one who saw it. Remember, Anna made you a cake?"

"Like it was my birthday."

"It *was* your birthday, Em. You were reborn that day."

She drew up her knees. "Yeah, well, it didn't take. It only took two months for me to run away."

"Because you let yourself believe the voices in your head that say you are a thief. And broken. And unlovable. But love says something different. It says you're wanted. And valuable. And important. And that you belong."

From beyond her closed door, light filtered in, and voices lifted in the hallway of the penthouse. She walked to the mirror and stared at her reflection in the darkness, her wig off, her hair short and mussed, trying too hard in her silly silky dress.

"How long are you going to listen to the lies, Emberly? How long are you going to let your pride tell you that you are better off alone?"

Her eyes filled.

"And if you're wondering, God is love, so . . . feel free to substitute—*God* says you're wanted. And valuable. And important. And that you belong. He looks at you and says, 'That's Emberly, whom I love.' And since God loves you, you are safe. And most important, you're not alone. You never have been."

And just like that, Stein's words rocked through her. *"You didn't care. You went after Tomas on your own, not even a second to think 'Hey, I have backup.' Me. You had me."*

"I'm an idiot."

"Sometimes. But an idiot who is loved."

"Thanks for that."

"Listen. There is the intoxicating smell of cinnamon rising from the kitchen. I think I have an intruder."

"Wish I were there."

A beat. "I wish you were here too, Em. Not because of the rolls, but because Stein is a good man, and with him I heard you laugh. And saw you hope. I saw *you* again. By the way, I talked with Stein's brother Jack, and he thinks I need to buy a camper."

"A what?"

"Go fix this, Emberly. The man is crazy about you. Be brave. After all, you are a Black Swan. Unique. Beautiful. Unexpected. I'm going to find some nourishment. I have a long night ahead. Don't let me down—I need these people in my life. Love you." She hung up.

Emberly stared at herself. Great, now even the scant makeup she'd worn burned down her cheeks. She wiped her face with her hands and got up.

Walked to the window. *Emberly, the one Jesus*—she closed her eyes—*loves.*

She pressed her hand to the window, drew it away, and watched her handprint disappear.

And deep in her memory, the swell of a hymn stirred inside her. *"Amazing love! how can it be that Thou, my God, shouldst die for me?"*

Amazing love.

Outside, a million tiny lights burned. *"You're not alone. You never have been."*

Suddenly, the immutable sense of being *seen* rushed over her. She stepped back, shaking.

Seen. Known. And yes—
Emberly, the girl that I love.
She sank onto the bed, put her hands on her face.
"For God so loved Emberly that he gave his only son . . ." She nearly looked up, expecting to see Boz standing in front of her all these years later. But no, just the memory of him.
"If the son sets you free, you will be free indeed."
Oh, she wanted to believe that.
"I just . . . I don't know how, God." Her voice felt small, almost pitiful, but . . . even so, as she took a breath, a strength—no, *a presence*—seemed to fill her.
She sat on the bed and simply breathed it in.
"Not alone." The sense of it embedded in her bones.
Go fix this. Maybe Nim's voice. Maybe not. But Emberly got up and headed to the door.
Light bled down the hallway, across the four other bedroom doors, but she headed to the great room with the view of the city. She rounded through the kitchen to the office.
Logan Thorne stood with his back to her as she knocked, then came in.
He glanced over his shoulder, his expression dark.
"What's going on?"
He sighed, shut the laptop on his desk, and walked over to her. "You did really well tonight. Thank you."
"I nearly didn't." She made a wry face.
He gave her a grim nod.
"So, you got something off that phone."
"Yes. We got . . . a big something." He folded his arms. "For the past few years, we've been chasing down a rogue faction of the CIA. They were in league with Reba Jackson—"
"The VP-elect who was involved in an assassination plot."
"That was just the beginning." He offered her a seat on one of the plush, blue velvet chairs. She sat on the edge, her silk dress

puddling around her bare feet. "We thought—and still believe—that a faction of the Russian troika, the government leadership, wanted to pull us into a war. And they were using a branch of the Bratva to do this."

"The Petrov Bratva."

"Indeed. Two years ago, they created a bioweapon and tried to deploy it at an aero event in Florida."

She sat back.

"About the same time, they attempted another assassination on Air Force One, with the president aboard. This time with an EMP bomb."

"Creative."

"It gets worse. You heard about the near bombing in Lauchtenland last year?"

"No."

"Because we stopped it." He leaned against the front of the sturdy mahogany desk. "They had another bioweapon, this time one that would have spread radioactive waste across the country. They were going to deploy it during an American–European football game."

She realized her mouth had opened.

"And last year, the Petrovs broke into the crypobank in Montelena and stole two hundred million dollars. At first we weren't sure what it was for, but we realized . . . it was to buy an island."

"Mariposa."

"Yes. The world's largest stockpile of obsidian. Thankfully we were able to divert their shipment—"

"The operation Declan was on."

"Yes. He's been working with our organization for a while. Axiom wasn't exactly bait, but it became clear that's what they wanted." He drew in a breath. "And we're starting to wonder if you might have been part of their game plan."

She frowned. "I . . . what?"

"You were right. Luis is missing. And so are Mystique and Shep. And we dug into the connection between your Captain Teresa and Luis. They were together before you extracted him out of Krakow. And . . . we think Teresa worked for the KGB."

"So, the entire mission was . . . what? A fake?"

"He did give away troop movements, but perhaps that crime served as his cover."

"And all this time . . ."

"He's been playing the Swans."

She looked away, shook her head.

"The man at the center of all this, however, is not Tomas, or Luis . . . It's a man named Alan Martin. He's ex-CIA, and he masterminded, well, everything, we believe."

He picked up the cell phone. "And today this phone proved it. We found calls from Tomas to a cell here in the city, and Coco was able to ping it to a specific location. She ran facial recognition from the cameras in the area against any known Bratva contacts and . . . there he was. Talking to Tomas on a bench in the middle of Hudson Yards. Eating ice cream."

She stared at Logan. "So, this Alan Martin is behind . . . what, exactly? I talked with Nim. She said the program is intact."

"I know. Declan called me. But Nim thinks there might be a back door, which means somehow it can still be hacked."

"And Declan is still worried."

"He's going to ask the convention center to go offline during his demonstration."

"Right. No Internet, no hacking." She sighed. "Okay then, how can I help?"

He frowned, shook his head. "You're done, Phoenix. We'll take it from here."

She blinked at him. "What? No, this is a Swan operation."

"And you did your job. You secured Axiom. We got the virus—"

"Are you even sure it works?"

"Declan was there the entire time. He has the virus parked in his cloud server, even if Luis tainted the other one. We have Alan's phone and are tracking his GPS."

Are tracking . . . "Wait. Is Stein still here?"

"No. He and Colt and Tate left about a half hour ago." He got up. "Thanks again, Phoenix. You've been a big help. I guess you'll be needing a flight somewhere?"

Oh. "Um."

"You live in Lisbon?"

She nodded. So . . . dismissed, then.

She walked out into the kitchen, stood in the quiet.

Stein had left.

On his own mission.

Without her.

She walked down the hallway, pushed open the door, and for a second, thought maybe . . .

Maybe he'd be waiting, with a Snickers bar and that lazy smile.

But her room was empty.

"Come with me if you want to live."

She sank into the bed, curled her knees to her chest, and watched the moon, a shimmering ball in a black sky. And tried to tell herself that she wasn't alone.

His eyes had turned to sandpaper.

That had nothing on his mood, however. Steinbeck sipped black coffee, standing at the edge of the SAR exhibit, watching as the crowd gathered.

He now understood why Declan needed such a large exhibit space. He'd packed an entire make-believe village into the ninety-thousand-square-foot hall with the thirty-eight-feet-high ceiling. A village that very much resembled the destroyed island of

Mariposa after a landslide took out a terrible swath of the small community. Lumber, cement, rebar, steel girders, mud, and dirt, all constructed out of plaster. The exhibit felt just a little too real.

No wonder Declan had developed the SAR dogs. Made to mimic German shepherds, they stood in a row, quiet and intimidating under gleaming lights. Behind them hung an expansive wall banner with an actual photo of the rubble in Mariposa, the words "Transforming EMS Response with SAR AI Dogs" emblazoned in white against the chaos.

Smaller droids that looked a lot like the automatic lawn mower Jack wanted to buy sat in front of a banner with a background of burnt forest. This one advertised AI bomb-detection sweepers.

"Those were developed with help from our EOD expert, Sibba. She's from Slovenia—they still have unexploded ordnance from World War Two," Colt had said as they'd watched the rehearsal for the event that morning.

A red rope hanging between stanchions stretched in front of the dogs and the rubble, another in front of the bomb sweepers. Declan would take the podium in the middle, elevated on a short dais, his company's logo on the front: *Spectra Cybernetics: Empowering AI Innovation.*

A massive screen hung over the entire exhibit, where Declan would show his video before showcasing the dogs hunting for lost "people."

They'd run through the video this morning, and the rehearsal went off without a glitch. Stein and crew had spent last night with eyes glued to the strategically placed cameras from their station in Declan's rented greenroom. He'd even caught a few winks on the sofa between shifts.

So really, he had no reason for the buzz under his skin.

It didn't help that between the winks, Emberly had roamed his brain, and he couldn't purge the look on her face after she'd returned to the gala.

He'd hurt her. He knew it. And the longer it sat inside him, the more his chest ached, poison swilling his veins.

"This reminds me of when I attended my mother-in-law's presidential campaign event in San Diego," Tate said next to him. "I knew something was going to go down—I just couldn't untangle it. Turned out the sound guy had sabotaged the mics."

Steinbeck looked at him. "You checked the sound system?"

"Twice." Tate lifted a shoulder. "I'm glad Glo isn't here. I was always a little distracted with her in the audience." He glanced at Steinbeck. "But my girl wasn't some sort of super spy, so . . ."

Steinbeck's mouth tightened. "She's not *my girl*."

"Sure looked like your girl at the gala. And the way you pulled her off that rig—"

"She rescued herself, thank you, and I was just . . ." He swallowed, shook his head. "She can take care of herself."

"Black Swans work alone."

Tate nodded, took another sip of coffee.

"Tae said she enjoyed shopping with her." Colt threw his cup into a nearby trash can. "I probably shouldn't have brought Tae on this trip, but"—he folded his arms—"she's good for me." He offered a slight smile. "I can get a little unhinged. She's smart and calm and patient and . . ." He sighed. "But yeah, I'll never forget when she was held hostage by those jerks in Florida."

"Hostage?" Stein said. He'd been watching a delegation of Chinese scientists as they read a brochure and talked with one of Declan's sales reps.

"At an air show in Florida. The Petrovs were going to deploy a smallpox toxin. That's where I met Fraser Marshall."

"On the princess's detail?"

"Yeah. He worked for Ham Jones's outfit before he was injured in a security op gone south in Nigeria. He leveled up with his new gig. Then again, it's his brother Creed who really got the long stick.

Although I'd guess that God has a good plan for everyone. Oh, it looks like it's showtime."

Stein nearly didn't hear his last words, stuck on *"God has a good plan for everyone."*

Maybe that was the struggle. Stein had thought he'd landed on a plan. And Emberly had blown that up. *"This is what I do, Stein."*

He should have paid attention instead of dreaming up some happily ever after for them, walking away into the sunshine.

"Come with me if you want to live." Yeah, right. His gut tightened. He threw away his cup as Colt left him to take a position opposite the room. Tate had moved away also, watching the back of the growing crowd.

Spectators had come from around the globe—Russia, Nepal, Thailand, Indonesia, Brazil, Turkey. Stein's gaze ran over all of them, searching for trouble.

Declan walked out from behind the exhibit, followed by a handful of staffers.

"You guys in position?" Logan's voice thrummed in Steinbeck's earpiece.

"Aye," said Steinbeck quietly.

"Roger," added Tate and Colt.

At the front of the room, Declan took the stage to thunderous applause. The man seemed on fire today, imbued with a sort of energy that probably came with seeing a dream birth to life.

Steinbeck nearly pressed against the ache in his chest.

Declan raised his hands to quiet the room.

"Good morning, distinguished delegates and fellow innovators. My name is Declan Stone, and I am the CEO of Spectra Cybernetics, where we are committed to advancing the frontier of artificial intelligence not just to meet the future but to build it."

Steinbeck kept scanning the room.

"He was right there in the lobby and I . . . I didn't want to lose the opportunity to . . . Did you hear me? I got his phone!"

Aw, Emberly needed to get out of his head.

"At Spectra, we believe that AI is more than just technology. It is the key to unlocking solutions to some of the world's most pressing challenges. From improving disaster response to cleaning up some of our most war-torn countries, AI has the potential to transform lives across the globe."

"Good job, Phoenix. Clearly you're the thief we all thought you were."

Wow, he was a jerk.

"Imagine a world where AI can predict natural disasters with incredible accuracy, giving us vital hours to evacuate, save lives, and reduce damage. Our bomb sweepers can detect and neutralize explosive threats with precision and speed that far exceeds human capabilities. This technology not only saves lives but also ensures that post-trauma zones can be rehabilitated more quickly and safely."

"I was really hoping you meant it when you said you'd quit the Swans."

Maybe that had been unfair of him. Even if she had suggested it. Maybe she'd been trying to fit into his world. His dreams. Or at least what she thought they might be.

"Our AI applications are designed with the philosophy of 'AI for Good.' But the power of AI also comes with great responsibility. At Spectra, we are dedicated to developing AI that is not only powerful and efficient but also safe, transparent, and accountable."

"What am I going to do with you?" In his memory, he was pulling her close, her voice in his ear.

"Maybe . . . don't let go?"

Except he'd done exactly that, hadn't he?

So much for keeping promises.

"Ladies and gentlemen, as we stand at the cusp of a new era, the choices we make today will define the future of our planet and humanity. At Spectra, we choose to lead with innovation, integrity, and an unwavering commitment to the betterment of society through AI."

Stein's gaze fixed on Declan, but he heard the man from the beach—Judah. *"The failure of the disciples was that they looked at themselves and said . . . 'Not enough.' But Jesus asks us to look at Him and hear . . . 'By My strength.'"*

"Thank you for your attention, and I look forward to forging paths of collaboration and innovation together." Declan stepped off the stage and walked over to his SAR droids.

Maybe Phoenix—*Emberly*—hadn't been the mission.

Maybe the mission had been about him, and about trusting God with a woman he . . . he loved.

And longed to protect.

He stared out again at the crowd, searching it for trouble. *Lord, I'm not sure I'm up to the task, but . . . I give You who I am. And if You want me to step back into play . . . whatever that means . . . I surrender.*

And even in the midst of the murmurs of the crowd as one of Declan's techs fired up the droids, Stein heard the words. *"Stand back and see what I will do."*

It was a memory, but it steeled through him.

Up front, Declan told the dog to find. The animal moved over to the rubble.

"The dog has been programmed to search for the scent of blood or sweat or other human odors." He stood back and nodded to the tech to release another dog. The other two animals sat, as if waiting.

The first two dogs disappeared into the rubble.

Steinbeck's gaze fell on a man—thin, dark hair, glasses, wearing a hat and a leather jacket—holding a phone.

Not taking a picture, but . . . *texting?*

Maybe taking notes.

Stein turned back to the demonstration just as one of the dogs returned, climbing out from a blackened space, a sensor in its body beeping.

The tech walked over and pulled a screen from the back of the dog's neck.

"This is a GPS route. It indicates where the dog has located the specimen. The AI will then map the route for the rescuers. The uniqueness of this program is that while searching, the dog also collected X-ray information about the debris—type, location—and has created possible routes with a technical plan for extraction." He turned to the dog. "Good dog."

The crowd laughed as the animal wiggled its nubby tail.

"He doesn't require any dog treats, by the way."

More laughter.

"The Internet is offline, right?" This from Tate.

"Affirmative," Logan said. "There are two other symposiums meeting right now on this floor, but they're panel events—no need for Internet. We have a tight window, however."

So far, so good. Maybe they'd shut down the intrusion event.

The other dog returned, also beeping. The female tech lifted off the GPS device. "We'll load these coordinates into our system. The dogs also come equipped with a storage area." She opened up a back panel. "We can fill it with water or first-aid supplies and send the animal back with communications abilities to assist the injured while they wait for rescue."

"See the guy in the hat?" Colt's voice, in comm, from the other side of the room. "Dark shirt, leather jacket?"

"I saw him before," Stein said. "Texting." He searched for him again. Something about him had lodged inside . . . *Wait.*

"I don't have eyes on him, but he looks familiar." Stein, moving now as the tech in front fired up another dog, this one smaller.

"We'll ask Champ here to hunt for hot spots, potential fires." The tech deployed the animal.

Meanwhile, the other two dogs had stopped beeping.

Stein searched the shifting crowd, the crazy buzz under his skin now moving to his gut. Something—

A murmur rustled the crowd. He turned, searched for the source.

Doggy number one had woken up, its eyes reddened.

"Guys—" Stein started.

It launched out into the audience amidst screams, growling, slamming into spectators.

And then the second animal came to life.

Declan's staff scrambled to shut down the animals as the third and fourth dogs turned on the crowd, now stampeding toward the entrance.

Stein spotted the man in the hat, which had been knocked off by a fleeing participant.

Luis.

"I have him," Stein barked into the comms and took off, shouldering through the crowd.

"Get control of those droids!" This from Logan, but Stein ignored him, pushed around people as he barreled after Luis.

He lost him for a moment in the rush, spotted him again just as the man pushed out into the hall.

And was gone.

Stein forced his way out of the room and stood in the middle of the corridor, now packed with screaming participants, his heart hammering. "I lost him."

Security from the other areas slammed into the room, against the flow of escapees. Participants surged through the doors to the adjoining exhibit rooms, more people running down the escalator.

Shots barked in the air.

"Who's shooting?" Logan's voice.

Stein had whirled around. "I've got nothing!"

More shots and shouting.

"Close the exits!" Stein said, pushing into the other exhibit hall. "He might have taken the escalator down." *Wait.* "Pull the fire alarm!"

"What?"

Stein ran against the tide, shoving his way through, searching. "Last time the water shut them down!"

In a second, sirens blared, and just like that, water shot out of the sprinklers above.

More screaming, and the spray saturated the hallway, the carpet, the walls. People flushed out of the other exhibit hall, shoved past him.

And he stood in the middle, the water casting over him, saturating him, and it hit him.

This wasn't . . . "Something isn't right."

"No kidding!" Logan said. "It's not working. The dogs aren't going down."

"Then activate the virus!"

"We're connecting with the Internet now!"

He stopped in the hallway, staring at the other exhibit room. Signs outside explained the panels inside, the doors closed.

"Why infiltrate an *exhibit*? If Alan Martin and the Bratva are behind this, wouldn't they use the AI for something more deadly?"

More impactful?

The vertical banner outside the closed door of the exhibit hall caught his eyes.

Princess Imani of Lauchtenland, Britta White, daughter of the US president, Princess Madeline of Montelena, and a number of others he didn't recognize—a panel of female youth leaders.

And the door was shut.

He ran over to it. Locked. The terrible buzzing inside congealed, turned to ice.

"Logan—can you get ahold of Secret Service? Make sure they have eyes on Britta White?" He stepped back and his gaze fell on a fire-extinguisher cabinet, and the axe inside. "Guys, Declan's dogs weren't the target. They were the *distraction*. I need you in Exhibit Hall 3 *right now*."

Then he broke the glass and grabbed the axe.

ELEVEN

SHE KNEW IT. JUST . . . *KNEW* IT.

"Get down, Britta!"

Emberly stood close enough to the female secret service agent to hear the thrum of urgency in her voice. The woman positioned her body over Britta's as water splattered down into the exhibition room. They'd retreated to the back greenroom area.

Okay, so no time to congratulate herself on her brilliant instincts—which had resulted in obsessive sheet-twisting insomnia—last night as she'd sorted through Logan Thorne's story and pieced it together from different angles.

She just couldn't believe that attacking Declan's exhibition would rattle national security. So what if a billionaire inventor's creation had glitches or even infiltration into his AI program? Sure, that meant that some rogue government could attach a virus to the AI program, thwart its intended target's national security. In fact, that had been her mission—to secure the world from the threats of Axiom.

Except . . . *Luis*. What if he'd been using the Swans all along? He'd been the one to suggest the creation of the virus over a year ago. Had been the one who offered to create it if she could get her hands on Axiom.

It all fit—but she'd been too focused on the Skynet/*Terminator* angle to see the fine details.

No wonder Tomas had come after her following her little foray into the ladies' room with Princess Imani—who had told her about today's event . . . with President White's daughter, Britta.

Now, Emberly stood in the hallway to the back exit, garbed in the staff security uniform she'd nicked from the rental-security's staging area.

She'd gotten lucky too—found the badge of a woman who looked enough like her to pass scrutiny. Dark hair—the wig from last night, now cut shorter and under a cap—and a uniform that included a stun gun. She'd passed all the checkpoints and taken up a position against the wall, watching the panelists take the stage. Princess Imani, Princess Madeline, and of course Britta White. The panelists also included a woman from Nigeria and another from Thailand.

One by one, they'd given short inspirational speeches behind a podium, then taken their places at a long sturdy table, answering questions from the audience.

When chaos had erupted, the table had been pushed over by one of the secret service agents, an attempt to protect the ladies before herding them into the greenroom.

Funny, all the comms coming off her walkie focused on the chaos in the other exhibit hall. And yet, inside the greenroom, Pippa and the other security, especially the Secret Service, were on their phones, calling for assistance.

Tomas had somehow gotten past all the security the team had set up around Declan's exhibit. It didn't surprise her, really. Luis would have figured out a way to get past the shutdown of the Internet.

"We need to evac." This from Pippa, who joined Emberly at

the back entrance. She glanced at Emberly, then at the door and back again.

"Phoenix? How'd you get here?"

"I figured it out."

Pippa frowned.

"Later. This door leads out to the back hallway and stairs that go down all the way to the service area."

Pippa's hair was plastered to her head, the water dripping down her face onto her black suit. She leaned into her cuff mic. "Fraser. For the love, come in."

"If you're connected via the Wi-Fi, it's out."

Pippa gave her a hard look. "No, it's a cell connection."

"Could be jammed."

A secret service agent stepped out of the greenroom. "We're cut off too. We need to move Starlight, now."

Oh. Britta.

"I know," Pippa snapped. "But let's all calm down and get some eyes in the hallway before—"

The back door opened. Security—wearing the same uniform as Emberly—streamed in, a handful of men and a woman, holding handguns, AR-15s strapped over their shoulders. Pippa stepped back into the room, took a position in front of Imani.

The three secret service women drew their weapons.

"We're building security. Let's go." This from one of the older men, salt-and-pepper hair, a seasoned look on his face. He spoke with an accent, maybe Hispanic, and he held open the door as his men entered the room, ushering the others out.

Emberly stayed back, suddenly aware of her uniform, the fact that—

"Who are you?"

She turned and faced one of the men, who glanced at her badge, back at her.

"Can't you read?" Then she walked into the greenroom. "Okay, everyone, just head down the hallway, down the stairs."

Pippa shot her a frown just before she exited, her hand on Imani.

Yeah, something didn't feel right.

And then . . . *Wait—*

She ran after Pippa, grabbed her arm right before she got to the door. Pippa had hold of Imani, pulled her back.

"What if these guys did the same thing I did? What if—"

"Keep moving." The command came from behind her, a voice that . . .

No.

She turned, and of course Boris stood behind her. He'd clearly found another bull-bodied man from whom to filch his uniform, and now he startled, his gaze on her.

"Run, Pippa," Emberly said quietly and took a step toward Boris. "Round three?"

Behind her, Pippa had grabbed Imani around the waist for protection and now ran toward the exhibition hall.

Boris took a step toward Emberly, who raised her hands.

"This is going to go badly for you," Emberly snapped. He smiled and reached for her.

She dodged him, ran out into the exhibition hall.

The white pops of smoke bombs exploding made her hit the carpet.

Somewhere in the clutter, Pippa and Imani had vanished.

Boris hauled Emberly up by her arm. "Trying to run, little rat?" He pushed her toward the exit. She stumbled, hit the wall, turned back to him, her stun gun out, and lunged.

He slapped the gun away, but she rolled and lunged again.

The gun hit his hip and his leg buckled.

He fell and she rounded back toward the door to the hall.

Gunshots in the hallway stopped her. A scream added to the chaos.

She turned.

Britta's secret service agent lay in a puddle of blood.

Oh no, no—

And then—*yep,* she should have guessed—Igor appeared, holding his AR-15. Pointing it at her.

Boris still writhed on the floor, cursing, but he managed to climb to his feet. He staggered out, and Igor motioned with his gun.

No. No way was she ending up in a gulag in Russia.

Then Boris turned and smiled, something in his grip.

A chill shook through her.

Grenade.

"Don't—"

He pulled the pin, still smiling.

"Don't!"

"Phoenix!"

She stilled, whirled around.

No—no!

Steinbeck appeared through the gauzy smoke, running. "Phoenix!"

"Get back! Grenade! He's got a grenade—"

Igor grabbed her arm and yanked, and she fell against him as he headed toward the stairwell. She fought him—

Boris tossed the grenade past her, into the exhibition hall.

"Stein, run!"

Igor slammed her through the doorway, into the hall, just as the door exploded out and hit the wall. She landed on the concrete, heat bursting through her shoulder, her head slamming against the floor.

She lay for a moment, just . . . *What? What—*

Steinbeck!

Igor growled, then rolled to his feet. Hauled her up by her vest and dragged her down the hallway.

Smoke cluttered the doorway, billowed out of the room.

Steinbeck. Not again—she couldn't leave him again. She slammed her foot into Igor's leg, but he just turned and cuffed her across the face.

Pain exploded in her cheekbone, and her nose instantly bled, hot as he dragged her down the hallway, past another secret service officer, down the stairwell.

Screams echoed from below, maybe Britta and Madeline fighting their captors.

Igor practically pushed Emberly down the stairs, and she stumbled, hitting the wall with her injured shoulder. Then he grabbed her up and pushed her the next flight down. She kept her feet, scrambled ahead of him, breathing hard.

"Keep your head."

Mystique, in her brain, clearing it.

"Don't think of Steinbeck. Broken. Bleeding . . . Dead."

She hit the landing, spotted Britta and Madeline below. Madeline struggled in her captor's hold, her red hair out of its twist, her blue eyes flashing as she kicked at the man.

He slammed her against the wall, leaned in, and snarled something.

Madeline spat at him.

Oh boy.

Britta had taken a different route. Simply dropped, unmoving on the floor, her body a knot as the man tried to dislodge her.

He grabbed her hair and pulled. She screamed, fell to her back, kicking him, but he finally forced her up.

Madeline bore a welt on her face.

Now Emberly joined them at the bottom of the stairs, near the building's loading dock.

Madeline's captor shoved her against the concrete wall, grabbing her hands. She fought him, twisting, leaving a scrape of blood on the wall, but he managed to get zip ties onto her.

Britta tried to hard-jaw her tears, but she lowered her head, sobbing as her captor secured her wrists too.

"Leave her alone!" Emberly rushed him, pushed him hard, and he slammed against the door.

"Grab her!" This to Igor, who cuffed Emberly on her shoulder blade.

She grunted, fell, and tucked his stolen pepper spray into her vest.

Then she turned, and before Igor could hit her again, she put her wrists together, side to side. "Just calm down. No need to get rough."

Igor snapped on the flexicuffs.

"We should leave her," said Boris, finally down the stairs. "Shoot her here."

"No. We can use her." The voice jerked her, turned her hollow.

Tomas stepped into the area, dressed in a suit, a tie. He looked at Emberly, smiled. "This just gets more interesting."

Then he jerked his head, motioning them out the door.

The loading area held a few pallets, a forklift, and a delivery truck parked near the far door. Emberly did the math. If the men got them inside the truck, they would be in the wind.

Not. Happening.

She bumped up against Madeline as the men herded them down the stairs.

"Get ready to run."

Madeline shot her a look as Emberly caught up to Britta. "Be brave."

Britta looked up at her, horror in her eyes.

That's when Emberly tripped her.

Britta screamed, falling, and as she did, Emberly slammed her cuffs against her body, snapped them off, grabbed up the pepper spray, and deployed it, right into the eyes of her captors.

Madeline ducked and peeled off, also snapping her cuffs—

clearly the Bratva needed to update their equipment—and scampered behind a stack of pallets.

Coughing, Boris palmed his gun.

Emberly dove for Britta, hauling her up. "Run!"

But—*aw,* Britta tripped again, her ankle clearly turned in the fall. And Boris was shooting, still blinded.

Tomas, however, had come out last, the spray missing him, and now he also pulled a gun. "Stop, Emberly."

She grabbed up Britta, stepped in front of her. "Let us go, Tomas. I promise you, we'll meet again."

He shook his head. "I am so tired of you Black Swans."

Then he pulled the trigger.

His ears rang.

Steinbeck rolled out from behind the overturned table where he'd leaped after Emberly's warning.

Seeing her had stopped him flat. Probably saved his life, really.

As for the others still catching up, he'd shouted "Grenade!" just in case and curled into a ball, covered his ears, protected his head.

The grenade had exploded. A flash-bang. He'd stayed down, eyes closed, and when he rose, he spotted Colt and Tate appearing from the back.

"I think they took the president's daughter." He headed toward the entrance, his brain still rolling over—

What was Emberly doing here?

He stopped at the entrance to the back hallway, then rolled out. "Clear."

Colt and Tate filed behind him.

"Blood," said Colt, and Stein looked down to see drips and then a swath on a wall on the lower landing. The pungent odor of the smoke bombs and the acrid stink of gunpowder burned the air.

A gunshot echoed up the steps, a scream in its wake.

Stein motioned down and took point. Hit the first landing, peeked over. "Clear."

He headed to the next, and did the same, all the way to the bottom.

A shot popped and he hit the wall.

Another scream and he glanced at Colt, Tate. They nodded and he edged out.

Two bodies lay crumpled on the concrete floor of the parking garage. More shots and he spotted a handful of men in position behind pallets, a couple barrels.

The gunshots had popped from behind a truck.

His gaze fell on a man in a suit, and his jaw tightened. "Tomas, eleven o'clock, behind those barrels."

A bullet pinged off the doorframe, and he turned, spotted a security officer—clearly not, but *whatever*—hunkered down behind the loading platform.

Stein ducked back inside, glanced at Colt. "People down near the truck. Looks like building security, but my guess is that they're with the Bratva."

"How do you—"

Another ping into the stairwell, and a peek out showed Tomas running hard behind a uniform toward a forklift. A few more men were on their feet now, firing toward whoever stood behind the truck.

Emberly?

"Go," Stein said.

Colt stepped out and neutralized the shooter by the loading dock.

Steinbeck followed and dropped another man, this one turning on Colt.

More gunshots, these aimed at the men behind a barrel. Stein had a better angle, but it was Tate who shut them down.

Tate moved down the stairs. At the bottom, he crouched and took out another man, who'd risen for a try.

The shooters behind the truck focused on a bigger man who held position behind a dumpster.

Maybe it was Steinbeck's imagination, but it seemed he'd seen the big fella outside Nimue's house in Melbourne Beach.

"It's the Bratva."

"No duh," said Tate, who'd dropped behind the loading dock, over the man Colt had eliminated. He pointed to a star inked on the back of the shooter's neck. "I know these guys. Bratva for sure."

Tomas and another man hunkered down behind the forklift.

Steinbeck spotted a woman with red hair behind a stack of pallets. *Madeline Ribaldi.* He remembered her from the gala. She was pointing to the bodies on the floor.

He frowned. He could see one of the uniformed security officers, wearing a vest, but even as he looked, someone was struggling from beneath—

Britta White. Shaking, her hair bloody, trying to crawl out from—

His knees nearly left him.

No, no—

Emberly wasn't behind the truck, shooting at the enemy . . .

He took off toward the bodies, but a shot nearly clipped him. And that was *Just. It.*

He turned and unloaded on the two behind the forklift, all the way until he reached Britta. Then he hauled her up and carried her, one arm around her, to the truck. Shoved her into the back. "Stay down."

"I got her," said a deep voice behind the truck.

He turned and stilled. "Shep?"

"Get Emberly." Shep held a Glock, clearly abandoning his sidelines-only position. He glanced at Britta. "You shot?"

"No." She wrapped her arms around herself, shaking.

"Stay put," Shep said and glanced at Stein. Nodded.

Then Steinbeck stepped back around the truck.

A barrage of shots—somebody behind there had a semiautomatic—peppered the room as Stein ran out toward . . .

Not *the body*.

Please be alive!

Emberly lay, her face in a puddle of blood. He grabbed her vest, pulled her along the concrete floor like . . .

Not a rag doll. Not a *corpse*.

He dropped behind the truck and pulled her into his arms, turned her over.

Her beautiful eyes were closed, and blood smeared her face, her nose clearly broken. *Please be alive, please—*

Her pulse thumped under his fingers at her neck. But her breath shuddered in and out, as if struggling.

More shots, and a shout, but he ignored them as he laid her down, searching for the wound.

She wore a Kevlar vest—*good girl*—and he found where the bullet had made a terrible dent in the casing on her right side, torso. He unzipped the vest and opened it.

No blood, and yet she still struggled.

"Sorry, babe." He lifted her shirt. Deep red-purple stained her skin, evidence of internal bleeding.

"She must have broken ribs when the bullet hit," Shep said, standing close enough to see the damage.

"She saved my life," said Britta, her arms around her updrawn knees. "She just stood there, right in front of me, and let him shoot her!"

"Okay, okay"—Shep held up his hand to Britta—"just breathe."

Steinbeck, too, clung to Shep's advice. *Just breathe.*

Just breathe, Emberly!

"Listen," Shep said. "You back up London—I'll take care of Emberly."

Stein looked up, past Shep. London stood behind the open passenger-side door of the truck, well-armed.

"She's not leaving here without Tomas. This is personal," Shep said.

Yeah, well, for him too, and the thought galvanized him. "Don't. Let. Her. Die."

Shep's mouth tightened, a thin line that Steinbeck refused to think about.

Stay with me, Emberly. He scooted up along the truck and opened the driver's-side door.

Glanced at London through the truck. She wore a black hat over her blonde hair and had a dark expression. "Any ideas?"

He found Colt and Tate and motioned to them. Colt got up, scuttled over to Madeline behind her pallet, ducking as a shot whizzed over his head.

Tate pulled off a shot, but it pinged against the forklift as the shooter vanished.

If Steinbeck had time . . . He glanced at Tate, met his eyes.

Tate nodded and hunkered down in position. Gave just the slightest bob of his head.

"Look alive," Steinbeck said to London.

Then he got up and stepped out from behind the car door. He took off at a run, nothing too fast, but fast enough.

The Bratva shooter took the bait. He rose just a little and—

Tate sent him sprawling back behind the forklift.

Stein skidded behind a row of barrels.

"It's over, Tomas!" London shouted. "There's no escaping. Surrender now and give up Alan Martin and you have hope of not being executed for attempting to kidnap the first daughter."

Steinbeck peeked out. Spotted Tomas behind the forklift.

And saw him put the gun to himself—

The door to the garage jerked open. There were shouts, and a tactical assault team swarmed in from the garage door, from the stairwell, descending on Tomas.

Steinbeck stood just as Fraser Marshall grabbed up the man, disarmed him, and threw him facedown onto the grimy concrete.

Someone was a little hot that his princess had been attacked.

Yeah, well, Stein too. He took off toward Shep, spotted him motioning to one of the tactical guys.

"What?"

"I think one of the ribs punctured a lung. She can't breathe because her chest cavity is filling with air." Shep didn't sound panicked, but he had opened up her shirt, taken off her vest. "If we don't relieve the pressure, it could shut down her heart." He leaned back, shouted toward the tactical guy, "I need that chest-decompression kit!"

The veins in Emberly's neck had started to swell, her body whitening, her fingertips turning blue. She was gasping even while unconscious, but only one side of her chest was moving.

Stein dropped to his knees. "Shep—"

"I know!" Shep put his fingers to her throat. "She's in tachycardia—"

An ambulance screamed in, and Stein hit his feet, took off to the parking lot. The vehicle barely stopped before Stein opened up the back. "I need a decompression kit!"

"Just calm down." The male EMT, mid-thirties, reached for a med bag.

"Oh, this is calm. You don't want to see me not calm," Stein said, his voice lowering. He put up a hand to stop the EMT from exiting. "I'm going to need that kit."

"Hurry!" Shep shouted.

Stein stared at the man and put intent in his eyes. "He's a medic. Trying to save my girlfriend's life."

The EMT turned back inside and handed him the kit.

Stein ran it back just as Shep leaned over to give Emberly breaths.

No, no—

Stein dropped the kit beside Shep.

"Help her breathe," Shep said.

Stein fell to his knees on the opposite side, blew out a couple quick breaths, then leaned over and met Emberly's mouth.

Breathed life into her.

Please, Emberly.

Again.

Please.

Shep pulled on gloves, ripped open antiseptic wipes.

London landed beside Stein. "How can I help?"

Stein kept breathing into Emberly. "C'mon, Phoenix. Don't die. You're tougher than this."

"Clean the insertion site." Shep indicated the space between her ribs. He handed London the wipes.

Stein breathed again. Only one side of Emberly's chest rose, and just barely. He could hardly find air for himself.

Please, God. Please.

"That's good, London." Shep handed her gauze. "Take these and catch the blood that runs off. Stein, hold up."

Stein leaned back and only then realized that Tate and Colt and Logan and Fraser stood behind him, around him.

Colt put a hand on his shoulder, squeezed. And as Stein watched Shep feel for the space between Emberly's ribs, the one place that might save her life, he picked up her hand, held it.

He didn't care that his eyes filled, that his voice emerged small and broken. That the guys might hear him. "I'm holding on, Emberly. Just like I said. I'm sorry I let you go. I was selfish and scared and stupid. And it will never happen again. Just don't . . . don't leave."

Shep shoved the needle in, and she jerked as if in response to pain. Then air sloughed out of her through the large-bore needle. Shep pressed fingers to her neck.

"Compressions, London."

He said it quietly, and Stein stared at him as London bent over and started CPR.

No, no—

"Breathe, Stein."

He looked at Shep.

"For her. Breathe for her!"

Right. London stopped compressions and Stein leaned over, sent air into Emberly's lungs. He tasted salt on his lips as he took a breath and delivered another one.

"Compressions," Shep said, and London kept pumping.

A crowd gathered around them.

"Twelve, thirteen—okay, breaths, Stein."

He leaned over, breathed into her.

Nothing.

Again.

She remained white, and London started again. Behind him, Britta started to sob. Madeline came up and held her, arms tight around her. He glanced at them, back at Emberly.

No. It was not supposed to end like this. They were supposed— well, they weren't supposed to be anything. The thief and the Boy Scout. Yeah, it was a crazy fairy tale, but it was theirs. Oh, he wanted it to be theirs. *Please, God. I've got nothing but You.*

The blood London pumped through Emberly had started to flush her face. But still, she lay, unmoving, her face broken, and Stein closed his eyes, listening to London count. *Nine. Ten. Eleven—*

"Stand back and see what I will do."

His breath caught, the words nearly thunder, ripping through him. He opened his eyes.

Emberly's chest moved, a breath captured. Then another.

"That's good, London."

"We have oxygen," the EMT from before said, delivering—finally—an O2 tank. He affixed a mask over Emberly's mouth.

And she breathed.

Somehow Shep got hold of a stethoscope, and he pressed it to her chest. "Yeah, her other lung is working. The air is leaving her pleural cavity."

Colt had both hands on Stein's shoulders now and squeezed hard even as Stein sat back, his body shaking.

He grabbed Emberly's hand.

She squeezed it a second before she opened her eyes, searched the room, and what might have been panic flashed in them.

"You're okay, babe." He leaned up then, held her gaze.

She stared at him, her voice nearly inaudible as she spoke. He leaned close to her lips. "You're not dead."

He met her eyes. "Not yet."

"I thought—" She reached up to move the oxygen, but he caught her hand.

"I know. You thought you left me behind in a pile of rubble."

Her eyes filled.

"Been there, done that. Do not recommend."

She closed her eyes, then started to sob.

What?

"Em. You're okay. I'm okay. Tomas is . . ."

"In custody," said Fraser.

"It's over. Except, how did you . . . I mean . . . how did you even get here? In . . . this?" He gestured to the outfit.

And it occurred to him then that if she hadn't been wearing the vest . . . *Oh.*

"C'mere," she whispered, and he leaned over.

"I'm a thief."

He pulled back, searched her face.

She smiled and then . . . *winked*?

Oh, and the laugh just pressed out of him, a huff that released the brutal coil inside him. "Yeah, you are." And he didn't want to sound sappy, but . . . she'd completely stolen his heart.

"We need to move her now." This from the EMT who'd brought in a backboard.

Steinbeck moved away but kept hold of her hand.

"Sir, you'll have to let her go."

He looked at the man.

A beat.

"Never mind."

They put her on the board, strapped her down, and started an IV, and as Emberly drifted into sedation, he was right there.

Holding on.

TWELVE

MAYBE SHE WAS DEAD.

At least, that was the crazy thought that punched through the darkness as Emberly forced her way up, out of the soft layers of darkness, cotton, the sense of something carrying her as she drifted . . .

And surfaced to light.

So much light. It streamed in through the windows of . . . *Oh, a hospital.* She lay in a bed, an IV line strapped to her arm, blankets warming her, the room big and bright and—

She spotted a uniformed officer through the strip of glass in the door. But no Steinbeck. Not that she'd expected him to stay—oh, who was she kidding?

He'd said things. She remembered them landing sweetly in her heart. Something about holding on, or begging her not to leave. She scrolled back through her most recent recollection. *Oh yeah.* Tomas had shot her. From about ten feet away.

Maybe she *was* dead . . .

Except, she wore an oxygen cannula under her nose, giving off the slightest hiss, and with the presence of a heart monitor beeping . . .

Alive, yes. But alone.

She blinked, her eyes burning. *Sheesh,* what was her problem? She'd been alone most of her life.

Besides—Black Swans worked . . .

She closed her eyes. *No.* Not anymore. And maybe never, because a memory eased in, words recently remembered.

"You're not alone. You never have been."

Right. She opened her eyes. Stared out the window. The New York skyline, buildings, blue sky. *Thank You, God, for not letting me die.* The prayer rose, took hold.

And right behind it, words tremored through her.

"Come with me if you want to live."

Her breath caught. *What?*

Outside the room, laughter drifted down the hallway. She leaned back, closed her eyes. The door opened.

"Oh good. She's still sleeping."

Really?

Footsteps, and then a warm grip slipped into hers.

She opened her eyes.

Stein froze, blue eyes wide.

"You were going to pretend you were here the entire time?" she said.

Behind him stood—*wait*—"Nim?"

Her sister came over, leaned past Steinbeck, and kissed her forehead. She wore a pair of baggy floral pants and a tank. "For the record, he *has* been here the whole time. Look at him. He's a disaster."

Emberly gave Steinbeck a hard look. Bloodshot eyes, wearing a pair of scrubs, a delicious growth of dark-blond and copper whiskers on his face, and maybe he seemed a little underslept.

Steinbeck shrugged. "I only scooted out because I was on an important foraging mission." He reached into his pocket and pulled out a Snickers bar.

She reached for it. "You're my favorite."

"Yeah, it's for me. Nothing but soft pudding and broth for you there, Miss Two Broken Ribs and You Scared Us All to Death by Nearly Dying."

She cocked her head at him. "I'm starved."

"I'll split it with you." He smiled.

"You are so annoying."

"But helpful. I mean, someone had to give you mouth-to-mouth."

"That's so unnecessary," Nim said. "And a little gross. Listen. He's right—soup for you. But I do have people wanting to see you."

"People?"

"Well, aside from a grateful nation, and perhaps the president—"

"The president? Of the United States?"

"No, of Argentina. Yes, of the United States. You did save his daughter's life. And not to mention Princess Madeline of Montelena."

"Are they okay?"

"Other than needing therapy and maybe some Krav Maga lessons, yes. I think Britta said she wants to be just like you when she grows up."

"Maybe she and I need a little chat about that."

"I think probably you need to talk with"—and her voice fell—"Mystique first."

"Mystique is here?"

"Yes," Nimue said. She made a face. "She's a little intense."

Emberly laughed. "Okay."

Nimue walked to the door, motioned outside, then came back. "Let's be clear. I don't like you going off-grid and scaring me like that."

"Me either." The stern voice came from Mystique, who walked into the room, her hair pulled back, a grim look on her face.

Shep came in behind her, nodded at Stein before turning back to Mystique. "You should talk. I was really worried."

"Long story." She wove her fingers into Shep's and looked at Emberly. "Let's just say that it's a good thing Shep has my back. Luis had set a trap for us with the Bratva. We had to go dark for a hot minute . . . Anyway, I want to know how you ended up in that room with Britta White."

"It was impulse. I just kept thinking about the Bratva and how whatever they did with Declan's AI program wasn't . . . it wasn't something that could drag the US into a war. So I thought . . . what *could* do something like that? And then I remembered Princess Imani telling me how excited she was to meet the president's daughter, and it just . . . clicked. The death of someone that important . . . It could rock a nation."

"Smart."

"I mean, it was either that or they'd figure out how to take over all the AI-controlled drones and attack the capital."

Stein stilled. "That could happen?"

"I don't know—I mean, what happened in the exhibit?"

"The dogs turned on us. Just like before."

She nodded. "I thought so. But how? Didn't you shut down the Internet?"

He nodded.

"But not the cell phones," Nim said.

He glanced at her. "Declan's AI is too big of a program to be controlled by a cell-phone signal."

"But not a satellite signal," Mystique said. She glanced at Nim. "I don't know why we didn't think of that. G5. It connects to satellites. And then the signal is sent from the low-orbit satellite to the computer. Or dog, as it were."

"Someone was sending the inputs via cell phone," Emberly said.

"They wouldn't even have needed to be on-site," Mystique.

"Except Luis *was* on-site. I saw him. Or at least I thought so." Stein scrubbed his hands down his face. He did look tired.

"Okay, well, in other good news," Nim said, "I found the back door to Axiom and gave Declan the information. He's tidying it up."

"And," Mystique added, "the virus worked. We downloaded it and deployed it successfully. What we need to do is add it as a component to every AI program. A simple command could self-destruct the system."

"The other good news is that we have Tomas," Shep said. "And Logan is developing a task force to hunt for Alan Martin. It's time he was caught."

"And Luis?"

Mystique made a wry face.

"Luis is in the wind," said Shep.

"We'll find him," Nimue added. "I'm looking."

"Don't worry about Luis." Mystique set a hand on Emberly's arm, squeezed. "Now, will you please take some serious time off? This was too close."

Oh.

"Okay then." Mystique looked at Steinbeck. "You need some sleep."

Stein nodded. "I can't wait to get out of here and get home."

Shep shook his hand as he and Mystique headed out.

Emberly swallowed. Looked at Nim. "Any news on your house?"

"Other than that the insurance is completely ripping me off? No."

Emberly sighed. "So I guess it's back to Lisbon—"

"Are you kidding me?"

She looked at Stein, who'd leaned forward, anger on his face. *Oh no.* She'd seen this before. "What?"

"You're not going back to Lisbon."

"I live in Lisbon."

"You haven't lived in Lisbon for the better part of a year."

"I like Lisbon."

"I don't care if Lisbon is your favorite place on the entire planet, you're not going there." His mouth made a tight line.

"You're not the boss of me."

"Really? I think maybe I am, there, partner."

"We're not . . ." But she closed her mouth.

And he smiled.

"Fine. Then where am I supposed to—"

"With me, Miss Please Pay Attention. You're injured. And I'm not letting you out of my sight. And besides, my mom makes amazing cinnamon rolls."

She stilled.

"He's not lying," Nim said. "They are amazing cinnamon rolls."

"You're coming back with me to the King's Inn."

She gaped at him. "Oh, Stein. I don't . . . I can't . . ."

"You can. And you will. Declan is flying us back as soon as you're discharged."

She looked away and then heard the door close, and when she turned back, Stein stood alone.

"Where'd Nim go?"

"She probably doesn't want to hear what I'm going to say to you."

"Why not?"

"Because it's . . . sappy. And she's protecting my man card."

"Please. She cares nothing about—"

"I love you, Emberly." He stepped up to the bed, sighed, took her hand. "And Nim saw me . . . Let's just say I was tired—"

"Did you *cry*?"

He looked away, toward the ceiling.

"Steinbeck Kingston, you are many different people—arrogant and annoying, and tough and bossy, and—"

"Incredibly hot, irresistible—"

"And sweet."

He gave a wry grin.

"Let's go back to the I-love-you part."

His impossibly blue eyes met hers. Oh, he was handsome. The kind of rugged, interesting, intoxicating handsome that made a girl want more of him every day.

"I love you. I love the person who is Phoenix, girl who always rises from the ashes, who isn't afraid of . . . anything."

"That's not true. I'm afraid I'll never get half of that Snickers bar."

He sat down on her bed. "And I love Emberly, with her feisty, hot exterior but is soft and beautiful and fits in my arms."

"And Ashley?"

"Oh, she has all the moves. But truth is, I love all the versions of you, and anyone else you want to be. I love your creativity and your smarts and the fact that when I'm with you, I know I'm on mission."

"What mission is that?"

"To love the girl that Jesus loves."

Then he leaned down and lifted the oxygen cannula off her nose.

"I might suffocate."

"I'll bring you back to life. I know mouth-to-mouth resuscitation."

And then he proved it. Slowly, perfectly, and exactly, and indeed, she was very, very much alive.

• ——————————— •

And he was back to chopping wood.

Steinbeck brought the axe down on the perched log, and it splintered down the middle. He set down the axe and ripped the rest of the log in half with his gloved hands.

The sun baked his skin, splinters on his ratty flannel shirt, but somehow the action, the focus, had settled him.

They were safe. *She* was safe.

"We have a splitter."

He glanced over and spotted Jack emerging from the garage. He wore his greasy overalls, working on one of the UTVs that had died this week.

That wasn't all that had died. Steinbeck had returned to a different Jack. A Jack he thought had been beaten, now skulking back.

He'd asked Doyle about it as they sat on the porch last night at the Norbert. Emberly had sat tucked against him on the porch swing, a blanket over her, healing.

"Dunno," Doyle had said. "He came home from Harper's house a few days ago, slammed his door, and emerged later as The Beast."

Interesting.

But Stein understood the frustration of loving a stubborn woman. Emberly was an impossible patient, refusing to stay in bed since they'd arrived from New York City. Two days they'd been here, after four days in the hospital, and yesterday he'd found her in the kitchen of the King's Inn, albeit on a high-top stool, watching his mother roll out pie dough.

And last night, she'd walked out to the dock, sitting on the end, soaking in the sunset. Such a normal, benign thing, but the simplicity of it had trumpeted into his heart.

Oh, he loved her. He'd joined her, folded her hand into his, watching the sunset as his frustration died a little.

So maybe she was mending. Earlier today, she'd insisted on going to church with the family. He'd sat in the pew, listening to the sermon on Isaiah 30, on the rebellion of Israel.

And for some reason, the words about faithfulness had sunk in, embedded in his soul. *"Although the Lord gives you the bread of adversity and the water of affliction, your teachers will be hidden no more; with your own eyes you will see them. Whether you turn to the right or to the left, your ears will hear a voice behind you, saying, 'This is the way; walk in it.'"*

He'd glanced at Emberly, and she'd met his eyes and smiled at him, and never had he felt more sure about anything.

Yes, he was still on mission.

"I like the sweat," Steinbeck said now to Jack.

"Suit yourself." Jack picked up a few of the fallen logs and set them on the woodpile.

Steinbeck did the same. "You all right?"

Jack glanced at him. "Why?"

"Bad Jack is back."

"I was never Bad Jack."

Steinbeck raised an eyebrow.

Jack shook his head, picked up a couple more logs. "If you're looking for something to do, the front garden needs weeding."

"I think *you* need weeding. C'mon, bro—did something happen between you and Harper?"

Jack only paused for a second before lifting a shoulder and throwing the last of the logs on the pile. "We timed out."

Steinbeck just stared at him. Jack slapped off his hands. "She's moving to Nashville. Pursuing a new job."

"She is not."

He held up his hand. "Scout's honor."

"No. Harper has loved you for . . . *sheesh,* since she was in pigtails."

"I don't want to hear it." Jack turned away. "I need to shower. Mom wants us to have a family dinner tonight. She's making a roast."

Stein caught up to him. "So, what—you're not going to stand in her way?"

"No. Why would I do that?"

"Why would you—*are you kidding me*? Because you love her and you thought you had a future together!"

Jack stopped. "I would go with her, but she didn't ask me to."

"Did you ask her to stay?"

A muscle pulled in Jack's jaw.

"Wow."

"Listen, I was going to propose, okay? A couple weeks ago and then . . . I don't know why I didn't, and now it's too late."

"It's not too late." Steinbeck shook his head. "Too late is when the woman you love is lying on a concrete floor and you're breathing life into her, praying desperately that God will give you a second chance. *That* is too late. Or almost." He let out a shaky breath, put a hand on his chest, shook the moment away.

Jack met his gaze. "That's what happened?"

"That's what happened. And I realized that nothing—not my pride, not my frustration, not even her sometimes reckless behavior—was going to keep me from . . ." He sighed. "Well, from being her teammate."

"Teammate?"

"Just . . . yes. Teammate plus, maybe."

"Some people might call that marriage."

Stein shrugged. "We'll get there."

Jack smiled then, the first cloud break in the darkness. "No 'plus' without the ring, pal. But good for you." Then he sighed, the smile dissipating.

"Bro. I've never seen any two people more meant for each other than you and Harper. And you know it. So . . . what's holding you back?"

Jack considered him. "Dad said something the day Boo got married that's been rooting around my head for the past eight months. That we were created to experience the overwhelming love of heaven. And if we just would get out of the way, stop trying to lead with our own wisdom, and let God be in charge, then that's all we'd need. We'd wake up every day on mission—the one that says we trust God."

"Dad said that?"

"Something like that. But the most important part here is that we have to get out of the way, Stein. You think you know what you want . . . but God knows you better. Just . . . listen to his voice." Jack drew in a breath. "I'm thinking of selling Flo."

"Flo?"

"The bus."

Huh. "Really?"

"I took the bar exam. And maybe I didn't pass it—I don't know yet—but I do know that I don't want to travel without Harper. Maybe I'll head back to Florida . . ."

"Or maybe you stay here. The King's Inn is in good shape. Maybe better than when Doyle was groundskeeper. The table is amazing."

Jack just stared at it.

Stein couldn't help but put a hand on his shoulder. "Get out of your own way and let God save you here, bro."

"Is that what you're doing with Emberly?"

Oh. "Yes."

"You think she's the right girl to spend your life with?"

Steinbeck frowned. "If you're referring to Austen's words—"

"About being dangerous, and trouble?"

Right. "I think God is up to something with Emberly."

Jack considered him for a moment, then nodded. "Just don't get hurt."

"I think we're beyond that. It's part of the job description, isn't it?"

"What job description?"

"To love well."

A beat. And then Jack smiled. "Glad you're back. And sticking around."

"I didn't say that."

Jack frowned.

"But for now . . . yes. Maybe."

Still, the frown. "Are you guys in any danger?"

Oh. "No. I mean, yes, Luis and maybe his partner, a woman named Teresa, are still on the lam, but there are people on it. No, we're safe here. I promise, I didn't bring trouble back to the King's Inn."

"Good. Because I just got the place in shape. Mom scheduled a couple days of cleaning this week while the inn is empty. I'll shoot you a list."

"Fabulous." But Stein smiled as they turned and headed into the house.

The kitchen smelled of garlic and thyme, the roasting meat in the oven. He guessed his mom was baking potatoes over at the carriage house or in the King's Inn kitchen.

He went through to the kitchen in search of a glass of water.

And that's when the conversation from the porch drifted in to him. He peeked out the window to where Emberly and Austen sat on the porch swing. Nimue was out by the lake, walking the shoreline.

"I've only ever been a Swan."

"That's not true." Austen had her legs crossed, her back to Stein. "You're a sister. And a daughter. And Emberly, the one Jesus loves."

He moved away from the window, not wanting to eavesdrop, totally wanting to eavesdrop.

"At the core of it, whether you want to admit it or not, in God we live and move and have our being. Every step we take is under His watchful presence. And the more aware you are of that, the more free, the more alive you will feel."

Silence. Then Emberly's voice. "Today, with Stein, in church, it seemed that . . . I don't know. Maybe this was all . . . part of the plan. Meeting Steinbeck three years ago, and then again, and . . . But you don't really know me, Austen. You have no idea what—"

"It doesn't matter. Jesus hung on the cross, and next to Him the thief believed in Jesus. He asked Jesus to remember him when

He came into His kingdom. He asked for mercy. And you know what Jesus said?"

He glanced at her. Emberly frowned.

"'Truly, I say to you, today you will be with me in paradise.' See, Em, it's not about what you are, but who Jesus is. The Redeemer. The payer of our debt, fulfilling our death sentence, and the victor over the battle between good and evil. And you . . . you belong with the redeemed. Anyone who belongs to Christ is a new person. The old life is gone, a new has begun. Maybe you're no longer a Black Swan. But just . . . a swan."

Steinbeck closed his eyes.

Silence, just his heartbeat.

And then, "Yes," Emberly said quietly.

"Yes?"

"I believe you."

"Good. Want to tell the Lord that?"

Stein opened his eyes, smiled. Austen, his twin. A warrior of the heart.

He walked away as Emberly's voice drifted up, wound around him . . .

"Lord, I'm sorry I ran from You for so long . . ."

He headed upstairs.

Maybe the mission was over.

Maybe not.

All he had to do was listen.

• —————————— •

"You weren't really thinking you'd leave without saying good-bye?"

The voice at the door made Harper look up from where, yes, her suitcase lay on the sofa, clothes piled on the chair, the coffee table. Open boxes sat on the floor for long-term storage.

Her mother had already moved out most of the upstairs office as well as her own clothing, which she'd packed up and taken with her yesterday to Boston.

"Hey, Boo," said Harper.

Her friend came in, her dark hair short, wearing an oversized Duck Lake Storm sweatshirt, leggings, and Converse tennis shoes.

"I didn't know you and Oaken were back."

"He did the Utah State Fair last weekend. We're headed to Oklahoma's state fair on Sunday."

"Busy."

Boo came over, picked up a tie-dyed T-shirt. "I remember this one. VBS, seventh grade. It can't possibly still fit."

"Believe it or not, yes, which is a really sad state of affairs. I sleep in it."

Boo handed it over, put her hands on her hips, surveying the place. "So, your mom is really selling the place."

"Yeah. She's contacted a Realtor. They're going to stage the house and get it on the market. She gave me until the end of the month, but . . . I need to go."

Boo moved the stack of T-shirts and sat on the overstuffed chair. "No, you don't."

"The rest of those are for Goodwill." She pointed to the box on the floor.

"Really? This one is from when we went to the Ben King concert. What were we—fifteen?" She held up the concert tee that featured the singer emblazoned on the front.

"It's in the past. I don't need it."

Boo tossed it at her suitcase. "What you don't need is to be packing at all."

"Boo—"

"My brother Jack is not in a good way, Harper. He's . . . dark and crabby again and . . . well, I blame you."

Harper turned, her eyes wide. "What?"

"You broke the poor man's heart."

Boo wasn't kidding by the solemn look on her face.

"Boo. I don't want to leave. Are you kidding?" She sank down onto the sofa. "I've cried for a week straight." Her voice wobbled. "I've loved your brother since I was . . . I don't know—"

"Twelve years old."

"Yes. At least. But . . ." She shook her head. "It appears we want different things."

"Like what—a family, a home?"

"That's what I want. He wants . . . I don't know what he wants. He took the bar, Boo. Without telling me."

Boo nodded. "Maybe he was afraid he'd fail."

"Oh, I've seen him fail before. It doesn't scare me."

"It might scare him."

"You know what scares him?" She stood up, grabbed the stack of T-shirts, and dropped them into the box. "Proposing."

"What?"

She rounded on her. "Not that I would know, because he hasn't. And—"

"You're mad because he didn't *propose*?" Boo stared at her.

"When you put it like that . . . no. But . . . fine, yes. Sort of. I don't know. I guess . . ." She frowned. "Why did you come over here? To make me feel like a total jerk?"

"Is it working?"

"A little."

"Good. We're having a family dinner. Steinbeck is back, along with his"—and she finger quoted the word—"'girlfriend.' Although I think they actually *are* together. He's all weirdly doting on her and . . . Anyway, since we're all in town at the same time, Mom wants us to have family dinner."

"Great. Have a lovely time." And she didn't mean for the words to emerge so sharp, even brittle.

"You're part of the family, Harper."

"No, Boo. I'm not."

Boo stood up. "Yes. Actually, you are. You've always been. And for the love, will you just talk to him? Sheesh—you're the one who's supposed to be good with words."

Harper apparently wasn't done crying. She wiped her cheeks. "For the record, I wasn't going to take this job. But he told me to."

Boo arched an eyebrow. "He did not."

"Stood right there, and when I asked him why I shouldn't take it . . . he had nothing. Said it was an opportunity of a lifetime. So . . ." She shrugged, quick and sharp.

"Okay. That was . . . weird. But love is patient and maybe you should give him another chance."

"For him to destroy me in front of your entire family? He laughed at me, Boo. *Laughed*. Again."

Boo stepped up to her, took her shoulders. "He's not laughing now. I promise you, my brother looks like he's lost his best friend. And frankly, so do you." She pulled Harper close.

"I still have you. That counts."

"That does count." Boo held her away. "I remember telling you right before my wedding that I'd learned that God had good things for those who trust in His love for them. God loves you, Bee. I know you know this. But sometimes we're not the easiest people to love. And if he doesn't give up on us, maybe we shouldn't give up on others."

Harper sighed.

"If you come to dinner, I'll tell you a secret." Boo smiled. Put her hands on her tummy.

Harper's breath caught. "Really?"

"Mm-hmm. But only my mom knows. Oaken and I are announcing it at dinner. You don't want to miss that."

Harper sighed. "No, no, I don't."

"Then how about you change out of this—what *are* you wearing?"

"What? You don't remember this shirt?"

Boo paused. "That's my shirt. My Scooby-Doo shirt."

"And you're not getting it back."

Boo looped her arm through Harper's. "C'mon. I promise, it'll be okay."

"Doubtful." But she slid on her sandals and followed Boo up the trail, across the yard to the King's Inn, and then past it, over the lawn to where the family had congregated. The chrysanthemums bloomed along the front of the porch, and it was hard to miss Jack throwing a football to Steinbeck and Doyle in the yard. Conrad and Oaken drove up in the UTV with firewood, then got out and added it to a stack of logs. Clearly a bonfire was on the agenda.

She'd probably be back at her house by then, packing her car.

"Bee!" This from Austen, who came down the stairs of the porch, her auburn hair tied back. She hugged Harper. "Jack told me this terrible story about you leaving for Nashville."

She glanced over at him. He appeared as if he was trying very hard not to look at her. *Shoot,* he looked good in a pair of jeans and a T-shirt that stretched over his shoulders, his torso.

Don't look.

She climbed the porch stairs and went into the kitchen, where Tia was mashing potatoes. "Hey. I didn't know you and Doyle were back." She didn't know Tia well—mostly through Tia's sister, Penny. Dark hair, pretty, tan, smart, and in Penny's opinion, a little bossy, but then again, she was the older sister.

Penny came in carrying an oversized jar of pickles. Set it on the counter. "Okay, this was the last jar in the cellar."

"That's the one," said Mama Em, and she glanced over at Harper. "Thank you for coming."

Oh. Harper nodded. "How can I help?"

"Get the guys to set the table."

She sighed, then went outside and stood on the steps and called them in.

Stein ran over and up the stairs. "I'll check on Emberly." He moved past her.

Conrad came in and headed to the kitchen, came out with placemats and a stack of dishes. Doyle went in, maybe for glasses.

And then there was Jack. He came up the steps, stopped.

He glanced at her. Gave her a tight smile. "You haven't left yet."

"Tonight." *Or tomorrow. Or right now.*

He nodded. *Oh,* he did look rough, but then again, she was wearing cutoff shorts and a Scooby-Doo shirt, so . . .

She didn't want to leave it like this. Didn't want to leave at all, but . . .

"I—"

"Leave it, Harper." He held up a hand. "We'll get through this dinner and maybe someday figure out a way to . . ." He shook his head. "Whatever."

He started to walk away, toward the door.

Conrad stood in front of him.

"Move."

Penny came out behind him, holding a tray of pickles. Looked at Jack, then at Harper. "For Pete's sake, will you two have a conversation?"

"We did," Jack said. He took the pickles from Penny. "It's done."

Boo had come up, holding Oaken's hand. "It's not done. Harper spent the week crying her eyes out."

"Hey. That was private information."

"Jack is about as friendly as a mule," said Doyle, sliding out from behind Penny.

Jack shook his head.

"Just . . . propose to the woman already." This from Boo.

Harper might have worn the same look as Jack. "Boo!"

"Well. That's the problem, right?"

Jack frowned. Cocked his head.

Austen had come out of the kitchen carrying the bowl of potatoes, Tia behind her. She stopped at the roadblock by the door. "What did I miss?"

"Jack is going to propose to Harper," said Conrad.

"I am not!"

And Harper had never felt more slapped. She recoiled, caught her breath. "Sorry, Boo." She turned, headed down the stairs.

And nearly plowed over Declan Stone. He stood in her way, and she stared at him. *Right.* Austen was dating the billionaire.

He reached out and steadied her. "You okay?"

"No, she's not okay," said Tia. "Apparently, Jack won't propose."

Jack rounded on Tia. "What?"

She held up her hands. "I'm just catching him up. It's good for everyone to have all the information so they don't walk into something unprepared."

Declan gave her a look.

She smiled.

"Okay, for the record, I'm very busy, and clearly you and Doyle figured it out." Declan looked at Austen. "Help me out here."

"Oh no. I agree. It's important to communicate, especially when you have feelings for someone." She smiled. "Otherwise, they could, I don't know, think they're just the hired help."

"I'm wondering if I got invited to the right party."

"Hey, Dec." Steinbeck stood at the door, Emberly leaning on his arm.

"What happened?" Harper said, her gaze on Emberly. "Are you okay?"

"Long story," Emberly answered.

"It might involve saving the life of the president's daughter," Stein said, and they were clearly together, because the way he looked at the petite redhead . . .

Jack had looked at Harper that way, once upon a short time ago.

And it hit her then. Why . . . How did they get here?

Maybe it hit Jack too, because his gaze was on hers, hard. She couldn't move.

Oh, Jack. This wasn't how it was supposed to end.

Another woman came out behind them. Olive skin, dark hair, pretty. She carried a casserole and set it in the middle of the table. "This is quite the table."

"I made it," Stein said.

Jack broke her gaze and looked at him. "I made it."

Stein held up his hand. "Okay, I helped."

"I made it because Mom wanted our entire family to sit around it." Jack turned to Harper. "All of us."

She just stared at him.

He took a step toward her. "Is there anything . . ." He drew in a breath. Closed his eyes.

"C'mon, Jack," Stein said softly.

Silence, and her heart thudded.

Jack opened his eyes. "Is there anything I can say to make you stay, Bee?"

Austen looked at her, then Jack, back at Harper.

Boo, behind him, was nodding.

The words simply formed, fell out. "You . . . could ask me to marry you."

Oh no, had she really said that? Silence fell, thick around her.

Oh, she was an idiot. She turned.

"Are you kidding me?"

She rounded on him, her eyes wide. "No. I'm not kidding you." Her mouth opened, then closed, her eyes filling. "I . . ." She wiped her cheeks. *Oh great, in front of everyone too.* "I know it sounds stupid, but . . . I thought—"

He took a step toward her, so much in his eyes she couldn't read—anger? worry? pain? "It's *not* stupid. And when I asked if you were kidding me, I meant . . . *of course.* I was going to propose two weeks ago and then, I'm not sure what happened."

"Your stupid joke happened," Conrad said.

Jack ignored him.

Harper glanced at Conrad. "What stupid joke?"

"I was going to ask you that night on the bus and then, I don't know. It wasn't perfect, and I panicked, and the next thing I know, Conrad is telling me that you got a job in Nashville—"

"I thought you saw the letter—and that's why you didn't propose."

"What letter?"

"The letter that—never mind." She glanced at Penny, back at him. "Why did you take the bar without telling me?"

"You took the bar?" Doyle said.

Jack held up his hand. "I took it so that . . . if you wanted to stay here, I could . . . I could give you that."

"But . . . what about . . . Flo? I thought . . ."

He stepped down one stair. "Flo is a great adventure. But I thought maybe . . . maybe someday you'd want to come back here. And I don't know . . . Except, you're moving, so . . ."

"My *mom* is moving. And I wasn't going to take the job—but then you came in and told me to take it—"

He took another step. "No, I didn't."

"You did. You said it was a great opportunity."

"It *is* a great opportunity!" He stepped down another step. "You should take it."

"Oh no," Conrad said. "Here we go again."

"But I don't want it—I mean, I do, but . . ."

Jack looked slapped as he drew in a breath.

"Stop." Austen came down the steps. Faced Harper. "Bee. Do you love my brother?"

She cocked her head at Austen. "Seriously?"

"Right. Jack." She turned to her brother. "Do you really want Harper to leave?"

Jack clenched his jaw, shook his head.

"Then will you two idiots please make up so we can all live happily ever after?"

"Austen, Harper is not an idiot," Jack said. Then he looked at Harper and smiled. "I am."

"About time," said Stein.

Austen patted him on the cheek and headed back up the stairs.

Which just left Harper and Jack, standing there, in the grass, the family on the porch.

And Jack bending to one knee.

Wait—"I was kidding."

"No. You weren't. And I'm not either." He took her hand. "Harper. You are . . . my best friend. And the love of my life. And the woman I can't live without. And . . . just, please, for the love, will you marry me?"

She caught her breath. Stared down at this man, their future in his impossibly blue eyes. And nodded.

Jack smiled. Then he stood up, caught her to himself. "Wow, I was miserable without you."

"Yeah, you were," she said, holding on, her face in his neck.

He laughed, then he set her down, took her face in his hands. And in front of his entire family, he kissed her.

Sweetly. Perfectly.

But when he lifted his head, a spark shone in his eye. "That's for now." And he winked.

When she looked up, the family was setting the table, but Mama Em stood holding Grover's hand, grinning.

"Now it's a family dinner," she said.

They laid the table, pulled out chairs, and sat down to a pot roast, mashed potatoes, rolls, green beans, salad, and prayer.

Jack held her hand under the table and squeezed.

They began to pass the food, Doyle and Tia asking Declan about an exhibit, and Oaken and Boo talking about his concert tour, and Steinbeck asking Conrad about training camp, and then the woman beside Emberly said, "Who's Flo?"

A few smiles all around, and Stein passed her the beans. "Flo is—"

And that's when the King's Inn blew up.

THIRTEEN

FIVE MINUTES AGO, EMBERLY HAD BEEN SUNK into the delicious Kingston family chaos, the back porch magical with the laughter, the proposal, the . . . family.

The long oak table had stretched across the weathered boards, piled high with Mama Em's pot roast—juicy, thyme-laced, the meat falling apart under her fork, gravy pooling rich and dark on her plate. Mashed potatoes had steamed in a chipped blue bowl, their buttery warmth slicing through the crisp September air, while cinnamon rolls oozed sticky sweetness, the scent curling up to tangle with the bite of frost and the rustle of dry leaves skittering across the cool lawn.

Fall had draped the Minnesota dusk in fiery golds and deep reds, the sky a bruised canvas stretching over the compound, chrysanthemums along the steps glowing amber in the porch light's flicker.

Jack had lobbed a roll at Doyle, who had ducked, his laugh barking over the clatter of plates and forks scraping their plates. Steinbeck had sat beside her, his broad shoulder brushing hers, his hand—warm, rough, a lifeline she hadn't known she'd needed— sneaking under the table to squeeze hers. Her ribs had throbbed beneath the tight wrap, but his touch had dulled the ache, made it something she could carry.

Across from Emberly, Nimue had perched, picking at green beans, her brown hair catching the light, freckled nose wrinkling as Conrad razzed Oaken about his latest sold-out show at the Utah State Fair, the country star's tenor laugh rumbling.

Emberly had wanted this, more than she could voice, and maybe had communicated that in a glance at Steinbeck.

He'd smiled back at her, those blue eyes landing, stirring, igniting.

Oh, she loved him, and that thought had spread through her in a warm, delicious heat.

Emberly had speared a chunk of roast, the gravy thick and savory on her tongue, and smirked as Boo teased Oaken about recent swooning fan mail.

It had been loud, messy—family, real and raw, perfect.

Maybe this was it. The end, the beginning. No more slipping through shadows, living on edges and longing for perfect moments. Here, with Steinbeck's blue eyes crinkling at her, she didn't itch to bolt. She wanted this—him, this loud, sprawling tribe, whatever it looked like. A life with Steinbeck, his hand in hers, his gruff voice growling "I've got you" when the world caved in. She loved him—God help her, she did. His steady heart, his unshakable faith in her, in them, the way he'd chased her into the darkness and dragged her back.

Then, the thunderous *boom* had shredded the night.

The blast punched the air, rattling the porch, shattering the inn's kitchen windows a hundred yards off. Flames erupted, a jagged orange beast clawing the dusk, glass spraying across the grass, glinting in the fading light.

Mama Em screamed, and the entire family hit their feet.

"Em—call 911!" Grover shouted, even as Jack and Conrad sprinted off the porch, Doyle behind.

Emberly jolted, ribs screaming, her fork clattering to the plate, gravy splattering the table like blood. Steinbeck's grip tightened, pinning her hand to the wood. "Stay here!"

Then, of course, he vaulted the railing, leaves crunching under him as he sprinted toward the blaze.

"Hoses—extinguishers—move!" The shout came from one of the guys as Doyle snagged a red canister from the UTV.

Austen had followed them off the porch, along with Declan. Boo charged into the house after her mother, Tia standing there, frozen just before she glanced at Penny.

Then Tia, too, ran off the porch, charging through the haze.

Conrad had hauled out a hose and Oak held another, water jetting in wild arcs, the spray catching the firelight.

"The sprinklers are on!" Grover, a bold outline against the flames, directed Conrad to the side door. "Side door—stop it spreading!"

Mama Em ran out. "Fire Department on the way!" Her voice cracked, fierce and raw, over the chaos.

Emberly had risen, but Nimue grabbed her wrist. "Stay here. You don't need to get more hurt. They got this already." Harper and Austen and Declan had gone inside, maybe to haul out furniture or art or to close doors to keep the fire from spreading.

"Stay here."

Yeah, she couldn't just stand here.

She couldn't run—not with her ribs—but she headed toward the stairs. "C'mon, Nim—we have to help!" Pain stabbed at her, the cold mist slicking her skin, soaking her jeans, and chilling her to the bone.

Closer, smoke clogged the air, the inn's kitchen a furnace, flames licking the frame, black plumes billowing into the sky, thick and choking. The sprinkler inside sprayed, water hissing against the inferno, steam mixing with the acrid stink of burning wood, melted wiring, and scorched paint.

Grover gripped Mama Em's arm. Her face was etched with terror, tears cutting tracks through the soot on her cheeks as she watched her home burn. And all around them, the family fought—Steinbeck's silhouette swinging an extinguisher, foam dousing the black smoke, Jack wrestling another hose, water slashing the siding in desperate arcs. Conrad and Oaken sprayed the porch, and Declan, Austen, Tia, and Harper carried out artwork, furniture.

Nimue pushed porch furniture away from the flames, her form silhouetted against the blaze.

Emberly stared at the chaos, her gut twisting, sharp and hot, a thief's instinct kicking in . . .

This wasn't right. The inn didn't just blow up—not tonight, not with everyone here, laughing and whole. Her gaze scanned the chaos, the flames too fierce, the timing too perfect.

Wait—a shadow flickered near the Norbert's porch. Lean, moving through the darkness, and behind it, another figure—slighter, slinking low.

A glint of something metallic sparked in the firelight. A gun's barrel?

Her breath hitched. This wasn't random. This was a hit—a distraction, loud and brutal, to pull the family away.

She found Nimue, still moving furniture off the apron porch onto the lawn, and biting against the pain, she ran to her. "Nim, this is a hit."

Nimue rounded on her. "What?"

"We need to get inside." Emberly yanked Nimue toward the Norbert's back door, her boots slipping on the wet boards. The screen slammed shut, the kitchen dark, air heavy with the fading warmth of potatoes and the creeping tang of smoke seeping through the cracks. She shoved Nimue toward the counter, her own breaths ragged, pain lancing her side. "Stay low. Something's wrong."

Nimue stared at her. "What—no, we need to help—"

"The fire is a decoy!" Emberly grabbed a butcher knife from the block, her ribs throbbing as she pressed against the wall. "Too big, too fast. Look outside—someone's out there."

Nimue's eyes widened. "Who? Bratva?"

"I don't know yet." This felt personal, a blade aimed at her new life. "You've been digging—anyone you've tagged lately?"

Nimue swallowed, eyes darting. "Luis. His Bratva threads. I've been close, tracking his moves. But I covered my tracks—"

"Not enough." Emberly peeked through the window, the inn a tragedy—flames, smoke, the family fighting for their home.

From the edge of the porch, that lean shadow moved again, closer now, weaving through the haze. A woman's frame—*Teresa?*—slunk behind, her walk too smooth, too predatory, the gun glinting again in the firelight. Then the taller figure turned, the glow catching a familiar jaw, stubble sharp against the flickering orange—*Luis.*

Her stomach dropped. She knew it. "It's him. Luis. And Teresa."

Nimue's breath hitched, her voice a whisper. "Here? Now? Why—"

"You're the threat. Tracking him. He wants you gone." Emberly gripped the knife tighter, ribs a white-hot ache. "And me? Leverage—or payback. Whatever." She glanced at her. "Hide. Behind the island. Now."

Nimue scrambled back, sneakers squeaking. "Em, you're hurt. You can't fight them—"

"I can." Emberly's voice cut sharp, fierce. "I'm done running. God's got me here—Steinbeck's got me. I love him, Nim. I'm not losing this—not you, not any of it."

Not again.

Footsteps thudded outside. Heavy. Deliberate. Not family.

She moved behind the island.

The back door rattled, then exploded inward, wood splintering, hinges shrieking. Luis stormed in, dark eyes wild. Armed. Teresa came in behind him, pointed her weapon at Emberly.

Stay down, Nim.

"Phoenix," Luis growled. What had happened to the terrified computer hacker from three years ago in Krakow? Maybe he'd never really existed. A persona, meant to deceive. "You should've ended up in Siberia."

And it hit her then.

He'd been behind all of it. Masterminded her heist of Declan's program, including planting Captain Teresa—if that was her real name—on the boat to copy the program. And then the setup of creating the virus to secure it for the Bratva.

And now, what? Covering his tracks as he disappeared, only to sell the program and its defense to the highest bidder?

Emberly didn't blink. "I should have left you in Poland." She flicked her gaze to Teresa, "What's this, Luis? Kill my sister, grab me, vanish with your girlfriend?"

Teresa's smirk widened, silk over steel.

"Where's Nimue?"

"Gone." Emberly edged left, drawing him away from Nim. *Run, Nim.* She didn't look at her, but *please, Nim,* please read her mind.

He laughed, cold and jagged. "Liar."

He lunged at her. Emberly dodged, slashing his forearm—blood sprayed, hot—but her ribs burned, slowing her. He backhanded her jaw and she crashed into the counter. Her knife skittered across the floor.

"Em!" Nimue cried.

"Stay down!" Emberly shouted, scrambling up.

Not fast enough. Luis grabbed her hair, yanking, and jammed his gun into her spine. She elbowed his gut, but he dragged her toward the door.

Nimue bolted—*yes!*

Teresa slammed into her, and Nimue hit the wall. Teresa snagged her, wrenching her up. "Gotcha."

"No!" Emberly thrashed, kicking Luis's shin, but her searing ribs shut her down.

Luis's arm choked her, the gun barrel digging against her ribs. Outside, the fire roared, smoke thick, family shouts faint. "Move."

Teresa hauled Nimue out behind her, gun at her temple, then headed off the porch, leaves crunching as the women's shoes hit the grass.

Think!

It wasn't going to happen like this. Emberly had formed a plan even before Luis pushed her down the stairs. Hitting the bottom, Emberly went slack, rolled, screamed, and came up tackling Teresa.

"Run!"

Teresa stumbled, and Emberly slapped the gun away from Nimue—

A shot.

She rounded and slammed her hand into Teresa's nose. The woman shouted, blood gushed, and Emberly lunged for the weapon.

Luis tackled her, slamming her into the ground. Her breath whoofed out, her body turning to fire—

Nimue screamed and Emberly spotted Teresa grabbing her sister's hair, pushing her to the ground. Nimue struggled, kicking, fighting.

Attagirl.

Luis had found his feet, pointed the gun at her. "So much trouble." He shook his head.

She couldn't breathe, couldn't move—

God, please—

She put her arms over her head, closed her eyes.

Shots shattered the air.

How had this happened?

Steinbeck stood in the inn's kitchen doorway, extinguisher gripped tight, staring at the flames clawing up the walls.

The September night had been crisp, perfect—family laughing on the porch, the lake glinting under the stars, the scent of Mama Em's pot roast still lingering.

Now, smoke choked the air, thick with the acrid bite of burning timber and melted wiring, the sprinklers' hiss a weak sputter against the inferno.

Faulty wiring? A gas leak? The questions gnawed at him, but he shoved them down.

He swung the handle, foam blasting out, cutting through the black haze. The fire snarled, spitting embers that stung his face like shards. His tennis shoes slipped on wet grass, leaves crunching, the lawn slick with mist, the lake's glassy surface reflecting the orange blaze. Sweat soaked his shirt, arms burning as foam billowed into the heat. Jack wrestled a hose beside him, water jetting wild, slashing the siding.

"Keep it steady, Stein!" Jack shouted, voice hoarse.

Doyle charged in with another hose. "Left side's spreading—hit it!"

Conrad had hauled in a third, spray shimmering.

Steinbeck pushed forward, foam arcing, the blaze hissing back an inch. "We've got this!"

A flicker caught his eye—movement. Not flame. He squinted past the cottonwoods toward the Norbert's porch, shadows shifting, dim against the light. He glanced again, longer, the spray faltering.

A scream ripped through the chaos—high, desperate, and . . . *hers.*

"Emberly?" Steinbeck's head jerked, the canister slipping, thudding to the grass. He turned—and everything inside him went hot.

Through the smoke, he spotted—*no, what? Luis?*—standing over a figure on the ground.

And just like that—yeah, he got it. Luis had set the fire, a distraction to pull them away.

Steinbeck had brought trouble home.

He took off, even as Luis loomed over Emberly.

"Luis!"

The man jerked, glanced toward the house.

A gunshot cracked. Searing heat grazed Steinbeck's arm. He stumbled, crashing to one knee, wet earth soaking his jeans, leaves sticking, but he rolled, found his feet, and scrambled behind the family UTV.

A glance out showed Luis dragging Emberly toward the dock. And with him, a woman had hold of Nimue, stumbling, fighting. *Teresa.*

How did—why—

It didn't matter.

He glanced back at the burning house, then at Emberly. She kicked at her captor, but she seemed to be weakening.

Her ribs had to be on fire.

Beside her, Teresa gripped Nimue, a gun jammed to her neck.

And that's when he spotted the boat—a small skiff—listing at the end of the dock, hull rocking against the pilings.

They'd sneaked in via the lake, silent, unseen by the family as they ate on the porch, bypassing detection from the house, and somehow ignited the kitchen. Probably the same way they'd ignited Nimue's kitchen—Molotov cocktail, slow-burning, giving them long enough to plant and escape.

If they got the girls to the boat, they'd put out across the lake and . . .

Vanish.

Yeah, no. He wasn't losing Emberly. Not again.

Not ever.

He took off after them, nothing for a weapon but his bare hands, but this—this was . . . what he'd been made for.

"Luis, let her go!" he roared, hitting the dock, planks thudding under his shoes.

Luis spun, dragging Emberly, her knees buckling. "Back off or she's done!" His gun swung up.

Teresa shoved Nimue forward. "Move or I shoot!"

Emberly twisted, voice hoarse. "Steinbeck—get Nim!" She slammed her elbow into Luis's gut, and he stumbled, just enough—

Steinbeck launched himself at him, slamming him off the dock's edge. They crashed into the lake, the cold water swallowing them. The shock tried to punch out Steinbeck's breath, but he held on, his head clearing, his legs around Luis.

And sank.

He could stay here all day. Luis thrashed, fist cracking Steinbeck's jaw, blood bursting, metallic on his tongue. But still, he held. Lungs locked, breath held, muscles coiling.

Heat sliced his leg—he jerked. Another stab to his arm, enough to loosen his hold.

Luis jerked free and Stein kicked away, surfacing.

He cleared the water from his eyes in time to see Luis flash a knife.

Since when did Luis have skills? Except, maybe he always had. Who knew how far the man had played them?

Luis lunged at him, and Steinbeck jerked back, the blade barely missing his throat. But the movement jerked him off balance. The man landed on him, Steinbeck grabbing his wrist, fighting the knife hand.

Down they went, Steinbeck without a fresh breath, and this time Luis wrangled himself atop Stein, kicked his knee into Stein's gut.

Air whooshed out. He fought, but his lungs burned, aching, the world spotty—

He couldn't be the guy who drowned in his parents' backyard. He fought to find the bottom, to dislodge Luis, Stein's grip still on Luis's wrist—

But blackness swept over him.

Hands broke in from the surface—and grabbed Luis off him.

Another set of hands grabbed Stein's shirt. Steinbeck surged up, breaking the water, gasping, the cold air knifing his lungs. Conrad stood in front of him, waist-deep in the lake, breathing hard. "You're okay—you're okay!"

Jack's arms locked around Luis while Declan wrenched his knife hand back. Jack and Declan wrestled Luis to the shallows, pinning him against the muddy shore. Luis thrashed, swearing in Russian. Fighting.

Declan hit him, and he went still. "That's enough," Declan said. He glanced at Jack. "Got him?"

Jack nodded, and Declan turned, searching the darkness. *Emberly.*

Steinbeck staggered up, coughing, also searching.

A boat motor fired up. *No—*

Teresa hit the engine, and the skiff peeled away across the lake. "Stein!"

He found her, crawling across the dock, gasping, holding her ribs. Nimue stumbled behind her, trying to help her.

Steinbeck sloshed over to the dock, lifted himself onto it, walked over, and picked her up.

Just like that, into his arms. "You okay?"

She trembled against his wet frame, her hands gripping his soaked shirt, nails digging in, anchoring him, her green eyes locking on his, fierce. "You came for me."

He cupped her face, thumbs brushing blood from her cheeks,

her skin cold and damp but alive, lake water dripping from his fingers. "Get used to it," he said, voice low.

Sirens whined in the air, distant.

Her beautiful eyes filled. "Someday you'll get tired of rescuing me."

"Nope." Then he leaned down and kissed her. Gently, but his arms tightening around her. *Never.*

The sound of sirens swelled, a high-pitched wail rolling over the grounds, red and blue lights pulsing through the haze. Tires crunched gravel beyond the trees, headlights slicing the night. The inn stood, soggy and scorched but intact—smoke thinning, flames doused to smoldering embers, the air heavy with wet ash and smoke.

He spotted Doyle and Oaken dousing the house, the porch, Austen and Tia still pulling out furniture.

Behind him, Conrad sloshed out of the water, shirt clinging, hair plastered to his forehead, exhaustion carving lines in his face. Jack and Declan hauled Luis up, his hands secured with Jack's belt.

Conrad trudged up, wringing his shirt, water pooling at his feet, a tired grin breaking through. He turned just as Penny ran down to the shore. She launched herself at Conrad.

"I didn't even see you. Where—"

"Had to help out my brother." He glanced at Stein, winked.

"The house—" Stein started.

"We got it," Penny said. "The fire department is here, but the flames are out."

"I'm okay, Stein. You can put me down." Emberly said softly.

She might be, but he wasn't. *Still,* he let her go, his arm still around her.

A smile tugged her lips, and her hand tightened on his, warm against his chilled skin as they headed up to the house.

They stood with his dad and mom, holding hands, and Conrad and Penny, and Doyle and Tia. Jack and Declan dragged Luis to a cruiser that had pulled up. There'd probably need to be some explaining there.

But for now he stood watching the fire department trek into the kitchen, check for flames.

"It's going to take a hot minute to clean this up," his mother said.

"That's what family is for," Doyle said, and glanced at his mom.

"Stein," Emberly whispered, tugging on his hand, and he turned to her. Her fingers moved to palm his chest. "I love you."

He raised an eyebrow.

"And . . . just so you know, I'm not going anywhere. Not unless it's with you."

He leaned in, forehead resting on hers, breaths mingling, smoke and lake water fading under her scent—alive, fierce, *his*. "I love you—every dangerous, intriguing, crazy, annoying, beautiful part of you," he said. "And to be clear, you couldn't ditch me if you tried."

Then he kissed her—slow, deep, tasting salt, fight, her lips cold but softening. She melted into him, a soft sound of happiness in her throat, hands tightening, drawing him in, her warmth seeping through his soaked shirt, his heart thudding against hers.

He lifted his head and she stepped into his embrace, watching as Jack and Declan returned, stood with the family, Austen and Declan holding hands, Harper in Jack's arms.

"So," Boo said. "Is now a good time to mention we're expecting?"

Laughter erupted—Jack's bark, Doyle's wheeze, Conrad's low chuckle—shattering the night's weight. Their mother gave a delighted shout and embraced Boo. Followed by Austen and Tia and Penny.

And Jack grabbed Oaken's hand. "You dog—congrats!"

And right then, Stein saw it—the chaos, the love, the soggy, stubborn family, the yesterday, today, and tomorrow God had given him.

This was the crazy, beautiful, perfect rest of his life.

Bonus Epilogue

Thank you for reading *Steinbeck*. I hope you loved the story. Find out what happens next with a Bonus Epilogue, a special gift, available only to my newsletter subscribers.

This Bonus Epilogue will not be released on any retailer platform, so scan my QR code to get your free gift. You acknowledge you are becoming a subscriber to my newsletter. Unsubscribe at any time.

Continue the Epic Romantic
Adventure with the next series...

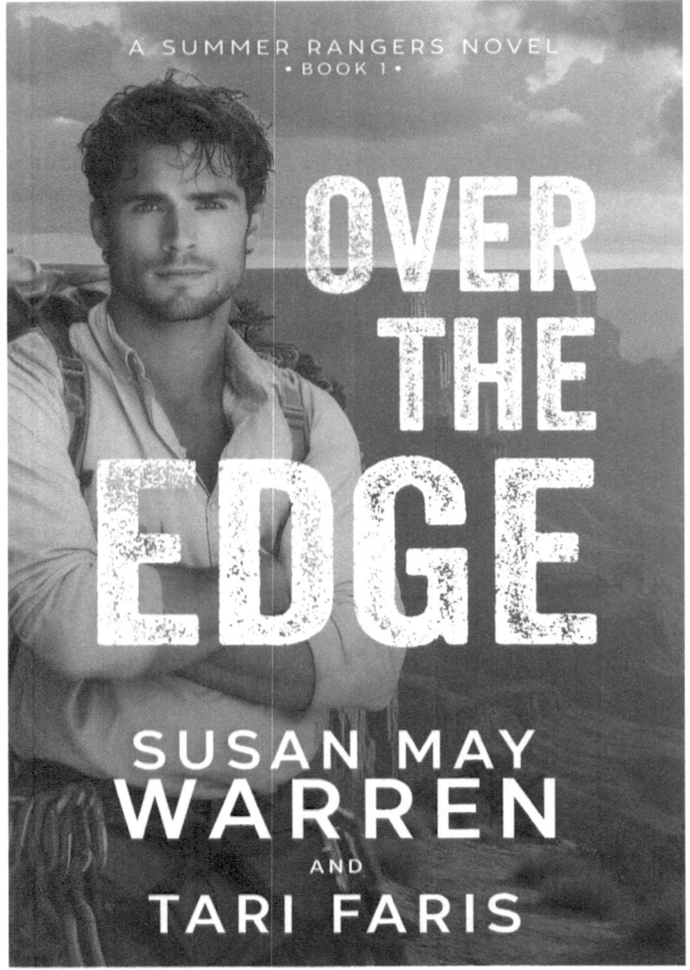

When a woman running from the mob
meets a ranger haunted by his past, the
Grand Canyon's dangers might be the
least of their troubles.

Tech-savvy hacker **Nimue Hart** has mastered the art of staying invisible, living off-grid in her Airstream and hiding from the Russian mob who want her silenced. But when a rescue mission forces her into the spotlight, her carefully constructed world begins to crumble.

Grand Canyon Backcountry Ranger **Liam Kingsley** buried his heart in the Swiss Alps a year ago after a tragic climbing accident. Now he keeps tourists safe and his emotions locked away—until a mysterious woman with secrets of her own makes him question everything he thought he knew about safety.

As their worlds collide, Nimue and Liam must navigate more than just the treacherous canyon trails. With mobsters closing in, a dangerous treasure unearthed, and lives hanging in the balance during a catastrophic flash flood, their growing trust in each other might be their only lifeline. But when Nimue's past catches up with them at the canyon's edge, Liam faces his worst nightmare all over again—this time with a woman he can't bear to lose.

Perfect for readers who love their romance with a shot of adrenaline, OVER THE EDGE delivers **heart-pounding action, breathtaking rescues, and the sizzling chemistry** between a protective ranger and a brilliant woman on the run.

Out in June, 2026!

ONE

NOT AGAIN. LIAM KINGSLEY PRESSED HIS chest against the scorching sandstone, peering over the northern rim of the Grand Canyon. June didn't even start until tomorrow, and here they were—minutes from the first statistic of the season.

Eight feet below, on a ledge barely wider than his Bronco's bench seat, a girl—maybe ten—sprawled on her back, one leg twisted beneath her. Terror bleached her face, but at least she was still breathing.

Thank heaven for small miracles.

Dark braids spilled across the sandstone, the colorful hair ties—purple and pink—a stark contrast against the ancient rock. Her Disney princess T-shirt was torn at the shoulder, revealing a nasty scrape that oozed blood. One sparkly tennis shoe still in place while the other lay somewhere in the rocks below.

Her eyes—wide and brown as a doe's—tracked his movement above. Her bottom lip quivered, but she hadn't cried. Yet. Brave kid. Or maybe too shocked to process what had happened.

"Kristen, my name is Liam." The two boys had been shouting

her name when he'd found them. "I'm a ranger and I'm here to help." He forced calm into his voice while his gut churned. That ledge was nothing more than fractured sandstone, spiderwebbed with cracks that could give way any second. One wrong shift, one deep breath, and she'd plummet another hundred feet to the jagged rocks below.

She whimpered—a sound that gutted him—and nodded faintly.

Up until now, he'd been enjoying the view as he patrolled the rim trail. The canyon stretched endlessly before him, layer upon layer of red sandstone and purple shadow carved deep into the earth. Pine-scented air filled his lungs—crisp, thin, carrying the faint mineral taste of ancient rock. Beyond where he lay, the world simply . . . dropped away. Two thousand feet of nothing but sky and stone.

A raven's call echoed off the canyon walls, the sound bouncing between the cliffs until it faded into silence so complete it pressed against his eardrums. The sun warmed his shoulders through his ranger shirt while a cool breeze whispered up from the depths.

Gorgeous but lethal. Especially to untended children hiking away from a nearby campsite.

Liam twisted toward the two boys hovering behind him—twelve and fourteen, maybe.

The younger one clutched a half-empty water bottle, his knuckles white against the plastic. Sweat darkened his Batman T-shirt despite the cool morning air, and his sneakers—definitely not hiking boots—were already caked with red canyon dust.

The older boy stood a head taller, all knobby elbows and gangly limbs he hadn't grown into yet. His sandy hair stuck up in every direction and dark circles shadowed his eyes, and his mouth pressed into a thin line that screamed guilt louder than any confession.

Brothers. Had to be. Same stubborn chin, same way of shifting their weight from foot to foot when cornered.

"Is she your sister?" Liam kept his voice steady, though his chest tightened at the fear radiating off them in waves.

The older boy's Adam's apple bobbed as he gave a slight nod. "W-we didn't know she was following us."

Of course they didn't.

Reckless people got other people killed. Only this time, he wasn't to blame.

He turned back to the girl on the ledge below. He forced his voice to stay calm, easy. "We're going to get you home, but I need you to stay real still. Can you do that?"

She whimpered. Nodded.

The boys crept forward. One loose rock could trigger an avalanche. Liam shrugged off his pack, creating a barrier behind him. The younger one's chin trembled, and he swiped at his nose with the back of his hand. Fresh scratches marked his forearms—tough kid, clearly.

"What are your names?"

"I'm Michael," said the older one. "That's my brother, Eric."

"All right, Michael, Eric, you're doing great. Just stay back and let me work. She's going to be okay."

Please, let that be true.

Liam yanked the radio from his belt and turned his back to the boys. "Base, this is Ranger Liam Kingsley, North Rim, sector Delta-7. I've got a juvenile female, approximately ten years old, stranded on unstable ledge eight feet below the rim. Possible leg fracture, hundred-foot drop below. Need helicopter and backup immediately."

Eden's voice crackled back instantly. "Copy, Liam. Chopper's committed elsewhere—thirty-minute ETA minimum. Noah's en route, twenty minutes out. Can you secure?"

Twenty minutes. The ledge might not survive twenty seconds. "I'll secure. Out."

Liam unhooked his sixty-meter climbing rope from his pack,

uncoiled it, and carried it to a sturdy juniper a few yards from the edge.

"Hey, Eric!"

The younger boy jumped.

"See that trail?" Liam wrapped the rope around the trunk twice, threading it through itself to create a secure wraparound anchor, then tied it off with a double bowline knot for redundancy. He gave it a firm tug—solid. "My buddy Noah is coming. Watch for dust; wave and holler when you spot him. Stay close enough to see us, far enough to stay safe."

The boy nodded once, then took off.

"What about me?" Michael's voice cracked. The kid was clearly near tears.

Liam snapped his harness, pulled out his Petzl GRIGRI, and clipped it to a locking carabiner attached to the belay loop of his harness. "You're my eyes up here. See any rockfall starting, you scream 'Debris.' Kristen's life depends on your warning."

The kid nodded, wiped a hand across his face.

Liam threaded the rope through the GRIGRI, ensuring that the brake strand hung downward, then he double-checked the setup. He slung a small first aid kit onto one of his loops and tucked a lightweight Petzl Sitta harness—small enough to adjust for Kristen's tiny frame—into his pack, along with a roll of SAM Splint and some climbing tape. He pulled on a pair of leather gloves and stepped to the edge, facing the anchor tree, his heels just shy of the drop.

Christiana's face ambushed him again. Her final scream.

His lungs seized. Not today. Not this girl.

He leaned back, then walked backward down the vertical face, keeping his body perpendicular to the rock and his knees slightly bent. The rope glided through the GRIGRI, the device's cam ready to lock at the first hint of speed. His boots found purchase on every ledge, his eyes flicking between Kristen and the wall.

"Kristen. You're doing awesome."

The ledge looked worse up close—spiderwebbed with fractures that predated her fall. Yeah, this rock was one bad storm from giving way, and now with the added weight . . . No, no, he wasn't going to go there.

Except, too late, because suddenly Christiana's shattered body flashed through his mind and the scream he couldn't escape ripped through him, the memory of Christiana missing her grip, her anchors pulling out like a zipper—

Then silence. Bone-jarring, soul-deafening silence. The kind that could paralyze a man. Or make him run—

Focus!

His chest tightened, his breath hitching, but he forced it down, looked at Kristen as he landed beside her. Pebbles kicked off over the edge. He ignored them and the tiny pinch in his gut. "How's the leg?"

He clipped a quickdraw from his harness to a small horn of rock in the wall, attaching the rope as a backup anchor, then turned to Kristen.

"All right, we're gonna fix up your leg and get you out of here. You're super brave, you know that?" Liam kept his weight on the rope.

"Hurts bad." Her voice barely whispered. "Can't move it."

"Perfect. Moving it is off-limits anyway. Time to fix you up and fly you home." Liam extracted the SAM Splint from his pack. "Ever visit the North Rim before? We've got deer everywhere, sometimes a condor if you're lucky enough."

"Saw a squirrel." Her voice thinned as he straightened her leg to fit into the splint. She gasped, sharp and sudden.

"Almost finished, kiddo."

He molded the foam-and-aluminum splint around her calf and shin, secured it with climbing tape. "Pain anywhere else? Back? Neck?"

She shook her head. He let out a coiled breath. Still, he pulled out a neck collar and secured it around her neck. "We're not taking any chances."

Then he pulled his radio off his belt. "Base, victim is secure. Can you give me an ETA on Noah?"

"He's still fifteen minutes out, Liam. Ran into tourist traffic."

And right then, the sandstone ledge seemed to lurch. Could be his imagination. Could be his worst fears, coming true . . . again.

He looked at Kristen. "Ready to fly?"

Her eyes widened.

He pulled out the Sitta harness. "This is your superhero gear." Liam fitted the harness around her waist and legs, adjusting the leg loops to her tiny frame, cinched it tight, and clipped the tie-in points to a locking carabiner. "Keeps you safe while we fly up."

He unclipped his personal anchor, then connected Kristen directly to his belay loop with a second locking carabiner, locking both gates with a twist.

"It's you and me together now," he said, and winked at her.

She gave him a watery grin.

And right then—not his imagination, thanks—the ledge groaned. New cracks zigzagged across the surface.

"Arms around my neck, tight as you can squeeze." He pulled her arms over his shoulders. "I've got you."

Her grip surprised him—iron strong for such small hands. Liam reversed his rappel, walking up the wall, hauling hand-over-hand on the rope's free end, the GRIGRI managing the tension.

Don't look down.

He kept his voice easy, despite the strain on his shoulders. "So you saw a rock squirrel? Those little guys are everywhere. Probably a dozen watching us right now thinking we are nuts."

"Hope they don't think we're the eating kind of nuts." She attempted a giggle, but it failed on a whimper.

A sharp crack echoed below them just before a distant crash.

The ledge—

Kristen screamed, her arms clamped around his neck, tightening.

"Kristen," he said, gauging the distance to the top, "I'm going to need to breathe if we want to reach the top. Could you—"

She buried her head in his back, between his shoulder blades.

Okay, so maybe not.

"What is your favorite subject in school?"

"Art." Thread-thin voice.

"Outstanding. I drew my dog once—Mom thought it was a bowl of spaghetti with legs."

Another weak laugh. Liam clung to that sound. The rim was just above, a few feet.

"We're nearly there."

"Liam!" Noah's voice boomed from over the edge a second before he appeared, his broad frame silhouetted against the sun. "What do you need? Meg is here too."

"Almost home." Liam kept climbing. "Help me over the lip. Guard that right leg."

Liam's boots gripped the rock, the rope taut against the anchor. "You will like Meg." He lowered his voice. "She's a doctor and will know exactly how to fix you up. She's really nice. And between you and me, I think Noah's got a crush on her, but they're both too chicken to admit it."

Kristen giggled again. Some of her terror melted away.

Noah had anchored himself and reached down, grabbing Kristen's harness and pulling her over the edge. Liam followed, collapsing onto solid ground. His chest heaved as he unclipped her from his harness, leaving her secured to the rope as a precaution.

"You did awesome, Kristen." He brushed dirt from her hair. Her brothers rushed toward them, and Meg knelt over her leg.

Liam sat back, his hands shaking, the adrenaline crashing out of him. He closed his eyes. Pine sap and limestone dust filled his nostrils. The rope burn on his palms stung—he should have worn gloves. Canyon wind cooled the sweat on his neck while gravel bit into his spine through his jacket. His heartbeat thundered in his ears, drowning out Meg's gentle questions and the boys' chatter—all proof that everyone was breathing, talking, alive.

He glanced sideways, catching a glimpse of a bus in the distance—it looked almost like a converted city bus. Mint green with faded brown trim, the vintage beast sported safari-style windows and the unmistakable boxy profile of a 1970s city transport gone rogue. There was some dispersed camping just outside the park boundaries, but everything below the rim in this area, as well as a hundred feet from the edge, was National Park, and that bus was too close. Something about it nagged at him, but he couldn't focus on it. Not yet.

Noah's hand landed heavy on his shoulder. "Quite a save. You solid?"

Liam nodded, lying. Adrenaline had stirred up the coiled darkness inside. Christiana's face flashed again—the wide eyes, the scream—

Maybe he couldn't do this job if, every time he rescued someone, the past crashed over him, took him out.

He was just starting to learn how to stand again.

An SUV skidded to a stop. A woman launched out, tears streaming.

"Mom!" Michael bounced to his feet. "She's okay! The ranger saved her!"

"You should've seen him!" Eric rushed over as their mother collapsed beside Kristen. "Total hero!"

The word punched into Liam's chest. "Just doing the job." But his voice emerged thin, the words hollow.

Because they didn't know the truth.

Heroes didn't get their friends killed.

Please don't let them find me.

Except it might be too late. Because according to the encrypted chatter she'd intercepted yesterday, she was the target.

The certainty gnawed at Nimue Hart's gut like a parasite. Sure, the encrypted chatter had been faint, snatched from the ether via her satellite uplink under the wide Arizona sky, but she'd cracked it in under an hour. "New lead on target," it had read. "Mobilizing assets." No names, no specifics, just the cold efficiency of the Russian syndicate she'd been dodging since they'd tracked her to King's Inn eight months ago.

Nimue stretched out in the small mint-green seat of her converted city bus, pencil trailing across the page as she captured the shapes and shadows of the canyon through the side window. Her hand moved in practiced strokes—light for the distant rim, heavy for the shadows carved deep into sandstone. Drawing had always been her reset button, the one thing that untangled the knots in her chest.

The North Rim spread before her like a geological masterpiece—crimson buttes rising from purple depths, their surfaces carved into impossible angles by millennia of wind and water. Morning light painted the layered rock in shades of amber and rust, while shadows pooled like spilled ink in the crevices below. A condor circled somewhere in that vast emptiness, riding thermals between the ancient walls. But on her page, the vibrant canyon translated to stark grays and blacks, her pencil capturing texture and form without the fire of color.

The view should have been enough to distract her from yesterday's intercepted message, but her pencil kept pausing mid-stroke.

She'd told Emberly she wasn't running, which was true. Hiding, though? That was another story entirely. She'd found herself in her own game of cat and mouse, but until yesterday she'd believed she held the upper hand.

New lead on target.

She'd made the mistake of leaving a trail in her online searching. Rookie move.

At least if she was the target, no one else would get caught in the crossfire. She set her sketchbook aside and slid back onto the bench at the table, fingers flying across the keys of her setup. Three monitors flickered to life, casting blue light across her face.

The fold-down table that should have converted into a queen bed had become the permanent home for her digital fortress—three screens, her tower, a tangle of cables, and a keyboard worn smooth from years of use. She'd rather crash on the minicouch anyway. Sleep had sort of become a luxury after eight months on the run.

She scanned the encrypted chatter. Yeah, there it was, only updated: "Moving on target."

Her heart dropped to her stomach. She toggled through feeds from her perimeter cameras, each one a grainy window into the world around her. Nothing. Not even a swaying branch.

Were they moving on someone else?

She sagged against the seat back. Maybe this was the sign she needed to pack up and move again. But she'd chosen this place for a reason. The bus, parked in a dispersed camping spot just west of the Grand Canyon's North Rim, was her sanctuary and her fortress. Its mint-green exterior hopefully passed for an eccentric camper's ride.

No one would guess it thrummed with more computing power than the nearby lodge could dream of—solar panels feeding a battery bank, a satellite dish, and a network of cameras hidden in the surrounding pines. Moving meant starting over. Again.

The quiet peace of her solo trip had been nice at first. Now she hated it with every fiber of her being. But if keeping her sister—and the people they loved—safe meant living alone, she'd pay that price.

She secured the connection, then dialed her sister Emberly's number. The call disconnected. She tried again with the same result. She pushed back from the table with enough force to make the bus rock slightly before heading outside.

The stairs affixed to the back creaked as she climbed up to the deck the previous owner, Jack Kingston, had built on top. He'd probably envisioned romantic evenings under the stars with his fiancée, Harper, but for Nimue, the small deck made the perfect platform for her satellites and solar panels. The sides rose just high enough to hide her equipment from casual observers.

She stepped onto the wood decking, then walked over to Big Bertha. This dish had been her biggest investment—as large and powerful as the bus could handle without looking like a NASA facility. A small branch of leaves had fallen across the receiver. She tossed it over the side, then checked the alignment. No damage, thank goodness.

The North Rim of the Grand Canyon had more trees than the South Rim, which wasn't ideal for her signal, but the lack of hordes of tourists was a must. Besides, the canyon stretching south provided a wide enough sky to make up for the interference.

From her elevated perch, the world spread out like a masterpiece painted in stone and sky. Towering ponderosa pines and aspens crowded around her position, their branches creating a natural canopy that filtered the afternoon light. Beyond the treeline, the canyon yawned open—a vast chasm carved into layers of red sandstone, pink limestone, and cream-colored rock that told the story of the ages in geological shorthand.

The North Rim sat over a thousand feet higher than its famous southern counterpart, and the difference showed in everything from the cooler air to the thick forest that surrounded her. No crowds of tourists with their clicking cameras and chattering voices. No parade of tour buses belching diesel fumes. Just the whisper of wind through pine needles and the distant cry of a red-tailed hawk circling the thermals.

She was tucked with her back to the forest like a security blanket, but to her south, the canyon floor disappeared into purple shadows, the Colorado River nothing more than a silver thread winding through the depths. The far rim shimmered in the heat haze, a ribbon of gold and rust that seemed to float above the void.

This was why she'd chosen this spot. Isolation wrapped in beauty, the cover of the trees combined with a wide sky for her satellites. The nearest neighbor was the North Rim village, made up of a campground, lodge, visitor center, general store, and a couple dozen buildings for staff. But even that was miles away over winding forest roads. Out here, she could disappear into the landscape like smoke.

She tried the call again. This time Emberly answered on the second ring.

"What's wrong?"

Of course that was Emberly's first response. She'd lived the past ten years as an elite Black Swan, running ops and looking over her shoulder. Nimue had always been equal parts proud of and terrified for her sister. But after living just eight months on the run, she'd decided she should have been way more worried about Em.

Loneliness. Fear. Paranoia, even. No wonder Emberly was always moving, always changing her appearance. No wonder she wanted to hang on tight to the rare and surprising relationship she had with a former Navy SEAL. Frankly, the two were made for each other.

After Nimue's house burned down, there really was no place for her. But even if it hadn't, she wasn't safe there. She wasn't safe anywhere. More than that, anywhere she went painted a target on anyone around her. The Bratva wanted her dead—that much had been clear from the moment she'd stared down the barrel of

Teresa's gun. They wouldn't hesitate to take out anyone who stood in their way. They'd been lucky that no one had died during the Russian Bratva's attack at King's Inn. They might not be so lucky next time.

Leaving felt like the only way to ensure that her sister and her new life stayed safe.

But no, Nimue wasn't a Swan. Never wanted to be. She preferred home and family.

At least in her wildest dreams.

"I'm . . . fine." The lie tasted bitter.

"You don't sound fine." Emberly's voice shifted from ops leader to protective older sister. "What happened?"

"Nothing. Everything." She cleared her throat, hating how weak she sounded. "How did you do it? Live alone. Always looking over your shoulder. Never feeling completely safe."

A shiver ran down her spine, and she wrapped her free arm around her waist.

"This won't be forever." Emberly's voice softened. Always the big sister. Always trying to protect. "We just need to figure out what they want from you. Sure, you got into their servers and tracked them. But it has to be something in those files you downloaded. Have you cracked any of them?"

Nimue made her way back down the steps to her kitchenette, phone pressed to her ear. She poured herself a fresh cup of coffee, the rich aroma doing nothing to calm her nerves. "Some. I'm still working on it. But I've been going over the data I acquired. Most of it is benign. Old shipping documents, some bank transactions. I turned it all over to the Caleb Group for their hacker to decipher, but Coco doesn't have anything either. Maybe it's just revenge." She sighed. "Maybe I'm just overreacting. I could come back—"

"No!"

Oh, hello. Nimue took a breath. "Okay, Em. What aren't you

telling me?" Nimue set the mug down harder than necessary, coffee sloshing over the rim.

A beat, and her sister's voice cut low. "I'm pretty sure I saw someone watching us yesterday."

Nimue reached for a paper towel but froze. "What?"

"I don't know. It was quick. They were parked in an SUV down the street—not at all conspicuous in a community like Melbourne Beach. Stein was on the roof, and he spotted it first. I was inside, painting a wall, and by the time I got out on the porch, the SUV was pulling away."

"Could've been a lost tourist."

"Or it could've been the Russian Bratva, waiting for you to show up."

"You have to get out of there." Nimue's hand shook as she wiped up the mess.

"Trust me, Stein doesn't let me out of his sight. He even insists on running with me, though I know it's killing his knees." Emberly's voice carried a note of fondness that made Nimue's chest ache. "But after yesterday, we talked and decided that we'd rather have them watch us than you. However, Stein set up a security perimeter and scanned the house for bugs."

"You moved in yet?"

"No. I'm still living in the camper beside your house. Stein is at Win's place down the road."

"Wait—Winchester Marshall's estate? The actor?"

"Yeah. He's really suffering." She laughed. "But we use Win's pool, and it's got a beautiful view of the ocean on the beach side."

"You know, you could use your portion of the inheritance Mom left us and get your own beach house."

Emberly laughed. "Yeah, unfortunately, two mil, even though it's a nice nest egg, won't get me anything bigger than a cabin on the beach. No, I like your place for now—two blocks off the beach, cute, three bedroom—it'll be beautiful when we get it done."

"It's not my place anymore." Oh, she hadn't meant to sound bitter.

"It will be again, Nim. We'll get it sorted."

She sighed, but the memory of the fire burned through her. No, the Russian mob had taken her peace, her security from her. "We'll see."

A sudden whirring roar shattered the quiet outside—the unmistakable thump of helicopter blades slicing through air.

Moving on target.

"Helicopter." Nimue froze. "I've got to go."

"What—" Emberly was shouting even as Nimue's phone clattered to the countertop. Nimue lunged toward her tech hub. "No, no, no."

The sound thundered closer, vibrating through the bus's frame. No—she'd been so careful—rerouting signals, masking her location.

She flipped through her camera feeds, pulse hammering in her ears. Pine branches swayed in the wind from the rotors, but she couldn't see the chopper. The third feed caught it—a figure sliding down the drop line, black against the sky.

Her breath hitched. The bus could move, but not fast enough. She'd have to ditch it, grab her go bag, disappear into the canyon—

She clicked to the fourth camera and let out a sigh. A red cross blazed across the helicopter's side.

Medical team. Not Bratva.

She closed her eyes as adrenaline flushed from her system, leaving her limbs heavy and warm. The walnut frame of the bench creaked as she sank onto it, cushions shifting under her weight. She exhaled a shaky laugh.

Emberly's voice still yelled from the phone, tinny and distant.

She picked it up, wincing at her sister's sharp tone. "It's fine. Just a medevac. But we should end this. Secure line or not . . ."

She didn't need to finish. The Bratva had hackers working for them—maybe not as good as her, but close enough.

"I still say the Bratva wouldn't put this many resources on you unless you have something they want. Or want back."

"I'll go through the files again. But I really don't know what they're after."

"Stay safe, sis. And if you need us—"

"Love you." Nimue ended the call and leaned forward, pulling up the feeds again. Her cameras weren't just for security—they were her eyes, her connection to a world she couldn't risk joining.

She cycled through angles until one locked onto the scene—a jagged cliff edge with a cluster of figures in ranger tan at the top. The way the lip of the canyon snaked back and forth in this area, her east-facing cameras had a clear shot across a fifty-foot gap in the canyon.

Someone was injured. She rewound the footage, watching the fall unfold in reverse.

Her stomach dropped at the image of the small girl tumbling over the cliff. The helplessness clawed at her chest—sharp, familiar. The same powerlessness she'd felt too often as a child, watching bad things happen to people she couldn't protect.

She zoomed in as far as her lenses allowed, the grainy image sharpening just enough to catch the rescue unfolding.

A ranger in climbing gear rappelled down the cliff face, broad shoulders straining against his harness. Dark hair whipped in the wind, just long enough to look untamed. She couldn't make out his eyes from this distance, but his intensity cut through the screen—focused, unyielding.

Nimue held her breath as he reached the girl. His movements were steady, deliberate. He immobilized her leg, then her neck, before he secured her to his line. She clung to his shoulders as he pulled them both up.

At the top, another ranger—long blond hair tied back, full

beard—grabbed his arm, hauling them both over the edge. A woman in a medic's vest knelt beside the girl, checking the splint.

Two boys crowded around—brothers, most likely. The girl was safe.

And that's when the dark-haired ranger turned, his gaze locking onto her camera. Impossible—he couldn't know it was there, hidden in the branches. But the way he stared, head tilted, sent electricity down her spine.

He lifted his radio, lips moving in words she couldn't hear. Reporting her position?

Her pulse kicked up again—a different kind of alarm. Not Bratva, but someone had noticed her. Someone with authority. Someone who might ask questions she couldn't answer.

She pulled her keyboard closer. The bus's interior—warm mint-green walls, the scent of new cupboards—suddenly felt like a cage. She'd been so careful, blending into the landscape, but that piercing look told her she wasn't invisible.

Her fingers hesitated over the keys. She could hack the park's database, but that radio was analog. She pulled up her supply list, mental gears shifting. A scanner. She needed a police scanner. If the rangers were onto her, she'd hear it first.

She glanced around the bus—her home, her shield. Every inch engineered for survival. The cameras alone had taken her over a week to mount and position in the trees.

But survival wasn't enough anymore. If Emberly was right, the Bratva wouldn't stop until they found her. Having a digital report filed by a ranger was the last thing she needed.

Nimue powered down her monitors, screens fading to black. She grabbed a jacket—brown, nondescript, forgettable—and stepped outside the bus's front door, gathering the few items she had out there. Her gaze swept the cameras mounted in the trees. No time to collect them.

Maybe if she moved for a week, they'd lose interest. She could return later.

She climbed into the driver's seat, engine rumbling to life beneath her. As the bus rolled forward, dust kicking up behind her, the Bratva's message replayed in her head.

New lead on target.

They hadn't found her this time. But she had to stay one step ahead if she hoped to survive.

WANT MORE ROMANTIC SUSPENSE IN YOUR LIFE?

RETURN TO MINNESOTA AND DIVE INTO THE ADVENTURE
AND ROMANCE THAT IS THE MINNESOTA MARSHALLS!

Yeah, those Marshalls...
what have they got themselves into this time?
FRASER
THE MINNESOTA MARSHALLS
SUSAN MAY WARREN
JONAS
THE MINNESOTA MARSHALLS
SUSAN MAY WARREN
NED
THE MINNESOTA MARSHALLS
SUSAN MAY WARREN
IRIS
THE MINNESOTA MARSHALLS
SUSAN MAY WARREN
CREED
THE MINNESOTA MARSHALLS
SUSAN MAY WARREN
THE MINNESOTA MARSHALLS
SUSAN MAY WARREN
SUSANMAYWARREN.COM

AVAILABLE NOW

Note to Reader

Dear Amazing Readers,

What a wild ride this has been! From the depths of Minnesota to the far corners of the globe, Steinbeck's adventure has taken us places I never imagined when I first sat down to write. Watching him navigate international intrigue, face impossible odds, and ultimately find his way back to what matters most—family—has been absolutely thrilling to experience. 😊

This marks the end of our Minnesota Kingston adventures (though something tells me we haven't seen the last of this remarkable family!). What started as a local story has become a globe-spanning epic, and I hope you've loved every heart-pounding, jet-setting moment.

If Steinbeck's journey from danger to devotion, from distant shores back to home, captured your heart the way it did mine, would you consider leaving a review? Your words help other readers discover these adventures (although, don't give anything away!).

I'm endlessly grateful for my incredible team who make these wild stories possible. To my brilliant editor, Anne Horch—you somehow always know how to take my globe-trotting chaos and turn it into something that sings.

Massive thanks to my phenomenal Rel Mollet—my personal mission control! From tracking story details to keeping me on track with my deadlines and making sure readers get their books, you're absolutely invaluable.

Endless appreciation to my brainstorming dream team, Rachel Hauck and Sarah Erredge, who help me figure out how to get characters out of the most impossible situations across multiple continents. You two are creative geniuses!

To my wonderful husband, Andrew—thank you for your unwavering support through every deadline and for being an amazing cook who keeps me fed during those marathon writing sessions. You make this writing life possible!

Huge love to Emilie Haney for creating covers that capture all the excitement and heart of these stories, and to Tari Faris for making every page as beautiful as the adventures they contain.

Katie Donovan, you're absolutely amazing at catching every detail, especially when we're racing against deadlines with international adventures!

To my beloved readers—you've followed this family across oceans and through danger, and you've made every moment of writing worthwhile. I'd love to hear how Steinbeck's story touched your heart at susan@susanmaywarren.com.

For behind-the-scenes fun, sneak peeks, and all kinds of extras, visit susanmaywarren.com or scan the QR code below.

The Minnesota Kingstons have given us one final adventure, and what an adventure it's been! Thank you for taking this incredible journey with us. 😊

With overflowing gratitude and love,
Susie May

P.S. Jump into my next adventure –
Track of Courage! 🖤

More Books by Susan May Warren

Most recent to the beginning of the epic lineup, in reading order.

THE MINNESOTA KINGSTONS
Jack
Conrad
Doyle
Austen
Steinbeck

ALASKA AIR ONE RESCUE
One Last Shot
One Last Chance
One Last Promise
One Last Stand

THE MINNESOTA MARSHALLS
Fraser
Jonas
Ned
Iris
Creed

THE EPIC STORY OF RJ AND YORK
Out of the Night
I Will Find You
No Matter the Cost

SKY KING RANCH
Sunrise
Sunburst
Sundown

GLOBAL SEARCH AND RESCUE
The Way of the Brave
The Heart of a Hero
The Price of Valor

THE MONTANA MARSHALLS
Knox
Tate
Ford
Wyatt
Ruby Jane

MONTANA RESCUE
If Ever I Would Leave You (novella prequel)
Wild Montana Skies
Rescue Me
A Matter of Trust
Crossfire (novella)
Troubled Waters
Storm Front
Wait for Me

MONTANA FIRE
Where There's Smoke (Summer of Fire)
Playing with Fire (Summer of Fire)
Burnin' For You (Summer of Fire)
Oh, The Weather Outside is Frightful (Christmas novella)
I'll be There (Montana Fire/Deep Haven crossover)
Light My Fire (Summer of the Burning Sky)
The Heat is On (Summer of the Burning Sky)
Some Like it Hot (Summer of the Burning Sky)
You Don't Have to Be a Star (Montana Fire spin-off)

THE TRUE LIES OF REMBRANDT STONE
Cast the First Stone
No Unturned Stone
Sticks and Stone
Set in Stone
Blood from a Stone
Heart of Stone

A complete list of Susan's novels can be found at
susanmaywarren.com/novels/bibliography/.

About the Author

Susan May Warren is the USA Today bestselling author of over 100 novels with nearly 2 million books sold, including the Global Search and Rescue and the Montana Rescue series. Winner of a RITA Award and multiple Christy and Carol Awards, as well as the HOLT Medallion and numerous Readers' Choice Awards, Susan makes her home in Minnesota.

Visit her at www.susanmaywarren.com

www.ingramcontent.com/pod-product-compliance
Lightning Source LLC
Chambersburg PA
CBHW020654010826
48969CB00013B/1730